First Kill

Nonfiction by Michael Kronenwetter

Terrorism: A Guide to Events and Documents

Capital Punishment

The Peace Commandos

Prejudice in America

United They Hate

Michael Kronenwetter

First
Kill

Thomas Dunne Books

St. Martin's Minotaur ❦ New York

THOMAS DUNNE BOOKS.
An imprint of St. Martin's Press.

www.minotaurbooks.com

Library of Congress Cataloging-in-Publication Data

Kronenwetter, Michael.
    First kill / Michael Kronenwetter.—1st ed.
       p. cm.
    ISBN 0-312-34737-5
    EAN 978-0-312-34737-6
    1. Private investigators—Wisconsin—Fiction. 2. Journalists—Crimes against—Fiction. 3. Divorced fathers—Fiction. 4. Widows—Fiction. I. Title.

PS3611.R66F57 2005
813'.6—dc22

                                                                    2005046564

First Edition: September 2005

10 9 8 7 6 5 4 3 2 1

For my wife, Pat,
and our wonderful children,
Muffin and Jay

ACKNOWLEDGMENTS

I am extremely grateful to the extraordinary Ruth Cavin for selecting this book for St. Martin's Press. I'm also grateful to private-eye novelist Richard Helms for his role in bringing it to her attention.

I would like to thank both my daughter, Catherine, and my son, Jay, for all the helpful advice they've given me in preparing this book.

And my wife, Pat, who was unfailingly encouraging to my writing of this book.

Also John Bandock, a twice-wounded Vietnam veteran who provided me with helpful information about that war—although by no means about the kind of disgraceful episode described in this book.

Of course, it's impossible to be grateful for notorious criminals like John Dillinger, "Baby Face" Nelson, and Ed Gein, but each of them did, in fact, provide some of the historical incidents referred to in this book.

Finally, I'd like to express my tremendous appreciation of Isabelle Stelmahoske and the late Arthur Henderson—the two most inspiring teachers I've encountered in my entire life.

Part One

My Back Pages

—BOB DYLAN

1:15 Friday Morning, October 16

Jack Drucker didn't recognize his death when he saw it coming in the rearview mirror of his car.

At that time, Jack's sleek yellow '69 Stingray was parked on a twisting residential cul-de-sac just off Highway 51 in the town of Pinery Falls, Wisconsin. "Old 51" was the two-lane promise of adventure that the young Bob Dylan used to sing "ran right by his baby's door," from up Wisconsin-way down to no-man's-land. That is, all the way from the lake district of northern Wisconsin down to New Orleans.

Little River Road cuts off "Old 51" to snake the shoreline of the Wisconsin River almost a mile before coming to the turnaround that marks its end. About halfway along, both the road and the river duck behind a small hill that shields them from cars passing on the highway. The few houses perched on that hillside above the river are further protected by the thick growth of trees and brush that covers the upper third of the slope.

The people who live in those houses pay hefty premiums for both the view and relative seclusion. Because they can all afford excellent burglar-alarm systems, there are no streetlights out along the road, and on a clear night, when the moon and stars reflect off the surface of the river, residents looking out their windows can imagine themselves in the resort country fifty miles to the north.

In keeping with the rustic image of the neighborhood, there are no curbs on Little River Road. The Stingray was parked on the western shoulder of the road, the one that runs along the riverbank. The night was overcast and the dammed-up river was black and still. The paved road itself was only a paler ribbon in the enclosing darkness. There'd been an early freeze that night, so Jack had the Stingray's hardtop on, its engine running, and its windows rolled up against the cold.

Only one car had passed since Jack had been parked there, and it had headed out toward the highway. Two of the three large houses visible from the car were completely dark. There was a light in one window of the third, but there was no sign of human movement anywhere.

Jack was well into middle age, but most people who met him assumed that he was younger. His tall and well-muscled body could have passed for thirty and his chiseled face for not much older than that. His wavy blond hair—which, in this light, matched the color of the car—showed no sign of either thinning or receding. But it wasn't just his looks that fooled people; it was something to do with energy. With vibrations. All his life, Jack had given off vibrations of strength, vitality, and easy confidence.

He had been sitting there long enough to crave a cigarette, but that would mean either rolling down a window or coating the inside of his windshield with a smeary film of carcinogens. Besides, he didn't want the glowing tip of a lit cigarette to attract the attention of anyone looking out a window of one of the houses across the road. He wasn't exactly hiding—not in that car, he wasn't—but he didn't want some nervous householder calling the police, either. And besides, if the wrong person happened to notice him sitting out there in the dark, Jack's errand could turn out to be pointless.

If, he thought irritably, this wasn't pointless already.

He was beginning to think he'd been the victim of a hoax. He decided to wait ten more minutes, then roll down his window and have a cigarette. While he was smoking it, he'd decide how much longer to wait before giving up and going home to bed.

What the hell, *he thought.* Why wait?

He was just reaching for the pack of cigarettes in his jacket pocket when his death appeared in the Stingray's mirror. The high-beam headlights of another car came sweeping around the long curve a hundred yards behind him. As he watched their slow approach through the darkness, he wondered if this could be what he'd been waiting for. He watched with growing interest as the car slowed to a crawl, then pulled onto the shoulder and came to a stop a few car lengths behind the Stingray. The glare of the high beams still shielded the outlines of the car itself from his view. He wondered if he was about to be rousted by a cop on patrol. Had one of the householders called the police after all?

Then the headlights went off.

That couldn't be a cop.

Still semiblinded from the vanished brightness, Jack tried to blink away the phantoms that danced in front of his eyes.

The driver's door swung open.

A dark-coated figure emerged and began walking up the road toward Jack's car.

Jack rolled down his window.

Turning to face the newcomer, Jack felt the cold mouth of a gun barrel press against his forehead.

Speaking rapidly, the killer explained what was about to happen to Jack and why. It took only a moment, but during that time their faces were so close together that the white clouds of their breaths mingled in the cold night air.

Jack was not unnerved by fear. If anything, he was excited by it. After all, how could he be murdered? He was a man who lived a charmed life. He had faced possible deaths several times before and he was still alive. Even back in Vietnam, he had never really doubted that he'd come out of the chaos alive.

Slowly and dismissively, he turned his face away from the gun. He seemed more puzzled than afraid, and looked as if he were concentrating on working out an algebraic problem in his head.

Then he seemed to reach a solution and made a grab for the gun.

Before his hands ever reached it, the gun fired and the bullet slammed into his temple.

The echo of the gunshot rolled out over the river. As it faded away in the cold night air, the killer let go of the gun. It fell onto the lap of Jack's sagging body, bounced off, and came to rest between his right foot and the brake pedal.

There was still no sign of activity from any of the houses across the way.

No one had seen—or even heard—a thing.

1

I SAW HER AGAIN

—The Mamas and the Papas

Harry was driving me crazy. It wasn't his fault—he was just being a kid—but I couldn't take much more without some real relief. Having a six-year-old around all the time can be hard to take, particularly when your home is also your office and there's no escape from it.

It wasn't that I *disliked* having Harry with me. Just the opposite. I looked forward to his visits and hated those weekends when Sarah kept him with her. But this time, it was more than a weekend. It had already been a week since Sarah left town, and it would probably be at least another week before she returned.

It was the relentlessness that was getting to me. All that energy tearing around the place, crayoning on the walls, jumping on the furniture, inventing ways to make noise with things that had never made sounds before. And, worst of all, the constant demands—demands for food, demands for drink, demands for toys, demands for *Rugrats* on TV.

What Harry was really demanding, I suppose, was love.

Well, I loved him all right, and I longed to give him that love in a form that he could use. The trouble was that I'd only been a father for six years out of several decades, and a weekend father for most of those. What did I know about making a kid feel loved?

I wondered how Sarah put up with it. She's a hotshot executive at Mueller's Cheese Company these days and not the kind of person you'd expect to tolerate crayoned walls and creative noise.

On that particular midweek afternoon, my ex-wife was in Paris, of all places. She was there to negotiate the importation of Mueller's new line of tavern cheeses into France. Mueller's makes some of the best cheese in Wisconsin, which means some of the best in the world. And that's not just my opinion, either. In fact, that's not my opinion at all. I hate cheese. That's the opinion of people who know about these things, the judges who give out blue ribbons at big-time cheese festivals. (And yes, Virginia, there *are* such things as big-time cheese festivals.)

If Sarah pulled it off, Mueller's would become the first American company to have its cheese mass-marketed in France since the 1890s. (I told you it was good.) But the negotiations would take another week or two, and while she was gone, I had Harry with me.

Sarah and I had been divorced for five years, which was slightly longer than we'd been married. By the time of the divorce, our marriage had settled into a kind of tired bitterness that I think surprised us both. But then, who marries expecting to be unhappy?

For Sarah, the bitterness was tinged with indignation. She'd already had one unhappy marriage, which she blamed on the fact that her husband had been a creep. No argument there. I'd met him. But now she was unhappy in her second marriage, so that had to be her husband's fault too. And maybe it was.

The divorce was inevitable, or so I told myself. But before it came, we had Harry.

I'd never pictured myself as a father. Yet there I was with a baby in my arms. Incredible! I actually *enjoyed* getting up when he cried in the middle of the night. I'd give him his bottle and rock him back to sleep. I even sang him lullabies. That was a kick. I can't carry a tune, but Harry never seemed to mind.

Then Sarah left and took Harry with her.

It made sense. I mean, how could I raise a kid on my own? I'm a working private detective, a one-man operation. My hours are unpredictable and I'm in and out all the time.

It made economic sense too. My income is spotty at best. Sarah was already on the fast track at Mueller's, and she could provide for Harry better than I could. Besides, a young boy needs a mother in a way he doesn't need a father. At least, that's what people say.

The fact that it made sense didn't mean it didn't hurt. At first, it hurt a lot. It never *stopped* hurting altogether, but it wasn't long before I got comfortable living alone again. And why not? I'd lived alone for most of my life. So, while I always looked forward to Harry coming on the weekends, I always looked forward to him leaving, too. But now the easy and reassuring rhythm to his comings and goings was broken. I'd already had him longer than at any one time since the divorce, and it was wearing me down.

It was late afternoon Wednesday, and I was trying to get my expense records in order. If I didn't get the bills in the mail soon, the clients wouldn't get them before the weekend. That meant none of them would have a chance to put a check in the mail until the next week at the earliest, and my cash was getting even shorter than my credit.

Desperate, I'd sent the little dynamo out to play. That was great fun for him, but it turned out to be even worse for me. That was where I'd wanted him, of course, but once he was there I started to worry. Was six really old enough to be playing outside alone? You heard about kids who—

Relax, I told myself. *This is Red Maple Street in Pinery Falls, Wisconsin, not some crack alley in the South Bronx.* But the fact that this was Red Maple Street didn't mean that there weren't some real weirdos around. And it didn't mean there wasn't a lot of traffic a block away on Menard Avenue, either.

I went over to the front window. I was hoping to see Harry playing in the front yard, but the only thing out there was a beautiful fall afternoon. Most of the leaves in the park across the street had already turned and there was enough color to take your breath away. It was late afternoon, and the setting sun behind the trees gave the reds and yellows of the maples, the rust browns of the oaks, and the delicate golds of the birches a vivid chromatic glow.

Harry was probably out in back playing on the swing that I'd hung from a branch of the big basswood.

Probably.

But what if he wasn't? What if he'd wandered off and gotten lost? What if—

A gut-wrenching screech of tires came from Menard Avenue. My stomach flipped over.

Harry!

I told myself not to worry. There was nothing unusual about screeching tires on Menard, which used to be a part of Old 51. There's a bypass around Pinery Falls these days, but Menard is still the business route through town. A lot of out-of-towners misjudge the quick stoplight on the corner of Menard and Red Maple. Fender benders are pretty frequent there.

But where the hell is Harry?

What do I do now? I asked myself. Shoud I get back to work, trusting that Harry had stayed in the yard as he had promised to do, or run outside and check that he's OK?

Was this a parental instinct or a neurotic guilt? I was still standing at the window trying to decide when a red Sable wagon pulled up to the curb in front of the house.

Elizabeth Kermanski got out.

My stomach flipped over again.

2

HERE YOU COME AGAIN

—Dolly Parton

L ooking back on it, I shouldn't have been surprised.

Elizabeth Kermanski was Elizabeth Drucker now. Her husband had recently been murdered, and, judging from the news reports, the police were getting nowhere with the case. I was a private detective who had once been friends with them both. All things considered, I should have been expecting her visit.

But I wasn't.

A hand-painted sign directs clients to the front door, but Liz was coming around to the side door that faces the driveway. That was the door she'd always used in the old days—back when we were young and this house was just the house that I grew up in and not a place of business.

She was wearing white slacks and a blue sweater, and her light brown hair glowed in the sun. When she looked up and saw me at the window, she smiled. Once upon a time, that smile had the power to addle my brains. Maybe it still did. She'd already climbed the steps to the porch before it occurred to me to go to the door and welcome her.

"You used to walk right in," I said when I opened the door.

"I'm sorry." They were the first words Liz had said to me in decades.

"No," I said foolishly. "I just meant—you know, old times."

We were standing awkwardly in the open doorway. It had been so long since we'd seen each other that we didn't know who we were to each other anymore. At least I didn't. Old feelings were stirring, not all of them pleasant.

"I was sorry to hear about Jack," I said. It sounded even emptier than such sentiments usually do, but she nodded and swallowed hard. Her eyes teared up, and her hands reached out like those of a blind woman searching for something familiar. Without thinking about it, I moved in so close that our bodies touched. We put our arms around each other and she clung to me.

Her body felt both strange and familiar against mine. She smelled of floral soap; I could feel her breathe. We stood that way for what seemed like a long time. Anyone walking by would have thought that we were lovers.

"I thought about going to the funeral," I told her. "But I got drunk instead."

"I understand, Hank." Her voice was muffled against my chest. "I know how you felt about Jack."

If so, she knew more than I did.

After a while, her body relaxed. After another moment, we let go of each other. She reached into a pocket of her slacks, pulled out a Kleenex, and dabbed it against her eyes and cheeks. Liz has the most incredible eyes I've ever seen. They're blue, but such a pale blue that they hardly seem to have any color at all. Like a cat's eyes, they catch the light so well that they almost seem to generate their own. They generate something else as well, a kind of intensity that grabs you and pulls you into them.

After the tears stopped coming, she managed a smile. "May I come in?" she asked.

I'd almost forgotten that we were still standing in the doorway. After all these years, I could still get lost in those eyes.

"Of course," I said. "The house is a little different now," I explained, ushering her into my small living room. I gestured toward an open door in the far wall. "My office is in through there."

As she started to walk by me, I stopped her with a hand on her shoulder.

"Did you see Harry out there?" I asked.

"Harry?" She sounded puzzled.

"My son."

"Your son?" she asked, as if surprised.

She didn't even know I had a son.

"A little guy," I explained. "Six years old. He's wearing a Packer windbreaker with a hood. He should be in the yard someplace."

She shook her head. "I didn't see anyone. Maybe he's in the back?"

"Oh, hell. Look, I need to find him. Could you go on into the office? It'll only take me a minute."

"Don't be silly," she said. "I'll help you look."

She followed me back to the porch, where I called out Harry's name. That was all it took. Like an eager terrier, a small figure in a green-and-gold jacket came bounding around the corner of the house yelling, *"Da-deeeee!"* at the top of his lungs. He reminded me of the cartoons he watched on TV—a colorful blur of motion, ending in a little boy.

Bounding onto the porch, he flung himself up into my arms, totally confident that I would catch him. Which, of course, I did.

"Da-dee-da-dee-dadeedadeedadee," he chanted, clutching tight to me as if he'd been lost and I was home.

"Settle down, sport," I said. "We've got company."

"Com! *Pan! Neee!*" he proclaimed, squirming around to get a look at the unfamiliar lady standing beside us on the porch. "Whoooo?" he asked, making it into a cartoon owl sound.

"This is an old friend of mine," I told him. "Her name is Elizabeth Drucker. Liz, this is Harry. Harry, Liz."

"She is not!" he protested in mock indignation. "She's not *hairy* at all."

He exploded into giggles, and Liz laughed too.

Wriggling around in my arms, Harry pushed his hands against my chest to let me know he wanted down. Once firmly planted on the porch, he stood up straight and held out his right hand. "I'm pleased to meet you," he said with all the mustered solemnity of a little boy being polite. Sarah must have been teaching him manners.

"I'm pleased to meet you, too, Harry." Liz said, seeming as delighted by him as he was with her.

The formalities over, he turned to me. "Can I have a sandwich, Daddy? Please. I'm *hunnn*gry."

Harry was always *hunnn*gry. Or *thirrr*sty. Or both.

"Not right now," I told him. "Maybe later."

He was ready to argue, but I headed him off. "Listen, sport. Liz and I need to go inside and talk for a while. Can I count on you to stay in the yard until we're done?"

"Can I come, too?"

"No, you can't. This is grown-up stuff."

"'Cause you want to know why?" he went on, ignoring my answer. "'Cause I'll be really quiet. Honest, I will."

"No, Harry."

His face crumpled. Tears appeared in his eyes and inflated themselves like balloons. It was one of his best tricks.

"I know what," Liz put in brightly, squatting down so that her face was level with his. "Would you like someone to play with?"

His ravaged face morphed back to its usual shape. It even brightened. "Sure I would. You want to play with me?"

"Oh, *I'm* not much fun to play with," she responded. "But just you wait a minute."

She left the porch and took a few steps toward the front curb where the Sable was parked. Harry and I followed after her.

"Hey, Tommy!" she called, waving a hand in the air like a magician.

A head popped up in the backseat. The curbside rear door opened and the head emerged, followed by a young male body. "Yeah?"

"Come on over here and meet some people."

By his size, I figured him to be about twelve or thirteen. With his hands in the pockets of his baggy gangsta pants, he slouched through the leaves toward us. He moved sullenly, his eyes fixed on the ground in front of his feet, his body language resenting every step. But when he stopped in front of us and lifted his head, he was smiling pleasantly enough.

So, this was Liz's son.

And Jack's.

I'd seen Tommy around town a few times with one or the other of his parents, but always at a distance. I'd never met him, never heard him speak.

"This is my son, Tommy," she said, with obvious affection in her voice. "Tommy, this is Harry Berlin and his father, Hank."

"Hi, Tommy." I held out my hand. He took it with a grunting sound I took to be a greeting.

Liz suggested that Tommy entertain Harry while the adults talked.

"OK, sure," Tommy agreed. He wasn't exactly enthusiastic about it, but he wasn't grudging, either. He almost seemed to like the idea. "So, whatcha wanna do, Harry?"

"*I* know!" Harry exclaimed. "Let's us rake the leaves!" He made it sound like the world's most exciting recreational activity.

"OK. Sure," Tommy agreed. When Harry turned toward the backyard, Tommy looked toward his mother and shrugged.

Then the kids ran off around the house to look for rakes while the grown-ups went inside to talk about murder.

3

IT SEEMS SO LONG AGO

—Leonard Cohen

I want you to find out who killed Jack," she said. Liz was sitting in the smaller of the two client armchairs that face my desk. It's a comfortable chair, but she didn't look very comfortable in it. Her back was too straight, for one thing. Her arms were stretched out along the armrests, with her hands gripping the ends like those of a prisoner strapped into Old Sparky bracing for the jolt.

To tell you the truth, I didn't feel all that comfortable myself. There were ghosts in the room. Not just Jack's, but hers and mine as well—the ghosts of the people we'd been the last time we were in that room together.

That was near the end of the long, hot summer of 1968. Back before Canada. Back before a lot of things. This room hadn't been an office then but the living room of my family home. All three of us had been drinking beer and sharing fresh memories of our high school years and excitement about our immediate futures. We'd just graduated from high school that spring, and we'd be headed down to the university in Madison in the fall.

It was the night they told me they were engaged.

Ghosts.

Long-buried feelings were stirring, but this was business. At least, that's what I told myself.

"Why?" I asked.

The question seemed to startle her. "Why what?" she asked.

"Why do you want me to find out who killed Jack?"

"I—but that's obvious, isn't it? I want you to find out who killed him and why."

She looked earnestly into my eyes. "I want *justice*," she said.

"Sure. But finding killers is what the cops do."

"But they aren't getting anywhere," she protested. "Every time I call them, they say they're working on it, but I don't think they're doing anything at all. My impression is they don't know *what* to do."

That didn't surprise me any. With one or two exceptions in both directions, the Pinery Falls cops are OK. But they're still just small-town cops.

"Besides," she added. "I want you to find out something more. I want you to find out *why* Jack was killed."

I nodded.

"Who's the lead investigator?" I asked. Then, when she looked uncertain, "Who talks to you the most?"

"George Carlson." She smiled. "You must remember him."

Carlson had been our classmate back at Pinery Falls High. He was one of those exceptions I mentioned, by far the ablest cop on the Pinery Falls force. But he could be a real harassment too. And he usually was whenever I was involved. Back in high school, George had been one of those kids who loved being hall monitor. A stickler for the rules, he'd turn in anyone he saw smoking or checking a cheat-sheet during a test. His only redeeming feature was that he wasn't a hypocrite. He always obeyed the rules himself.

"Why did you come to me?" I asked. There were two other detective agencies in town, both of them better staffed than mine. But then, any agency with a secretary was better staffed than mine.

Liz looked embarrassed. She stole a quick look at the ceiling, then one at the floor. "It just seemed natural to come to you," she said.

Natural. Sure. Just like the old days. *Who ya gonna call? Ghostbusters—and good old Hank Berlin!* But she needed to know this wasn't the old days. More important, *I* needed to know that.

"I can charge by the hour or the day," I said brusquely. "It's plus expenses either way. Which is better for you depends on what's involved in the investigation. We can negotiate some, but there are no special discounts for old friends."

I chose that last word very deliberately.

She flinched at my tone but quickly dismissed the whole question of money.

"Of course," she said. "The fee doesn't matter. I've got money to pay you. But you'll do it, then? You'll find out who killed Jack?"

"If I can."

Her fingers released their grip on the arms of the chair. She seemed to relax for the first time since she'd entered the office. "I was afraid that maybe—because of everything that happened between us—that maybe you wouldn't."

"That was a long time ago," I said.

Sure it was.

"I'm glad," she said earnestly, leaning forward and fixing me with those electric eyes. "I never wanted to lose you as a friend, Hank. You must know that."

"Let's just drop that subject, OK?"

She flinched again.

"OK," she said.

She readjusted her position in the chair, sitting up straight and folding her hands in her lap. She looked about as prim as a good little girl in church, and about as comfortable as a condemned prisoner awaiting the eternal zap.

"I've never hired a detective before," she said. "So what happens now?"

"Now I need information to get started. As much as I can get."

I already knew something about Jack's murder, of course. Everybody in Pinery Falls knew about it. It was the biggest crime news to hit central Wisconsin since Miss Dairyland strangled her romantic rival in the parking lot of the Wausau Howard Johnson. Right after Jack was killed, journalists from all over the state had come to town to report on the violent death of one of their own, and the local TV stations had been playing it up big every day since. That would have been inevitable anyway in a town this size, but the coverage was intensified by the fact that Jack had worked for the *Pinery Falls Torrent* and that he was the son of its owner and publisher, Wesley Drucker. Mysteriously, however, the coverage in the *Torrent* itself had been oddly muted.

"Eventually, I'll need to know a lot of things," I said. "But let's start with the night it happened. I want you to tell me everything you know about the night Jack was killed."

4

A LOVER'S QUESTION

—Clyde McPhatter

It was hard to concentrate on what Liz was saying. I was too conscious of her physical presence on the other side of the desk, the almost chemical mixture of energy and vulnerability that had once drawn me to her like a source of heat in a cold room. I'd never been sure if other people felt it too, or if I was the only one. But everyone saw her beauty. You'd have to be blind not to see that.

Her features were not exactly small, but they gave the impression of being incredibly delicate, as if someone had taken great care in forming them. They looked breakable. Her eyes were the magic blue they'd always been, and her figure was almost as trim as it had been in college. She had the same light brown hair, with the same bits of blond mixed in, gifts from the sun that hid any gray that might be starting to appear.

As I said, it was hard to concentrate on what she was saying. I must have heard it, though, because I did manage to ask rational questions, and later on I even remembered the answers.

The police hadn't told her much more about the murder than they'd told the media. Jack's body had been found by a squad car on a routine patrol about 3:30 that Friday morning. Jack had been shot through the head with a single bullet. The coroner, who had gotten there within two hours of the body's discovery, estimated that Jack had been dead three or four hours at most. That meant Jack had probably been shot sometime between 1:30 and 2:30 a.m.

"The gun was on the floor of the car, near Jack's feet," I pointed out. "That suggests he might have done it himself, but from what the news says, the cops don't think so."

"Oh no," she protested. "Of course he didn't. I knew Jack. *You* knew him. He wouldn't do something like that."

I considered it. In the old days, I would have sworn that Jack hadn't killed himself. But that was decades ago. Who knew about now? Maybe Liz did, and maybe she didn't.

"It doesn't seem likely," I acknowledged. Except that I remembered that Jack had once idolized Hemingway and dreamed of emulating him. Hemingway had killed himself. Shot himself in the head, come to think of it.

"What else did the cops did tell you?" I asked.

"They didn't tell me anything, really. Mostly, they just asked me things."

"What things?"

"Well—whether I could identify the gun, for one thing."

"And could you?"

"I'm not very good about guns. The only guns I know anything about are Jack's."

"Jack's *guns*, plural?" I asked.

"He'd gotten to be something of a gun freak. He kept three hunting rifles and a small collection of handguns that he was very proud of. He called them his 'pieces.' Why do men use the same word for guns that they use for women they don't care about at all?"

"You got me," I admitted. "Did Jack often carry a gun?"

"Oh no. At least I don't think so." She frowned. "That's illegal, isn't it?"

"I wouldn't have thought that mattered much to Jack."

"He had a special display case for the handguns, with a made-to-order place for each one. Well, he always kept the display case locked, except when he took the guns out to show people. Or just to *fondle*." She made a face. "He did that sometimes," she added.

"Maybe some men use the same word for guns and women because they think of them both as things to fondle."

"That could be it," she said. "Anyways, all the guns that were in the case are still there." She brightened. "That's proof that he didn't kill himself, isn't it?"

"It leans that way," I said.

"Besides, the gun the police showed me was different."

"Different?" The news media hadn't said anything specific about the murder weapon, except that it was a handgun.

"From the ones in the case," she explained. "It was big and ugly, and it had a funny handle."

"Funny?"

"Funny peculiar," she said. "There was something really strange about it. When they showed me the gun, they held it up in a plastic bag, and I couldn't really see it all that well. I mean, I probably *could* have, but I didn't want to."

"Of course you didn't," I reassured her. "Don't worry about it."

It was about this point in the conversation that we took a break to go outside and check on the kids. They were doing fine. They had raked up the leaves, not only from my backyard but also from the neighbors' on both sides, and were in the process of constructing an elaborate maze.

"Coffee?" I asked when Liz and I returned to the office. "I still don't drink it myself, but I keep some around for visitors."

"No, thanks," she said, smiling. "Last time I was here, it was Point Special."

So she remembered too.

"That's right," I said. "Want some of that instead?"

She shook her head no.

"So," I began, after we'd resumed our places on opposite sides of my desk, and with them, our roles as detective and client. "What did the police ask you about besides the gun?"

"Well, about that night, mostly. They asked if I knew what Jack was doing out on that road so late. What I was doing when he was killed. Things like that."

"Did you answer them?"

She looked surprised. "Of course I did. They're the police."

"That's the best reason in the world *not* to answer them," I told her. "At least not without a lawyer."

"But why not?" she asked. Then it came to her. "Oh, you mean because they might suspect me? But why would a wife want him dead?"

"Who knows? Maybe he snored. Maybe he picked his nose at the dinner table."

She smiled, showing that she appreciated the effort to keep things light. Then I spoiled it. "Maybe you stood to inherit a lot of money."

She stopped smiling and looked at me in a new way. "Do you suspect me, too?"

"No," I answered. "But I have to ask the same sorts of questions the police do."

She nodded. "All right, ask."

"Did you?"

"Inherit a lot of money?" She shook her head. "Just a money market account."

"How much is in it?"

"I'm not exactly sure. Thirty thousand dollars maybe. Maybe a little more. And I have some rights to Jack's pension from the *Torrent*."

"Was there insurance?" I asked.

"Two hundred and fifty thousand dollars. But *I* don't get that any of that."

"You don't?" I was surprised.

"No, that goes to Tommy. We each had a policy in his name. For his education mostly, to give him a start. Of course, I'm his guardian, so I suppose I could grab the money and fly off to Rio. Do you think the police are watching the airport?"

I grinned. "I wouldn't think so. But why weren't you a beneficiary too?" I asked.

"There's no reason why I should be," she answered. "I don't need the money. I still have a little money from my father's insurance, and my job pays more than Jack's."

"*Your* job?" The fact she even *had* a job surprised me. I'd assumed that Liz Drucker didn't work. The thought must have shown in my face, because she grinned.

"I'm a vice president in charge of the Chippewa State Bank," she explained.

"I'm impressed," I said. And I was, too. Chippewa State, which was headquartered in Pinery Falls, was one of the largest independent banks left in Wisconsin.

If she was making more than Jack, she was definitely making more than me. Both Sarah *and* Liz, then. I'd never asked my current lady friend, Rachel, but she was probably making more than I was, too—and she's a junior high school teacher! It wasn't a thought I cared to dwell on.

"Getting back to the night Jack was killed," I said, "what can you tell me about it?"

"Not much that's useful, I'm afraid. It was just an ordinary night. We watched television in the living room until after the ten o'clock news."

"We?"

"Jack and I. Tommy was out. He had an overnight at a friend's house."

"On a school night?"

"There wasn't any school that Friday. The teachers had an in-service or something."

Then I remembered. That was the day Sarah dropped Harry off with me and left for Paris. They'd arrived early in the morning—

earlier than I'd expected. Sarah's eyes threw daggers when she saw Rachel in the kitchen munching on a piece of toast. Harry, of course, was delighted. Rachel and he were old friends.

"So, you and Jack watched TV until ten thirty. Then what?"

"I went upstairs to bed."

"Your bedroom's on the second floor?"

"That's right."

"Did you and Jack share the same bedroom?"

"Of course we did."

"The same bed?" It just came out. It was a defensible question. One that I might have asked any client in a similar situation. Sure it was.

She looked at me curiously. "Well, yes. Of course we did."

"Did Jack go up with you?"

"No. He stayed in the living room. He was going to read, I think, but I'm not sure about that. He just said he wasn't very sleepy and he'd be up later."

"So he wasn't planning to leave the house?"

"I don't think so. If he was going to go out on a story, he might not have told me. I mean, he never talked much about his work. But I think he would have told me if he was planning to leave the house, even if he didn't tell me why."

"Just how secretive was he? Do you know what story he was working on?"

Jack was an investigative reporter, and a good one. The fact that he was the son of the publisher gave him more time and latitude than most reporters ever get, even on papers a lot bigger than the *Torrent*. He put that freedom to good use, exposing several local scandals and at least one statewide one. A series he'd done on organized crime in Wisconsin had resulted in two members of Milwaukee's Carelli crime family going to prison and made Jack a finalist for the Pulitzer Prize. It seemed possible that something he had uncovered—or he was *about* to uncover—had led to his death.

But Liz shook her head. "No, I don't," she answered. "The police asked me about that too. But Jack almost never discussed the details of his work with me."

"Forget the details," I suggested. "What about the broad outlines? Do you have any idea what *kind* of story he might have been working on?"

She raised her hands in a gesture of helplessness. "I just don't know, Hank. The police might know. They took a bunch of his papers, notes and things, and they haven't returned them yet."

"Sure," I said. "And if they don't know, the paper will." I had some good contacts at the *Torrent*. One in particular. And, of course, I knew the old man.

"Let's get back to that night," I said. "What was Jack doing when you left him?"

"Reading. He was sitting in his favorite chair. The one where he always sat. Anyway, before I went up to bed, he said, 'Good night, sweetheart. I might be a while yet.'"

Her lips trembled, just a little. "That was the last thing he said to me, before—"

She shook her head, as if she was trying to shake the thought from her mind.

"Did you go right to sleep?" I asked quickly. She seemed a little fragile, and I didn't want her breaking down. She nodded, and the danger passed.

"Within fifteen or twenty minutes anyway," she said. "I've gotten to be an early sleeper these days. It seems to come with age."

"Did the police wake you up when they found the body?"

"Oh no. I mean, yes, the police *did* wake me up. It was about four thirty, I think," she said. "But that's not the *first* thing I remember. There was something in between."

"Oh?"

"The phone rang," she explained. "I was asleep, but the ringing woke me up. I looked over to see if Jack was going to answer it—the phone is on his side of the bed—but he wasn't there. I rolled over to answer it myself, but it broke off in the middle of a ring. I thought the caller might have just hung up, but Jack might have answered, too."

"Do you know what time this was?"

"Yes, I do. We have a little bedside clock radio, with one of those green displays. I always look at it when I wake up. It said twelve fifty-two. I couldn't believe that anyone was calling at that hour, but that's what it said."

"Did Jack usually talk on the phone that late?" I asked.

"Not 'usually,'" she explained. "But it wasn't all that *unusual*, either. If he was fighting a deadline, he might stay up even later. And"—she took a deep breath—"if he started really drinking, he might stay up until he passed out. Sometimes, he'd wake up for a while and drink some more before he came to bed."

That behavior pattern sounded uncomfortably familiar to me.

"Was Jack drinking that night?" I asked. The news reports of the autopsy hadn't said anything about alcohol in Jack's system, but the cops could be reserving it.

She shook her head. "I didn't see him drinking that night at all, and there was no dirty glass in the morning."

"You said you were groggy. Is it possible that you never really woke up? That you only dreamed that the phone rang, when it didn't?"

She shook her head. "I'd been asleep but I really woke up. And the phone really rang!"

A postmidnight phone call was unusual, but so was getting shot in the head. Maybe the two were connected. The phone call might have prompted Jack to leave the house and lured him, whether deliberately or not, to his death.

There were roughly a thousand other questions I could have asked her, but I didn't know enough yet to decide which ones might be worth the trouble. Besides, Liz was looking tired.

"You're a good client," I told her. "You know how to answer questions. Not everybody does."

"Thank you." She said it with a little duck of her head, as if she were literally trying to dodge the compliment.

The movement summoned the ghosts back and with them a moment from a warm summer night many years before. Liz and I had gone to a movie. Jesus, I could even remember what it was—*The Glass-Bottom Boat,* with Doris Day and Rod Taylor. Afterward, we were in my mother's Comet, parked at the curb in front of her parents' house. I had my arm around her and we kissed, then drew apart a little. There was a long, tingling moment of hesitation. *Should I kiss her again? Should I touch her breast? Should I put my hand on her thigh?* Instead of doing any of those things, I touched her cheek with the backs of my fingers.

"I love you," I said.

It was the first time I'd ever said that to anyone outside my family.

She'd given the same little duck of her head then, moving her cheek against my hand. She'd said the same thing too.

"I think that's enough for now," I said.

I got up and came around the desk. I held out my hand to help her out of the chair and she took it. It was the first time my hand had touched her flesh in—what? More than a quarter of a century? Her skin felt warm.

"I'll do my best," I promised her.

"I know you will, Hank." Her fingers squeezed mine, and there was an extra moment before our hands let go of each other.

The boys were chasing each other through the maze they'd constructed in the backyard. They seemed to be having a good time.

"OK, kids," I called out. "It's time for Tommy and Liz to go."

They stopped in their tracks and turned toward us. Tommy's face, which had been grinning with the game, went vacant. Harry's went livid.

"It's not fair!" he complained. "We just *started!*"

"Oh, come on now. You've been playing for—" I stopped. Arguing with him was a mistake I still made too often.

"Raking!" he protested. "Not *playing!* We just started playing right now."

"Cut it out, Harry," I snapped, giving him the look that meant business between us.

Liz took the cue. "Come on, Tommy," she said. "We've got things to do."

Tommy shrugged and shuffled off toward the front of the house. He was careful, though, to step over the neatly raked rows of leaves. The rest of us followed in his wake. Harry was scowling at me, weighing whether to resume his protest. He was a sharp kid, however, and he realized it wouldn't do any good. He had lost the battle, and he knew how to accept defeat.

"So long, Tommy," he called out.

"So long, kid," Tommy answered, climbing in the back of the Sable and promptly disappearing from view. I was a detective, so I deduced that he liked to ride lying down on the backseat. I used to ride that way myself when I was a kid. Of course, it was illegal now. It wasn't safe.

I thought about saying something to Liz about that but decided not to. It was probably a bone of contention between them, and it wasn't my business anyway.

"I'll call you as soon as I have something to report," I said, walking Liz to the car.

"Good-bye, Hank," she said, stopping on the curb and reaching out to shake my hand. "Thanks."

I took her hand in mine. It still felt warm.

We walked into the street and I opened the door for her.

"Call anytime," Liz said.

"I will."

I stood on the curb and watched the Sable pull away. Liz pulled out while there was no traffic on Maple Street. When they pulled up at the stoplight, she must have made Tommy put on his seat belt.

The light changed to green and the Sable turned left on Menard. I watched till it disappeared.

Elizabeth Kermanski was back.

Sort of.

And exactly how did I feel about that?

Years ago, I'd converted the front of my living room into my office. The back of the living room is hardly even big enough to be called a den, but it's dominated by what the Best Buys call a home entertainment center. This consists of a 37-inch TV that I watch mostly during slow evenings and the football season, a VCR/DVD player, a cassette deck, a CD player, an AM/FM radio, and two freestanding speakers. All that, plus an amplifier with more knobs, buttons, and levers than I still know what to do with.

When I'm doing paperwork in the office, I usually open the door to the living room, put the CD player on the shuffle, and jack up the volume. Most of my CDs are converted recordings from the sixties and seventies. I think it was Abbie Hoffman who said that each of us has the sound track of his own movie. Well, this was mine. Every cut on every album does something for me. Mostly, it summons up a time or place, and a whiff of what was then.

When I went back to work that afternoon, however, I turned on the TV. Then I gave Harry an apple and set him in front of it. That combination of exercise, food, and television calmed him enough for me to get back to my billing.

I still didn't get much done, though. The ghosts that still lurked in my office were nagging distractions—phantoms that danced at the edge of my vision, half-glimpsed out of the corner of an eye.

By then, it was too late to get the bills in the mail anyway.

To the three of us," I said, lifting a mug of beer. "The three musketeers!"

"Liz is a girl," Jack objected. "She can't be a musketeer."

"Male chauvinist pig," Liz complained, slapping him playfully on the shoulder.

"Besides, I'm no musketeer, either," Jack said. "I see myself as Scaramouche."

"Who's Scaramouche?" she asked.

" 'He was born with the gift of laughter,' " Jack quoted grandly. " 'And a sense that the world was mad.' "

"And me?" I asked. "Who am I?"

He grinned.

"You're Captain Ahab," he responded. "You're always searching for something, and when you latch onto it, you don't let go."

"That's not the way I see Hank at all," Liz protested. "He's more like some tormented priest. Who's a character like that?"

"Friar Tuck," I suggested, taking a Tuck-like swig of beer.

"More like the whiskey priest in The Power and the Glory," Jack said. "The priest with no name."

"And you?" I asked Liz. "Who are you?"

"That's easy," she said. "I'm Roxanne. From Cyrano de Bergerac."

5

OLD FRIENDS

—Simon and Garfunkel

For supper that night, I fixed Harry his favorite meal (macaroni and cheese, made with skim milk and mixed with canned tomatoes) and made myself a *sandwich jambon* with a baguette I'd picked up that afternoon at a bakery downtown. After we ate, I washed up, read Harry a story, waited outside the bathroom while he brushed his teeth, and then put him to bed, pulling the green-and-gold blanket with the big Packer logo on it up to his chin.

"I just love my boy," I told him, giving him a big hug.

"And I just love my *daddy*," he responded, flinging his skinny arms around my neck and holding on tight. I put up with it for a while before struggling free.

Going downstairs, I got a can of Point Special out of the refrigerator. It's brewed just down Interstate 39 in Stevens Point and I'd developed a taste for it during my senior year in high school. Wisconsin was an 18-for-beer state in those days, and my favorite beer bar had Point on tap. I'd missed it in Canada, and being able to get it again was one of the pleasures of coming back home in 1975. I popped the can and carried it to the living room, where I sat down on the sofa to await the inevitable.

"Daddy, I'm *thirrrsty!*

"Daddy, something's in the closet!

"Daddy, there's a bug in my bed!

The cries came about five minutes apart, like labor pains. Each time, I responded with a trip to Harry's room. It was the smallest of the three bedrooms on the second floor, the same one that I had when I was his age.

Did my own father make the same trek? Or didn't fathers do that kind of thing in those days? I don't remember my father tucking me in. In fact, I'm not sure if I remember him at all. I only have an impression of a face, of hard hands, and of the smell of cigar smoke. I can't even be sure if any of that is a real memory. Or is it just an impression I got out of old photographs, dreams, and subconscious longings?

The first couple of trips upstairs, I provided whatever reassurances Harry seemed to need. Then, when ten minutes had passed without a summons from above, I'd make the trip one more time, just to be sure. On this night, Harry was lying on his back. His arms and legs were flung this way and that in a wild asymmetry, like the limbs of a rag doll tossed on the bed. He was snoring—an endearing little sound, like the barking of a puppy.

A wave of sentimental tenderness washed over me. I pulled up the covers, then turned off the closet light that had been left on to assure him that no monster was lurking there, and went back downstairs.

On the way to the living room, I stopped off in the kitchen to grab another Point Special from the fridge. I thought about calling Rachel but decided against it. If I talked to her that night, I'd either have to *say* something about Liz hiring me or *avoid* saying something about it. I wouldn't feel comfortable either way.

I parked myself on the sofa, with the beer on an end table within easy reach, and tried to concentrate on my new case.

Most investigations boil down to one simple—but not necessarily easy—question. In this case, *Who killed Jack Drucker?* The way I usually approach an investigation is to break the big question down into a series of smaller questions that are easier to answer. A number of those smaller questions were already floating around in my mind. *What was Jack working on when he died? Who called the Drucker home that night? Did that call lure Jack to his death? What was "funny" about the handle of the gun?*

The trouble was that I kept being distracted by very different questions. Questions that had nothing to do with the murder. Questions like, *Why had she never called me even once in the decades I'd been back from Canada? Why hadn't Jack? Why hadn't I ever called* them?

There were other questions, too. Questions like, *Does she still have that sprinkling of freckles on her back? Does she still stutter when she gets sexually excited?*

When the Point Special can was empty, I went to the kitchen and got another one. I brought it back to the living room and stretched myself out on the sofa.

I realized, even then, that this investigation was likely to lead me deeper into the past than I really wanted to go. Liz's visit had stirred a trunkful of memories that I hadn't taken out and looked at for a long time. They kept teasing at my mind like those old songs that get in your head and won't go out again. Golden oldies. Blasts from the past. There was no point in fighting them, so I just drank my beer and let them come.

The three of us, Liz and Jack and I, all went back a long way. Jack and I met first. It happened in a city park one autumn day when we were ten years old. I was getting beaten up by a gang of seventh graders at the time. Bigger kids often took an instant dislike to me. I was an overweight, chunky kid whose insecurities took the form of cockiness. Bullies didn't see what I had to be cocky about, and it irritated the hell out of them.

On that day, Jack, who was fearless even then, weighed into the fight on my side. Of course, that meant that the bullies, who were at least two years older than we were, beat him up, too. But that wasn't important. What *was* important was that Jack and I became friends.

Before long, we were *best* friends, and we stayed that way all through high school.

It was an unlikely friendship. Jack was a popular kid, while I had trouble making friends. He was tall and athletic, while I was relatively short and stocky. Jack lived in a big house up on The Hill, where the town's old money hung out. I lived on Maple Street, in the same 1920s two-story that I live and work in today.

Jack's father was rich and powerful by Pinery Falls standards. Wesley Drucker was a one-man show—the owner, publisher, *and* editor of the *Pinery Falls Torrent*. My own father was already dead by the time I met Jack. He'd been an over-the-road truck driver before a heart attack killed him when he was thirty-six and I was five. He'd been a Teamster, so my mother got a decent pension (thank you, Dave Beck), and, once I was old enough to take care of myself after school, she worked as a secretary, so we did all right. But we lived in a different world from the Druckers.

Not surprisingly, being so different in background and personality, Jack and I disagreed about a lot of things, but we were the kind of friends whose arguments built bonds instead of walls. We honed our developing intellects on each other. He taught me to play poker, and I taught him chess. He introduced me to Dave Brubeck and Miles Davis, while I introduced him to Bob Dylan and Joan Baez. He was obsessed with London and Hemingway; I was enthralled by J. D. Salinger and, later, by Tolstoy and Dostoyevsky. We pressed our enthusiasms on each other without much success. But that didn't matter. We enlarged each other's worlds.

We talked endlessly about our dreams for the future. Of course, we didn't think of them as *dreams,* we thought of them as *plans.* Jack's stayed pretty constant. He was going to become a writer-adventurer. Mine were more protean. At different times, I thought I'd be a priest, a social worker, and a Supreme Court justice. Then, sometime late in high school, I realized that I didn't know what the hell I wanted to be or if I had the ambition to be anything at all.

Dreams weren't all we shared. For a time, we even shared a father—in my mind, at least. Having no father of my own, I took Jack's as a kind of surrogate. Maybe that was inevitable. Jack was the closet thing I had to a brother, so there was a logic in adopting his father as my own.

Wesley Drucker was still a relatively young man in those days, but he was already a defiant anachronism. He was an old-fashioned, fiercely independent newspaperman—a colorful and dying breed, even then. He smoked big cigars that were rumored to be real Cubans in a virulently anti-Castro age. His hair was prematurely white, and he wore white suits to match it long before Tom Wolfe made a New York fashion out of them. Strolling majestically through the downtown streets of Pinery Falls, he had the air of a misplaced time traveler, an antebellum plantation owner somehow transported to twentieth-century Wisconsin. A lot of people thought he was an oddball, but nobody mocked him. Not to his face. In a town the size of Pinery Falls, the power of the press could be very real. And very personal.

Looking back on it, Wesley Drucker was an odd choice for a father. Even for a fantasy one. From the time I spent in Jack's home, I knew firsthand that Wes could be a distant, forbidding, and sometimes even terrifying presence. Jack was always a little afraid of him and so was I. But, having no other model, I assumed that fathers were *supposed* to inspire fear in their children. Now, having a son of my own, I can't imagine wanting him to be afraid of me.

I never told anyone that I'd adopted Jack's father, not even Jack, and certainly not the old man himself.

Among the many differences between Jack's background and mine was religion. My family was Catholic, and my mother raised me to be a believer. Wesley Drucker, on the other hand, was an evangelical atheist of the kind that turns disbelief into the most dogmatic possible kind of faith. According to Jack, Wesley referred me as "the bead pusher." If Jack's mother had any religious views, Jack never learned what they were.

Even if we had lived in the same neighborhood, we would have gone to different grade schools. I went to St. Mary's Catholic and Jack went to La Follette Elementary. After seventh grade, I moved up to Holy Name Junior High. It was there that I went through a brief but intense wanting-to-be-a-priest stage.

For a while, I thought I had a real vocation. Looking back on it, I think that what attracted me was the *mystery* of it. I had a Catholic kid's consciousness of sin and grace, and the thought of spending my life wrestling with supernatural forces was seductive. In ninth grade, however, I had what Father Herbert called a "crisis of faith." In some ways, I suppose, that crisis is still going on.

My mother was having a hard time with the parochial school tuition, and, both half-reluctant and half-relieved, she agreed to let me switch over to the public school system. That was how, in our sophomore year in high school, Jack and I finally got to be classmates.

That was also the year that Liz Kermanski came into our lives.

I found her first.

Miraculously, without any warning and seemingly out of nowhere, she walked into civics class one day in late November and took the only vacant desk in the room—the one right next to mine.

She didn't really come out of nowhere, of course. Her family had just moved to Pinery Falls from Richland Center, a small town in the southern part of the state. There was nothing miraculous about her appearance in that particular classroom, either. Civics was required for sophomores in those days. But, for me, her sudden appearance in the middle of an otherwise ordinary school day was, if not miraculous, at least a little magical.

She was easily the most beautiful girl I'd ever seen, and I do mean *beautiful,* not just "pretty," or "cute," or even "sexy." That I could see the moment she walked into the room. Other things became apparent later. There was a glittering intensity about her that set her apart from all the other girls in my very limited experience. She was bright and friendly and caring—totally without that insistent sense of herself that consumed most of the good-looking girls in the school. A lot of the boys were naturally attracted to her. As for me, I was bewitched.

That first day, I spent the entire class hour watching her. If Mr. Hendricks had called on me, I wouldn't have known what the question was. I might not have known what class I was in.

At the end of the period, she actually turned and spoke to me, which was lucky, because it might have taken me years to get up the nerve to speak to her. She said that her next class was in 215B and she didn't know where that was. I told her it was in the old building and a little tricky to find. I offered to walk her there. She accepted with a gratitude that seemed completely real and unforced. And the rest, as they say, is history.

I fell in love that day in civics class and stayed that way until—well, until *when* exactly? Considering the way my stomach lurched when I saw her getting out of the Sable that afternoon, I wasn't prepared to answer that question.

Incredibly, this remarkable creature had once seemed to find me remarkable, too. I couldn't understand it. No girl ever had before. I didn't even find *myself* remarkable. I'd lost some weight since grade school and developed some muscle, but I was still a kid uncomfortable in his own skin, and a smart-ass to boot. But she saw something in me that she liked. In time, she even said she loved me. We discovered ourselves together, experiencing new emotions for the first time.

Moments, not always the most dramatic or even the most meaningful, came into my mind that night.

—Liz in our U.S. history class, where she sat one seat up and one row over. The sun streams through the classroom window, glinting off the blond sweep of her hair and the golden down on her left forearm.

—Floyd Cramer's "*Last Dance*" coming through the scratchy

speakers at Teen Town. Our bodies tight together, hardly moving on the dimly lit floor. The softness of Liz's body against mine. She feels my erection pressing against her. I'm embarrassed, but she looks up and smiles. I'm flooded with a new sense of myself. I'm an awkward and clumsy dancer, but it doesn't matter. This isn't dancing. This is lovemaking, and I am filled with a sense of awe and privilege that this wondrous being would share this moment with me, would even let everyone see that she and I are together.

—The Comet's windows are coated with our heat. Her tongue is darting against mine. My hand moves under her skirt, between her electric thighs, up and under her panties, straining to explore. Her hand on my hand. *Not now. Please. Not now.* Then, later, her fingers circling me, her mouth accepting me. No girl has ever done this before. *Oh, Liz. Oh, my God, Liz!*

—A warm autumn night in our junior year, in that same Comet, finally going "all the way." The first time for both of us.

—I round the corner on the third-floor corridor of the school. She's waiting there at my locker. She turns and her face lights up when she sees me. Epiphany. At that moment, I know that this is as close as I will ever come to complete and unmitigated happiness.

Of course, this couldn't last.

My secret fear had always been that she and Jack would be drawn together, which finally happened in the summer between our junior and senior years. Until then, despite the fact that the three of us were friends and hung out together, Jack had always maintained a respectful distance from her. That was respectful of me, I think. Of our friendship. He was never one to be particularly respectful of girls.

When it happened, there was nothing sneaky about it. Neither Jack nor Liz was that kind of person. She and I talked it over, sitting on the front porch of the house on Maple Street.

"I love you both," she told me. "I really do. But I love you in different ways."

"What good is that?" I asked.

"Then you *tell* me, Hank," she said. "Just tell me what to do."

"That's not fair. I can't do that. I love you. I can't *not* love you, no matter what."

She shook her head sadly. "It's all so confusing."

Her incredible blue eyes were burning, as if she was in some kind of pain. I watched her with the knowledge that I was losing her forever.

"Can you ever understand, Hank?"

I hoped I could.

I don't know exactly when I went to sleep, but when I woke up, it was two o'clock in the morning. There was an ache in my lower back and a seeming cotton ball in my mouth. Six empty Point Special cans had gathered up on the end table, along with one that was still half-full.

Is this middle age? I wondered idly, and not for the first time. *Or just one more stop on the road to alcoholism?*

Leaving the cans where they were, I headed upstairs for bed. My bedroom—which was originally my parents' and later Sarah's and mine—is at the far end of the upstairs hallway from Harry's. Before going to it, I looked in on him.

There was enough light from the hall to see that he was lying on his stomach, sprawled crosswise across the bed with his feet hanging over the edge. He'd thrown off the Packer blanket, and the top sheet was scrunched under him. As a baby, he'd slept through the night from the time he was a few weeks old, but in the past few years he'd turned into a restless sleeper. I wondered how much the divorce had had to do with that.

I picked up the blanket from the floor, then tugged as gently as I could at the tangled sheet. He stirred as I worked it out from under him, but he didn't wake up. Then I pushed my luck by trying to maneuver his body into a parallel relationship with the bed, so that I could cover him properly.

His little body jerked with surprising violence. A small arm thunked me on the head. I could hardly feel it, but the impact was enough to wake him. His eyes popped open in alarm.

"It's OK," I assured him. "It's me. Just tucking you in."

He shook his head in protest. "No covers, Daddy. I'm too hot."

"OK then," I agreed. "No covers. But scrunch over a little, so you won't fall out of bed."

He flopped around like a fish in the bottom of a boat until he'd reached a satisfactory position.

"Thattaboy," I said, leaning down to kiss him on the cheek. "Night, Harry."

He accepted the kiss but made a face as I straightened up again.

"Peee-you!" he exclaimed, pinching his nose between two fingers. "Your mouth *stinks*."

"Sorry," I told him. "It's jungle breath. I fell asleep downstairs."

"Jungle *beer*," he said. "You smell like jungle *beer*."

"That'll just happen sometimes," I said. "Sleep tight."

"Sleep tight, Daddy," he responded comfortably, rolling over on his side and hugging his pillow.

On the way out of the room, I realized that he hadn't complained about the closet light being off.

I guess the monsters were asleep.

6

YOU CAN'T ALWAYS GET WHAT YOU WANT

—The Rolling Stones

R achel calls me an unlikely detective, and I guess she's right. I'm not particularly big, or tough, or even hard-boiled. During Wisconsin's fanatic hunting season, my sympathies run with the deer, and I've always been more concerned with what's right than what's legal. Besides, I've never been big on authority or felt very comfortable around cops. After all, I spent some of the best years of my life in exile because of Vietnam.

Canada was good to me and I was reasonably happy there, but I'd never really felt at home. I jumped at the chance to come back to the States when the amnesty was declared in 1975. It was a great time to be a political felon in America, and not just for draft resisters, either. Ford had pardoned Nixon just the year before, and even old Spirochete Agnew managed to avoid doing any hard time.

I returned, not just to the States but to Pinery Falls, which seemed ironic to me even then. All the while I was growing up, my hometown had seemed small, provincial, and dull. Nothing exciting ever happened there, much less anything important. I'd always assumed that my *real* life would be lived somewhere else—in New York or Chicago or maybe even someplace foreign and exotic, like London,

Paris, or Tokyo. Then, after being away for a while and forbidden to return, I couldn't wait to get back.

To this day, I'm not sure why I returned to Pinery Falls. My mother died the year before the amnesty was issued (I wasn't able to go to her funeral because the FBI was known to haunt family funerals), and I had no close relatives left in town and no close friends, either. Maybe it was the same thing that made Jack come back after his stint in Vietnam, and then—even after he made a name for himself as a reporter and could have worked for any newspaper in the country—decide to stay.

Maybe it was something in the water.

My mother had left me the house I'd been raised in on Red Maple Street. I put off selling it and had the attorney who handled her will rent it out instead. Then, when I got the chance to come back, I told myself that it was only sensible to live in the place, since I already owned it free and clear. But I could have sold it and lived somewhere else if I'd wanted to.

For whatever reason, I returned home and started looking for a job. I'd worked a few jobs in Canada—driven a delivery truck, manned the counter at a Mac's Milk store, carted boxes at Canadian Tire—but nothing that struck me as a life's work.

I began looking for something that I could both do well and feel good about doing. After a while, I was ready to settle for either half of that.

I answered an ad in the *Torrent* for someone "with a combination of patience, imagination, initiative and stubbornness." When I dialed the number in the ad, a female voice answered, "Hanratty Agency." After she explained what the job was, I almost didn't bother to show up for the interview. But the reality was, I'd run out of other prospects by then and I figured, *What the hell?*

At that time, the Hanratty Agency was almost as small as my operation is now. It consisted entirely of Pat, its only full-time investigator, and his assistant, Hedy Salzmann, who handled the business side of the operation. Pat had been a policeman in Milwaukee for twenty-five years before he took his retirement and set up shop as a private investigator on the edge of the northwoods. At the time he placed that ad in the *Torrent,* the demand for his services was picking up, while Pat, who was already in his late fifties, was beginning to slow down. He decided that what the agency needed was young blood.

I think there were two reasons Pat hired me. The first was his son, Jared. Like most cops, Pat had been a hawk in the early days of the Vietnam War, and he'd passed his enthusiasm along to his son. Then Jared lost an arm over there. When he came home with bitter stories of what was going on in that war and joined the veterans' peace movement in Milwaukee, Pat rethought his position. He must have had some guilt about encouraging Jared to sign up and felt that he was atoning by hiring someone who'd opposed the war all along.

The second reason Pat hired me was my mother. It turned out that he had met her around the time I took off for Canada and the two of them had become friends. A cousin told me that Pat visited her in the hospital on the day she died. During the years I worked for him, I often wondered what *kind* of friends they'd been, but I never asked. The more I thought about it, the less I wanted to know.

Pat took an immediate and partly sentimental liking to me. He suggested that I help him out for a year or two. He'd pay me a fair salary and teach me the ropes while he eased himself into retirement. After that, I'd be on my own.

I had my doubts, both about whether I'd like the job and whether I'd be any good at it. Like a lot of my generation, my notion of private detectives came mostly from Mickey Spillane novels and old *film noirs*, and I didn't fit that mold at all. Even so, Pat assured me that I'd be fine in the job, and it turned out he was right.

I quickly learned that muscle is a highly overrated quality in a private investigator. It turned out that I have other, less tangible attributes. They include a knack for spotting when people are lying to me.

I'm pretty good at figuring out why they're lying, too. Pat says that that second talent is much rarer than the first.

Temperamentally, I was surprisingly well suited to the detective trade. I could plod with the best of them, and, because I was used to being alone, I didn't mind the long surveillances that drive most investigators crazy. On any given day, the work could be boring as hell, but I liked the variety and relative freedom of it. Each job was different. The romantic in me enjoyed the possibility of danger, while the rest of me was glad that the possibility was usually remote.

I didn't always feel good about what I did, but I didn't feel too bad about it, either. Most of the thieves and philanderers I nailed deserved nailing, and even those who probably didn't had dug their own holes. The Hanratty Agency did a lot of work for defense lawyers, so I occasionally got the satisfaction of seeing the evidence I collected prove some poor bastard's innocence.

Through it all, Pat was a mentor as well as a boss. He taught me the business and gave me as much experience as I could handle. Eventually we became friends.

Things worked out pretty much the way Pat predicted, although a little later than he'd planned. By the time he finally called it quits in the late eighties, the agency had four full-time investigators, including Pat and me, as well as a couple of part-timers we called on when needed. Pat offered to sell me the company on generous terms, but I didn't see myself as an employer, so I decided to set up on my own. Pat sold out to the On Guard Detective Agency, while I converted part of my living room into an office and (literally) hung out my shingle in the front yard.

In the meantime, I more or less stumbled into marriage. Then, a few years later, I stumbled out again. One of those philanderers I'd nailed had been married to a woman named Sarah, and the evidence I collected made it possible for her to divorce him. She was attractive, smart, and wounded—an irresistible combination for me at the time. I waited till the divorce was final and then asked her for a date. About a year later, we were married.

Sarah and I liked each other and maybe even loved each other. I thought so, anyway. But neither of us seemed to want what the other one had to give. Being a true son of the seventies, I was happy for my wife's success. I didn't want her to work, or even expect her to, but it didn't bother me when she did. The fact that she pulled in more money than I did was fine by me, too. It meant that we could take longer vacations in places that were warmer and farther away. But, being a true daughter of the seventies, she resented her success as much as I enjoyed it. Not the *fact* of it, just the utility.

The truth was that Sarah loved her job and everything about it. She loved working twice as hard as anybody else—and twice as well, too—and she positively devoured the appreciation she got for it. But she hadn't been raised to be the primary breadwinner, and she didn't like the role. On the other hand, she didn't want to live solely on my earnings either. What she would have liked most was doing exactly what she was doing but just as a hobby. Doing it for real spoiled the fun.

For me, the divorce was tinged with resignation. I was a Wisconsin-German Catholic, who'd once thought about being a priest. Even when I'd abandoned the Church, it never really abandoned me. Somewhere, deep down, I felt that I deserved the destruction of my marriage. I'd married a divorced woman.

I would have settled for a separation, but Sarah insisted on the legal finalities. No Catholic, Sarah. Not then, anyway. There would be no door left open for redemption with her.

After the divorce, I settled into my life as a small-town private investigator sliding easily into middle age. I can't say that I didn't have regrets—both about the breakup with Sarah and, most of all, about being so separated from Harry—but I came to terms with them. I can't say whether I was happy either, but I was more comfortable than I'd ever expected to be.

At least until that day I looked out the window and saw Elizabeth Drucker getting out of that Sable.

7

KIND OF A DRAG

—The Buckinghams

Thursday morning, I gave Harry some muesli softened with skim milk, and with a sliced banana and extra raisins thrown into the bowl. He gets no bacon and eggs at my house. I don't want my kid's arteries plugged up before their time. With his mother working for a cheese company it's a real struggle, but I do what I can.

Breakfast is not a habit with me, but that day I had some of the muesli to keep him company. It tasted surprisingly good. After breakfast, I dumped the dishes in the sink and got Harry ready for school. Mostly, I made sure he had his book bag—stuffed full and weighing a ton—along with him. He'd forgotten it the day before and, halfway there, we had to turn around to come back and get it. I think his forgetfulness was deliberate. Anything to avoid the terrible moment when he'd be confined to school.

First grade was still new to him and he wasn't sure how he felt about it. His teacher, Mrs. Hartwell, was "nice," but some of the kids were "mean." Meanest of all, he told me, was a hulking bully he knew only as "Rocky."

We climbed into my old red Sentra and set off for school. When people ask me why I have that car, I point out that an aging econocar doesn't draw a lot of attention to itself, which makes it handy for surveillance. It also costs relatively little to run.

Pinery Falls is built on the shores of the Wisconsin River. To get from the east side of the river, where I live, to the west side, where Sarah lives and Harry goes to school, you have to take one of the town's three bridges. That morning, we took the Chester Street Bridge, which is the southernmost of the three and also the shortest. It spans the river about a quarter of a mile below Tobacco Island. Just as we reached the other side of the river, I realized I'd forgotten to make Harry brush his teeth. There was no time to go back and have him do it now. I racked this up as yet another failure of my parental instincts.

Harry spent the ride slumped forward in the backseat, scowling at the expensive sneakers that his mother had bought him for the school year. I sensed a real tension behind his grimness. I couldn't tell whether it stemmed from the fear of Rocky or the fear of growing up. About halfway to the school, Harry straightened up as though energized by a new and exciting idea.

"Why don't I *not* go to school today?" he suggested brightly— almost as brightly as if he believed I'd take him up on his suggestion.

"It's a school day, Harry," I told him. "You have to go to school on school days."

"But it's the *morning*," he protested. "I don't want to go to school in the *morning*. Afternoons are OK, but I like being *home* in the morning."

Aha, I thought. It's fear of growing up after all. Last year, Harry had gone to half-day kindergarten, which was only held in the afternoon.

Even so, what he'd said gave me an absurd little glow. He'd referred to my house on Red Maple Street as "home." Harry kept surprising me with feelings I didn't expect. Unfortunately, that glow didn't change my role in my son's life, which is that of a perpetual spoilsport.

"You have to go to school," I told him as we pulled up in front of the school building. "It's your *job*. I've got my job, and this is yours."

He frowned but mulled it over.

"OK, Dad," he finally agreed, leaning over for a parting hug before climbing out of the car. I wondered how long it would be before he got too old for hugging his father.

I watched him trudge manfully across the schoolyard, book bag over his shoulder, heading toward a gaggle of classmates near the main doors. I tried to spot the behemoth known as Rocky, but they all looked normal sized to me.

Harry never looked back.

"Thattaboy," I encouraged him, speaking out loud, even though he couldn't hear me. "Go get 'em."

As he neared the group, a tiny girl with curly brown hair turned away from the crowd to greet him.

He broke into a run to join her.

I checked my watch. It was 7:55 a.m. and Harry would be in school until 2:50 p.m. That left me almost seven full hours to get to work.

8

HIGH FLYING BIRD

—Judy Henske

I knew exactly where Jack had died because I'd gone out to Little River Road that morning, as soon as I heard about his death. His body was already gone by the time I got there, but the Stingray was still parked on the grassy shoulder by the riverbank. Cops, news crews, and gawkers were swarming all over the place, so I didn't stop. It wasn't my case back then, and I had no morbid interest in the details of Jack's death—so why did I even go out there? To revisit something? To salute a lost friend? Who knows?

But this time was different. This time, I had business there.

I parked the Sentra as close as I could get to the place I remembered the Stingray had been. I figured that the driver's seat in the Sentra was a little higher than the one in the Stingray, so I slumped down. I had to suppress an atavistic twitch at the thought that my head was probably right where Jack's had been when the bullet slammed into it. From that position, I twisted my head right, then left, to test Jack's range of vision that night.

I drove the Sentra forward about thirty feet, then walked back. The day was bright and cool. The trees topping the hill above the river were ripe with autumn colors. Sunlight glistened on the rippling surface of the water, and the breeze that blew along the river was crisp and clean. It was one of those late fall days that make you glad you live in Wisconsin and wonder why anybody would want to live anywhere else.

The Wisconsin River is an enormous beast slithering down the center of the state before twisting west to join the Mississippi. The beast is tamed by a series of dams spaced out along its length, two of which span the river on either side of the southern tip of Tobacco Island, smack in the middle of Pinery Falls and about two miles downriver from the murder site. The dams regulate the flow of water over the twin falls after which the town was named. On that morning, both dams were open and the river was running fast and low. On the night of the murder, they had been closed. The river here must been silent and still.

The shoulder of the road I was standing on was wide enough to accommodate an SUV. From its edge, the riverbank dropped steeply down to the water about eight feet below. On the night of the murder, the water would have been higher, coming to within two or three feet of the shoulder. There was no barrier.

I got down on my hands and knees and crawled in expanding circles until I'd covered roughly twenty-five feet in every direction, including the slope of the riverbank.

It was useless, of course. An army of cops, forensic scientists, reporters, and curiosity seekers had been here before me. Anything I found was more likely to be their spoor than the killer's. Not that it mattered, since I didn't find anything at all.

As I got stiffly to my feet—my knees both cold and sore, and my abused joints reminding me that I was getting too old to be crawling around the ground—my eye was caught by a movement in the sky out over the river. I looked up to see Herman, which is my name for the solitary bald eagle who nests year-round somewhere in the vicinity of Pinery Falls. He's an extraordinarily large and beautiful bird I see every now and then, either patrolling the river or gliding over the town like a blessing. Just once, I saw him swoop down and take a fish out of the water. It made me forget to breathe.

Herman didn't seem to be fishing at the moment, just flying blithely northward, out for an eagle's version of a morning stroll. I watched him until he was out of sight, then climbed in the Sentra and drove it back to the murder spot. Getting out, I leaned down to the driver's side window. Was this where the killer had stood, or had the shot come from farther away? The news stories had implied that Jack had been shot from close range, but I'd learned from experience that news stories were often misleading.

Besides, how close was close?

The road was level, but just beyond the far shoulder, the land climbed steeply, rising to a wooded crest beyond which (unseen from here) was the old highway. Three large houses were visible from where I stood, each one set high on the hillside in the middle of a large, well-manicured lawn. They sat about two hundred feet from the road and were separated from each other by roughly the same distance. Each house was a different color and built to a different design, but there was an overarching sameness about them. They were all two-story one-family homes, equally expensive and equally unoriginal, and each was flanked by a two-car garage. They had obviously been built by the same builder and at the same time.

I crossed the road and scrambled partway up the lawn directly across from the car. About twenty feet above the Sentra, I sat on the steep slope and aimed my right forefinger at the driver's side window of the car. If it had been a gun and I had fired it from that angle, I might have hit the driver in the groin but never in the head. Not without putting a hole in the roof.

That didn't prove anything. Jack could have been sitting in some unlikely position. His head might have been sticking partway out the window, for all I knew. But if he was sitting normally, it was unlikely that the shot came from very far away. It had certainly not come from any of the houses on the hill. The angle was far too steep.

The ground was cold with morning dew, but I sat there for a while contemplating the scene from this new perspective. Whyever Jack had parked his car just there, it hadn't been to hide it. There was nothing along this whole stretch of road that would conceal a car from the view of anyone, either in the houses up above or along the road itself.

Nothing that would conceal a killer, either.

I could think of just three reasons Jack might have been out here that night. One, he was here to meet somebody, possibly summoned by the phone call whose ring Liz had heard. Two, he was on his way somewhere else but had stopped here. (Because he'd seen something? A stranded motorist? Something—or someone—lying by the side of the road?) Or three, he was surveilling somebody.

All at once another possibility came to mind. Could he have been parked out here with a woman? Middle-aged crazy, trying to prove he still could. I tentatively rejected that possibility. There were plenty of better places to park if car sex turned him on. But still—

A new question sprang to mind. *What was the* killer *doing out here?* Jack wasn't the only one who needed a reason to be on Little River Road in the middle of the night. The killer did too. Was Jack here because the killer was? Or was the killer here because of Jack? Or were they both here for some other reason entirely?

If so, could it have been the *same* reason? Was it possible that they came to this isolated spot, at that unlikely time of night, for two completely unrelated reasons? If so, how did that *coincidence* lead to murder?

And where had the killer come *from* anyway? Had he been waiting there beside the road, knowing that Jack was on his way? Had Jack driven the killer to this spot himself? Had the killer come in his own car? Had he come from one of the houses across the road? Or could he have come by boat on the river?

Another thought suddenly occurred to me. Was the killer alone? How many people were out here that night?

From my perch on the hill, I could see nothing that suggested an answer to any of these questions. That didn't bother me much. Not yet. As Pat Hanratty used to say, "At the beginning, a question is better than an answer. An answer might be wrong."

I got to my feet, stretched the kinks out, then climbed up the hillside to the southernmost of the three houses. Like its neighbors, it had two visible doors, one at the head of a little walkway at the front and the other within the open two-car garage at the side. That was probably the one the inhabitants usually used.

The welcome mat at the foot of the door had a smiley face and the words "The Holzmanns" imprinted on it. When I pushed the button beside the door, the muffled buzz was overwhelmed by a frantic barking that sounded like it came from a midsize dog confined to a room somewhere inside. Although I didn't see how anyone inside the house could have missed that racket, I waited till the barking died down and rang again. Still no human response.

The middle house didn't even have a dog.

The woman who came to the door at the last house reminded me of somebody's grandmother back in the days when grandmothers were a lot older than you were. She was a small woman, both short and trim. Her snow-white hair was thinning, but it was perfectly set in a fluffy style, and her slightly heavy makeup looked freshly applied. She could have been dressed for an outing, and she had that carefully turned-out look that older women of a certain class always seem to have.

She opened the inner door but left the screen door latched.

"Yes?" she asked, peering out at me uncertainly.

I didn't blame her for her caution. Knowing I was going to be scrabbling around on the ground that morning, I'd dressed in old jeans and a ratty camouflage jacket, and I must have looked pretty scruffy.

I held up my PI license and explained that I was investigating a crime in the neighborhood.

"That awful murder, you mean?" Hearing herself, she smiled self-consciously. "We always say that, don't we? That *awful* murder—as if there were any other kind."

Oddly enough, she seemed relieved to hear my business. She unlatched the screen door and pulled it open, ushering me inside.

"Please come in," she invited. "I'm Rebecca Schneider."

"Hank Berlin."

We shook hands. Her fingers were bent and twiglike, but her grip was surprisingly strong.

"I wondered about you," she admitted with an apologetic smile. "I noticed you out my front window, and your behavior did seem a bit . . . unusual."

I pictured myself as I must have looked from up here: a strange man, crawling around in circles like some demented dog chasing its tail.

Now that my "unusual" behavior had been accounted for, however, she was glad of the company. She welcomed me into a bright and spotless living room. Most of one wall was taken up by a large window that overlooked the river and the murder site.

"Please sit down," she offered, gesturing toward a sofa that was as white and immaculate as her hair.

"Thank you," I said.

"Would you like some tea?" she asked. *Tea.* This was too good to be true.

"No thanks," I said.

"Of course not," she said. "I should have known that you weren't a tea person. Coffee, then?"

"Nothing, really," I said.

"I'll bet you're a beer man, aren't you? Like my late husband." She beamed at me. "I've got some McKewan's Scotch Ale in the fridge. It's eight percent alcohol," she added astonishingly.

I looked at my watch. It was 9:15 a.m.

"That's really tempting," I said. "But I'd better not."

She seated herself in an easy chair facing the sofa.

"So, how may I help you?"

"The murder took place sometime after midnight, two weeks ago early Friday morning. Were you home that night?"

"Oh yes," she said. "I don't remember the last time I was away for the night," she added.

"Does anyone else live here with you?"

"No," she said, smiling ruefully. "My husband Ralph passed away several years ago. I've lived alone ever since."

"I'm sorry," I said. "Did you know Jack Drucker—the man who was killed?"

She shook her head. "No, I never met the man. Of course, I'd seen his work in the *Torrent*."

"Well, did you happen to notice a strange car parked down on the road that night?"

She shook her head again. "No. No one ever parks down there. Not unless someone is having a party and their driveway is full. Of course, if they did, I wouldn't know. I keep the shades down at night."

"And there was no party in the neighborhood that night?"

"I don't believe so."

"Were you still awake when it happened?"

"Oh no. I'm an early-to-bed-early-to-riser myself."

"So you didn't see or hear anything unusual that whole night?"

The media reported that the police had questioned the residents of Little River Road and that no one had seen anything suspicious, but the police sometimes reserve things. More often than not, in fact.

"I did, actually," she replied brightly.

"Oh?"

"But, it's probably nothing to do with your investigation," she warned.

"You never know," I said. "Tell me about it."

"Well . . ." She resettled herself on her chair and launched into her story, innocently pleased to have a tale to tell. "As I said, I usually go to sleep quite early, but I have a somewhat weak bladder and I often wake up in the middle of the night. I did so that Thursday, a little after midnight. When I entered the bathroom, I saw headlights out in the Masons' drive."

"The Masons?"

"Anthony Mason and his wife, Helen. He's an attorney, and quite prominent locally, I believe. Well, their driveway has a curve in it. When they drive up at night, the headlights sweep my bathroom window. It's quite unusual for anyone in this neighborhood to have visitors that late out here. People often *leave* that late, but they rarely arrive. My curiosity was aroused. I'm afraid that I pulled back the shade and peeked out to see who was there."

"Why afraid?" I asked. "You have a perfect right to look out your own window."

"Of course," she agreed, "but I felt like an old snoop."

I smiled.

"Did you recognize the Masons' visitor?"

She shook her head. "I did *see* him, though. The Masons have an outside security light. One of those that go on whenever a car drives up. He was very young. A teenager, I should think. He looked scarcely old enough to drive."

"What kind of a car was it?" I asked.

She gave a helpless shrug. "I'm afraid I don't know much about cars. It was a dark color, though. Dark blue or green, I suspect. And it had four doors."

"Did you tell the police about this?"

"Of course. But I don't think they were very interested."

"Oh? Why not?"

"Because of the time, I imagine. This was well before they say that the poor man who was killed even got there."

"When the boy arrived," I agreed. "But what time did he leave?"

"Almost immediately," she said. "At least I think so. After I finished my business, I went back to bed. It didn't take me long to drift off again, but before that I heard a car start up and drive away. But surely the police checked into that. They seemed to feel that there was no connection."

Leaving Mrs. Schneider and walking down the hill to my car, I remembered something.

I had been on this hillside before.

And so had Jack.

It hadn't come back to me earlier because we had been so young in those days and the landscape was so different now. The entire hillside had been woodland in those days, accessible only by boat from the river or on foot from the highway above the hill. It wasn't until years later that the road had been put in along the riverbank and the hillside above it cleared for development. I realized that the houses that currently dominated the hillside had been built while I was in Canada.

It was a hot and sticky afternoon in that magical summer between junior and senior high school, when tomorrow was a wrapped present and the future was infinite with possibilities. Biking out on Highway 51 (the bypass hadn't been put in yet), Jack and I stopped on the crest of that hill. Our legs were tired and the woods looked invitingly cool, so we hid our bikes in the brush and made our way into the forest on foot.

Muffled by the thick foliage, the sounds of the cars passing on the highway soon became no more than a distant and intermittent shushing. We hadn't gone far before we lost contact with civilization altogether.

The farther we went down the hillside, the closer the forest enveloped us, trees and underbrush, birds and scurrying things, and, down below, the ancient river making its way south. The hot sun made bright patterns in the shadows; the heavily shaded earth smelled damp and rich. This place had its own reality, at once protective and threatening, exciting and mysterious.

Giving ourselves over to this primal modality, we imagined ourselves Indian braves of the Tobacco tribe of the Huron Confederation—the first known inhabitants of the island that, two centuries after the Tobaccos disappeared, would be the site of the settlement that became Pinery Falls. The

Tabacs, as they were known to the voyageurs who roamed French Louisiana in search of furs, were a hard-luck band. Driven out of their native Huronia by the Iroquois in 1649, they had wandered vaguely westward for more than a decade, meeting hostility everywhere they went.

Roughly two thousand of them traveled over the Great Lakes, down the Mississippi River, then north up the Wisconsin. Eventually, they came to the twin cataracts after which Pinery Falls is now named. The island just north of the falls must have seemed like paradise to them. The waters that danced around it ran with fish, and the great forests that extended in all directions teemed with a rich variety of game, from squirrels to moose. Best of all, for this neighbor-ridden tribe, the island was uninhabited and there were no villages within many days' walk.

The Tabacs decided that this, at last, was home. They built their longhouses on the island, counting on the great moat of the river to protect them. They finished the longhouses just in time for the tribe to be decimated by the cruelest winter in Wisconsin history. Five hundred of them either starved or were frozen to death in their lodges that winter. Toward the end, those who remained stayed alive by eating the bark off trees.

Having survived a thousand-mile gauntlet of human enemies, the Tabacs got destroyed by nature.

Jack and I knew all this because we'd been told the story of the doomed Tabacs by a cheerful old lady with dyed hair and loose dentures on a school trip to the Wautauqua County Historical Society the previous spring.

The braves Jack and I had become, however, had no knowledge of the tragic future.

We were young hunters, stalking the hillside for worthy game, and we scored many kills that day. After a while, we started climbing the hill toward the place we had left our bikes, but we weren't ready to leave the woods just yet. About halfway up, the Tabacs in us spotted signs of other human beings. Not Indians like ourselves, but white-eyes, and not friendly voyageurs looking to trade in furs, but the new breed of white men who called themselves settlers. These were greedy, treacherous creatures, with spirits as tight as the coin purses they carried. They chopped down our trees to build their villages, and they stole our land to grow their crops.

Jack and I shared a single thought. We'd had enough of hunting game. We would become warriors today.

We had the advantage over the white-eyes because we had their trail. If we tracked them up and down the hillside, it was inevitable that we would find them before they found us. And so we did.

We imagined them a large party of at least twenty men, well armed with both pistols and long guns, while we had only bows and arrows. What did it matter? Superior weapons would be useless against enemies they could not see.

We used the trees for cover. Darting swiftly between them, we managed to pick off many of the white-eyes before the rest even realized what was happening to them. It was great sport. Much more fun than felling deer or elk or even bear.

Even when the white-eyes realized they were under attack, they still had no idea where the arrows were coming from. They began firing their guns at shadows. Their bullets spit harmlessly through the trees.

Courting danger, Jack let out a war whoop. Then another. I joined him, and soon we filled the forest with our cries.

The white-eyes turned their guns in the direction the sounds were coming from. A bullet sang past my ear and slammed into the trunk of a nearby tree.

Jack and I looked at each other and grinned.

Like the Indian braves we imagined ourselves to be, we stood on the brink of young manhood that day on that hillside. Like them, we had no fear.

Our childhood was over.

Our real lives were about to begin.

Yelping with delight and filled with a wild exhilaration, we turned and ran. We took to the forest as eagles take to the air—

Part Two

Taking Care of Business

—BACHMAN TURNER OVERDRIVE

9

I CAN'T GET NO
SATISFACTION

—The Rolling Stones

On the way to the newspaper office, I stopped off at the cop shop on Splinter Street. I was hoping to check with George Carlson, the captain who's next in line to the chief and who rates an office with a door. When I got there, it was closed. Not wanting to start things off on a bad note, I knocked.

"Come in," he growled—which was his way of warning whoever it was not to waste his time. When I entered, Carlson was going through the contents of several files that were scattered across his desk. He looked up, frowning. He frowned even harder when he saw it was me. "Yeah?" he asked.

Knowing that Carlson didn't go for chitchat, I got right to the point. I told him I'd been hired to investigate the Drucker case.

His frown turned thoughtful. "You got anything for me?"

"I'm just getting started. I was hoping you might fill me in. I'd particularly like to know—"

"I'm not paid to help with your job," he interrupted. "I'm paid to do mine." He picked up some papers from his desk. "If there's nothing else, I'm busy here."

This was vintage Carlson. I shrugged and turned to leave.

"Hank." He spoke just as I was about to close the door behind me. When I looked back, his attention still seemed to be on the papers.

"When you've got something, I might be willing to share a little," he said, without looking up.

Walking back to my car, I decided his last remark had been a confession of sorts. His earlier rebuff hadn't been a surprise. If he wouldn't talk to the widow, why should he talk to her hired help? Besides, as I've already mentioned, Carlson is a hard-ass. My visit had been mostly a discourtesy call, anyway, just to let him know I was around and interested. For real information, I had another source in the department, one I wasn't about to tap when Carlson was around.

Being a detective in a town like Pinery Falls is different from in a big city, especially if you grew up there. You know a bigger segment of the population, for one thing. Particularly those in your own age group. You went to high school with most of them, and that means you know them in a way you never get to know most of the people you meet later in life. For me, this was true of two members of the Pinery Falls Police Department. One was Carlson and the other was a uniform named Augie Bendorf.

It was also true of Keith Grabowski, the managing editor of the *Pinery Falls Torrent.* I'd expected the response I got from Carlson, but Keith's reaction surprised me.

At first, I thought I'd lucked out. Keith was not only at his desk, he was also alone and not on the telephone—a rare conjunction that usually meant he had time to talk. Keith's a good guy and a pretty good newspaperman. It's not his fault that the *Torrent* is a glorified house organ for the local powers-that-be. He does what he can. In the years since I took up the detective business, we'd traded information like two friendly handicappers, so I was stunned by his response when I asked what the paper had about Jack Drucker's murder.

"You working here, Hank? Or is this personal?" he asked.

"A little of both," I said.

"Well, it doesn't matter. Either way, I can't talk about it."

He picked up the pitcher of the ancient Mr. Coffee he kept on his desk and poured some of its contents into a mug.

Journalists are a strange bunch. It's their job to reveal information and most of them love to talk, but they pride themselves even more on their ability to keep a secret. They can be harder to pry information out of than a cop. They claim to operate according to an elaborate code they call 'journalistic ethics'—a code that varies from one of them to another. Some of it is comprehensible to ordinary mortals and some of it is not.

"I don't want any sources or confidential information," I insisted. "I just want to know what stories Jack was working on when he died."

Keith looked interested. "You think something he was working on got him killed?"

"It's possible," I said.

Keith shook his neatly shaved head.

"Doesn't matter why you want to know," he said. "The whole subject's forbidden. Off-limits. *Verboten.* The words 'Jack Drucker' cannot pass my lips."

"Forbidden?" I was astonished. "You're a newspaper editor, for God's sake. Who forbids you to reveal anything?"

Keith grimaced and pointed a finger in the air. Since his office, which we were in, is on the top floor of the *Torrent* building, I assumed the gesture was symbolic.

"Wes Drucker?" I asked.

Keith picked up the mug from his desk and examined its muddy contents.

"This stuff tastes like it was scraped off a crankshaft," he said. He sounded surprised, as if he hadn't been drinking the same stuff for at least two decades now. "You want some real coffee?"

Not waiting for an answer, he hefted himself off his chair and came around the desk.

"I'm going over to Sassy's," he announced. "You coming too?"

I followed him down the stairs and over to the diner-style restaurant across the street from the newspaper building. Sassy's is a hangout for refugees from the paper and also from the county courthouse building, which is located on its own city block a short distance away. It has tables instead of booths, so you can always see who's sitting nearby, and there's usually enough noise to make it hard for anyone to overhear a conversation. At that hour, it was almost empty. We took Keith's usual table in the back of the room.

"Let me guess," he said when we sat down. "You're on your way to a militia meeting."

It took me a second to realize he was talking about the camouflage jacket.

"Hunting snark," I answered.

We sometimes went to Sassy's when one of us had information to share, and I thought he might be planning to open up to me. But no such luck.

A waitress appeared. Keith ordered his usual coffee, black with sugar on the side, and I ordered my Diet Pepsi. There were three reasons for that—I don't like hot drinks, Rachel and my doctor both agree I should lose some weight, and Sassy's doesn't serve alcohol.

"The old man's passed the word," Keith explained as soon as the waitress left. "He doesn't want us discussing Jack with anybody. Period. We're not even supposed to cover the story any more than we have to. We can talk to the cops, and we can report what they tell us, but that's it. And even there . . ." He shrugged and let it hang.

So that was why the *Torrent*'s coverage had been so thin. There had been tributes detailing Jack's journalistic career but little hard information about the crime. Not at all what you'd expect from a paper whose star reporter had been murdered.

"That's crazy," I said.

Sassy—aka Helga Sasse, the cheerful middle-aged woman who owns the restaurant—brought our drinks to the table herself. This was an honor due entirely to Keith, whose naked head she delights in rubbing. I can't imagine anyone else getting away with that in public, but when Sassy does it, he practically giggles.

"Here you go, fellas," she said, setting the drinks down in front of us. Before she left, she ran her fingers over Keith's gleaming baldness, like a gypsy fortune-teller stroking a crystal ball.

"Jesus, I hate that," Keith protested, but only after she was out of earshot.

"Get a wig," I suggested.

He took a swig of his coffee. "It's just that simple, Hank. Wes wants us to leave it alone."

"And you *accept* that?" I asked.

"Hey, it's his newspaper. He pays my salary. Besides, this is a family matter with him."

"That's more reason to *push* the story, isn't it? Publicize the case, keep pressure on the cops to do it right."

"You'd think so, wouldn't you? But that's not what he wants, and I respect his wishes on this."

Sometimes you can play games with Keith. If you ask the same question in enough different ways, you'll find one he'll answer. But this wasn't one of those times. As far as he was concerned, the subject of Jack Drucker was closed.

But maybe not the subject of Wes Drucker.

"OK." I nodded, accepting his terms. "So that's what he wants. But why does he want it?"

"I don't know," Keith admitted, taking a great gulp of his coffee. Keith is no sipper.

"Doesn't that bother you?" I asked. "Not knowing?"

"Sure it bothers me. I'm a newspaperman. I hate not knowing things. When I was a kid, I hated having Christmas presents under the tree before Christmas morning. I wanted to tear them open right away. But the old man isn't biting a dog here. Stories get buried all the time. Sometimes for good reasons, sometimes for bad ones. Usually I argue, and sometimes I argue a lot. In this case, I don't argue very much. Jack was his son, for Christ's sake."

He downed the rest of his coffee. That was three trips to his mouth and the mug was drained. "Look, you want to talk about Jack with somebody else, you might try Charlie Cleveland." Cleveland was the main sports guys at the *Torrent*.

"Was he a friend of Jack's?" I asked.

"I don't know about friend, but they were drinking buddies. Most days, Charlie hangs out at the Wannigan after work. Jack used to join him there sometimes. I don't know what they talked about, but you might get something from him. Charlie's got a loose mouth when he drinks."

Keith looked at his watch and stood up. "Sorry to run, but I've got to get back."

Reaching in his pocket, he pulled out three dollar bills and tossed them on the table. That would cover what we owed, plus a tip. Sassy's is not an expensive place, which is one of the reasons a lot of *Torrent* people eat there.

"Sorry I couldn't be more help, Hank." He sounded like he meant it. "Good luck on it."

He headed for the door.

"Hey, Keith," I called after him. He turned and walked the few steps back to the table. "Someday I want you to tell me one of those good reasons for burying a story."

He grinned ruefully. "I'll see if I can think of one. In the meantime, if you come up with anything interesting, you let me know."

Finishing my Diet Pepsi, I thought about why Wes Drucker might want to put the lid on his paper's coverage of the murder. The obvious answer, that he was somehow involved in it himself, was too ludicrous to consider seriously.

But then why?

No other answer came to me.

Keith was an honorable newspaperman. Maybe he was no hero, but he was honorable. If he respected Wes's wishes in this, he believed that those wishes were honorable too. But the fact that he believed it didn't make it so.

I left Keith's money on the table, waved good-bye to Sassy, and headed back to the *Torrent* parking lot where I'd left the Sentra. I looked around for the old man's car. It was a scarlet Rolls-Royce with silver trim, the only one like it in Pinery Falls. Probably the only one like it in the state of Wisconsin. Maybe in the whole country. But it wasn't there.

That didn't surprise me any. From what I'd heard, he almost never showed up at the office anymore. But then, why should he? He owned the place.

10

DESPERADO

—The Eagles

I drove home and changed into regular clothes. While there, I checked the mail. As usual, it lacked balance. There were plenty of bills but no checks from satisfied clients. No checks at all, in fact.

I did a little paperwork, then, just before noon, fixed myself a sandwich made of packaged lean pastrami, low-fat mayonnaise, and ketchup, on low-cal white bread, and washed it down with a Diet Pepsi. I try to follow my doctor's advice at lunchtime. Then I don't feel so guilty when I ignore it later on.

My first stop in the afternoon was the public library. If I couldn't find out what Jack was working on when he died, I could at least find out what he'd published in the weeks immediately before. I went to the spot in the stacks where two months' worth of *Torrents* are left out to be accessible to casual readers. If one of Jack's stories had provoked his murder, I figured it would be there. An earlier story might have simmered for a while before exploding, but, if so, there was no way to tell how far back to go. Two months? Six months? A year? Six years?

I collected all the editions, up to and including the week after Jack's death, and lugged them over to a reading table. There, I methodically went through each one looking for any story with Jack's byline. This wasn't as time-consuming as it might sound. Like most daily papers, the *Torrent* is printed in sections. The first contains the two or three biggest news stories of the day, whatever they are, the rest of the national and international news, and the editorial page. The second has stories of local and state interest, and the third carries sports and business. Knowing Jack's beats, I only had to check the first two sections. My task was made easier by the fact that Jack was not only the publisher's son but the paper's star reporter. I could be pretty sure that any story with his byline would have pride of place. Most of Jack's stories would be found on the front page, or, at the very least, they'd be touted there. This meant that my examination of the rest of the paper could be pretty cursory.

Even so, I skimmed every page.

I left the papers with Jack's stories on the table and returned the rest to the stacks. When I returned, I counted nine stories in all. I'd read some of them before, but not with any particular attention. I subscribe to the *Torrent* and give it a daily once-over, but I only focus on stories that involve some aspect of a case I'm working on or catch my eye for some other reason. Jack's byline hadn't held any special interest for me.

The earliest piece was the account of the trial and conviction of a local grade school teacher named Sherman Beecher for abusing one of his students. It was straight reportage, with a few quotes from the victim's parents and the defense attorney thrown in for color. Child abuse had led to murder before, but, so far as I knew, never to the murder of a reporter who covered the trial.

One of the most recent pieces involved the local Hmong community. In the wake of the Vietnam War, roughly six thousand Hmongs and a thousand other Southeast Asians had been settled in Pinery Falls. That was a huge influx for a town with a population of less than ninety thousand people, almost all of whom were white and most of whom were at least fourth-generation Americans. Since then, Pinery Falls' Hmong population had nearly doubled.

Jack's story concerned a young woman named May Yang, who had come to America when she was about twelve years old (most of Pinery Falls' Hmongs had no birth records and so could only estimate their age), after a childhood spent in a refugee camp in Laos. Having had no previous formal education, she was mainstreamed into the Pinery Falls school system, where she caught up with her age cohorts in two years and soon passed most of them. After high school, she went on to the University of Wisconsin in Madison, and eventually to the UW law school, where she graduated second in her class. She was the first Hmong of either sex to graduate from a Wisconsin law school.

The occasion for Jack's article had been her return to Pinery Falls and hiring by the city's largest law firm, Fitzgerald & Stewart. I couldn't see any potential murder motive there. Things were not always smooth between the Hmongs and the old-timers, but Jack's piece was determinedly positive.

What I was looking for, to the extent that I was looking for anything specific, was some element in a story that might have led to murder. One of the most likely was money, and there was one story, published only a week before Jack's death, that reeked of that.

Headlined "SAUERHAGEN RESIGNS," the story concerned the ambitious effort to revitalize Pinery Falls' downtown area known as the Tobacco Island Development Corporation.

Left to its own devices, the Wisconsin River flows lazily into town from the north on its way to the Mississippi almost a hundred miles south. Shortly after reaching the city limits, the river splits into two narrower channels to sweep around the narrow, three-eighths-of-a-mile-hump of land known as Tobacco Island.

Just as they pass the southern end of the island, the two streams plunge twenty feet straight down into a roil of white water, where they rejoin to continue their journey south. Those two waterfalls powered the two sawmills that brought the first white residents to this part of the Wisconsin pinery. The mills were built on the island in the 1840s, and, with them, two dams to harness the river's power. Soon, men began to flood into the area. Germans, mostly, but many Scots, Poles, Swedes, and God only knows what else. Some of them came to work in the mills, some to fell the great white pines that provided the mills with raw material.

Before long, others came, plying the many trades needed to provide the loggers and millworkers with lodging, food, clothes, booze, and, of course, sex. Most of the new arrivals took up residence either on the island or on the riverbanks opposite the mills. Two bridges were built to allow them to get to and from their work. And so the town of Pinery Falls was born.

When the white pine ran out and the pinery turned into the cut-over, the original mills closed down. By that time, the town was able to survive without them. It even prospered. Paper mills opened up both north and south of town, which sent huge white and yellow clouds of malodorous smoke high into the air. When the wind was right, these blew out over the town, causing some visitors to wrinkle up their noses and others to become nauseous. Local residents got so they hardly noticed the smell. When they did, they regarded it almost affectionately, the way some people do their own farts.

Gradually, the island that had been the original working heart of Pinery Falls was abandoned. Most of the stores and other businesses that left the island relocated nearby on the eastern bank of the river. This new downtown business district grew and prospered for most of the twentieth century, while Tobacco Island was left to grow wild. In the past few decades, however, the downtown had fallen on hard times, thanks to the proliferation of strip malls and discount stores on the outskirts of town.

With the downtown business district dying, Pinery Falls had recently started building what amounted to a new downtown on Tobacco Island. The Tobacco Island Development Project was by far the biggest construction project in Pinery Falls history. And the biggest financial gamble too. When it was done, it would include an en-

closed mall, a sports complex, a theater, and a new community center, among other facilities. The mall would be financed by private
business interests, who would also contribute to the new civic buildings. The remaining costs would be borne by the city, which would
provide the needed infrastructure and loan guarantees, as well as the
full range of city services to the island—all on exceedingly favorable
terms.

The plan was more than a little controversial. On one side were
those who stood to suffer from the competition, along with the usual
collection of local troglodytes who automatically opposed anything
new—particularly any measure that seemed likely to raise their mil
rates. On the other side was almost everybody else. The local econ-
omy had been floundering for decades, and there was widespread
consensus that something big had to be done to rejuvenate it. Those
with a feel for the history of the place responded to the idea that the
city's birthplace would again become central to its existence.

Jack's story dealt with the sudden resignation of a city councilman
named Derek Sauerhagen, who was an outspoken opponent of the
project. According to the article, Sauerhagen had found himself increasingly isolated on the council. Following a roll call in which he
cast a vote against a city loan guarantee for a local developer, the frustrated councilman had stormed out of the meeting and announced
he was resigning. He complained bitterly that his fellow council
members were "rolling over" for the developers.

Jack's story balanced an angry interview with Sauerhagen with a
spirited defense of the project from Mayor Ray Mulkowski. From my
point of view, the indirect whiff of corruption that hung over the
piece was promising, but nothing in the story itself was new. All the
arguments expressed had been made before in other public forums,
including open city council meetings.

The rest of Jack's recent pieces were human interest stories in a series the *Torrent* was running under the general title NORTHWOODS
NEIGHBORS. Most of the *Torrent*'s reporters wrote occasional pieces

for the series. Jack's were not very different from the others, except in two respects. Like me, Jack was a local history buff, and he tended to use that history to fill out his stories. Also, the NORTHWOODS NEIGHBORS Jack chose to write about tended to be eccentrics, and his pieces often had an edge to them.

One of his recent subjects was a local Pinery Falls man who believed that he was the reincarnation of Abraham Lincoln. Another was a sweet-looking resident of a Wausau nursing home, who, in her youth, had been the mistress of one of Al Capone's lieutenants down in Chicago. Still another was a Stevens Point man who'd spent his youth as a geek, eating live chickens in the sideshow of a traveling circus.

The last of Jack's NORTHWOODS NEIGHBORS was one of the longest and, from my point of view, the most promising. Instead of the posed photographs that accompanied most of the others, this piece was illustrated by a grainy shot of its subject glaring at the photographer. Published the week before Jack's death, it read:

MOBSTER IN THE NORTHWOODS?
by Jack Drucker

Over the years, the Wisconsin northwoods have provided safe haven for outcasts and fugitives of every kind. There have been hermits on the lam from an intrusive and censorious society, criminals hiding from the law, and tormented souls fleeing the relentless demons inside themselves. Some of these refugees were harmless eccentrics, but others were desperate and dangerous men. All found solace, however temporary, among the sheltering forests of northern Wisconsin. Some still do. So it is that the very region that once harbored the likes of John Dillinger and his gang now harbors Tony Carelli, another figure associated, however innocently, with big-time crime.

Dillinger was the most notorious bank robber of an era when bank robbers were every bit as famous as, and even more genuinely popular, than movie stars. In his heyday, Dillinger was considered a Robin Hood by many Depression-era farmers who admired his daring, his panache, and, most of all, his practice of destroying the mortgages he found in the vaults of the banks he robbed.

The public may have admired him, but the nation's law enforcement officers regarded him as the worst kind of villain. In their eyes, he was a cop killer and a scofflaw who had to be put down at all costs. On the evening of April 22, 1934, a contingent of FBI agents, led by Assistant Director Hugh Clegg and Agent Melvin Purvis, entered the forest north of Minocqua, some seventy miles north of Pinery Falls.

They had received a tip that Dillinger and his gang were holed up in a tourist resort known as Little Bohemia. The agents fanned out through the trees and surrounded the lodge building, a large two-story structure that contained, in addition to other rooms, a restaurant and a bar where Dillinger and several members of his gang were, at that very moment, playing poker. Although the agents had no way of knowing it, more members of the gang, one of them the vicious killer known as "Baby Face" Nelson, were in a separate cabin only a short distance away.

Dillinger's gang was known to be armed, and its members were correctly regarded by the FBI as unpredictable and highly dangerous. The agents were more than a little nervous and inclined to be trigger-happy. When the front door of the lodge opened and three men came out and walked to a car, the agents opened fire.

Unfortunately for the FBI, and even more for the three men themselves, they were, in fact, innocent bystanders who had merely stopped off at Little Bohemia for a drink after work.

One was a local auto mechanic, and the others worked at a nearby Civilian Conservation Corps camp run by a New Deal program that offered healthy outdoor work to unemployed single men.

The FBI agents later claimed that they only intended to shoot out the car's tires. If so, the incident was a poor reflection on their marksmanship. All three of the innocent men were hit in the fusillade, one of them fatally. The two survivors scrambled out of the car and fled, one running into the woods and the other back into the lodge.

Warned by the gunfire, Dillinger and all his criminal companions managed to escape, leaving the embarrassed federal agents confused and angry. Later that same evening, "Baby Face" Nelson noticed that his getaway car was low on gas. Stopping at a rural gas station, he came face-to-face with three of the many lawmen that had been combing the area for the escaped gangsters. Nelson opened fire, killing an FBI agent named W. Carter Baum and seriously wounding both of the others. Then, adding insult to injury and death, Nelson stole their car. The incident completed a tragic symmetry: one dead, two wounded, a perfect tit-for-tat for the three innocent men who had been ambushed by the FBI at Little Bohemia.

The fiasco at Little Bohemia momentarily discredited the FBI, but it added immeasurably not only to Dillinger's notoriety but also to that of the Little Bohemia resort. To this day, the latter continues to cater to northwoods vacationers, most of whom, it must be said, are considerably more law-abiding than the Dillinger gang. Even now, visitors are drawn to the place less by the hearty food and drink served in its dining room than by the phantoms of the violent events that took place there on that April night in 1934.

Today, if an experienced hiker were to head due south-southeast from Little Bohemia, a long day's trek through the forest might bring him to a cabin on the shore of a small but picturesque body of water known as Deep Spring Lake. The cabin, which stands in the middle of a small clearing, is relatively large and comparatively new, but otherwise very similar to hundreds of other cabins throughout northern Wisconsin.

Five months ago, not just that cabin but Deep Spring Lake itself, plus a substantial part of the woodland around it, were all purchased by a hitherto unheard of entity called Deep Spring Investments. The deal was done quietly, but word of the transaction soon spread among residents of the Minocqua area, many of whom were suspicious of the unknown company's intentions. Unlikely rumors abounded. It was said that Deep Spring Investments planned to build some kind of amusement park on the land. That the property would become the headquarters of a white supremacy group. Even that Deep Spring Investments was carrying out seismic studies preparatory to drilling for oil.

Residents need not have worried about any of these possibilities. Deep Spring Investments is not, in any sense, an amusement company, nor does it have any connection to white supremacists, nor is it a mining or energy company. It is, in fact, a shell corporation, created solely for the purpose of hiding the identity of the true buyer of the property. That buyer is a 38-year-old Milwaukee man named Tony Carelli, who bought the property for the sole purpose of living on it, which he has done ever since the transaction became final.

Carelli is a man who values his privacy. No Trespassing signs have appeared around the perimeter of the property, and three out of the four private roads that lead to Deep Spring Lake have been barricaded, leaving open only a single lane dirt road that leads from Wisconsin State Highway 51 to Carelli's cabin.

Gradually, when there were no signs of unusual activity around the lake, residents of the area began to relax. Soon, the newcomer's Land Rover became a familiar sight on the streets of Minocqua, Woodruff, and other nearby towns. Longtime residents grew accustomed to seeing the new owner of Deep Spring Lake shopping for his food at the Minocqua IGA, or picking up do-it-yourself supplies at one of the local hardware stores, or having a quiet drink at Bosaki's Boat House.

In his limited personal contacts with the locals, the newcomer introduces himself simply as "Tony," but, thanks to the ubiquitous credit card, no man's surname can honestly remain secret for long. Tony Carelli's name is hardly as notorious as that of the legendary John Dillinger, but his associations are, in some ways, even less savory. For Tony Carelli is the son of Francis "Big Frank" Carelli, the real-life "godfather" of the Milwaukee crime family that is alleged, by law enforcement officials, to be responsible for most of the organized crime in the entire state.

Big Frank was convicted on five counts of racketeering and three of conspiracy to commit murder in 1990 and is currently serving a life term at Oxford Penitentiary in the southern part of the state, although the authorities believe that he still runs much of the family business from his prison cell.

For his part, Tony has never been charged with, much less convicted of, any serious crime. Except for a dropped charge of marijuana possession that resulted from his attendance at a pot party when he was in college, his police record is clean. Although both Milwaukee and federal authorities have suspected him of involvement in a number of criminal activities in the past, neither has been able to prove anything against him.

Detective Roger Anderson, a veteran of the Milwaukee Police Department's Organized Crime Division, believes that Carelli may have divorced himself from Big Frank's criminal enterprises. "I'm not about to give any Carelli a clean bill of health," Anderson says. "But I will say that Tony may be different. We haven't been able to pin anything on him, and, believe me, we've been trying for years."

Like a good son, Tony makes regular visits to his father at Oxford, but he denies any connection to the elder Carelli's criminal operations. How did Tony make enough money to buy an entire lake in a major tourist area? His explanation is a successful beer distributorship and a chain of car dealerships throughout southern Wisconsin and northern Illinois. He sold most of his interest in both businesses last year, and he claims to be retired and living off the proceeds.

Carelli's move to the northwoods can be interpreted as an effort to distance himself from his "family" background. More cynically, it can be seen as an effort to distance himself from the sophisticated law enforcement agencies headquartered in Milwaukee and Chicago. If the latter is his motive, Officer Randy Kramer of the Oneida County Sheriff's Department says that Carelli is making a big mistake. Kramer, who is disarmingly young to have such a deep sense of the area's history, explains: "During Prohibition, Dillinger and Capone's boys came up here to relax. This was the boondocks then. It was all dirt roads and party-line telephones, and the local cops didn't want any trouble. They knew those guys were out of their league, so they were like Sergeant Schultz. "I *see* nothing! I *hear* nothing!" Until the Little Bohemia thing, everybody felt safe. But that was a long time ago. It's a new day now. We've got paved roads and cell phones and computers that can access any data base in the country. We've even got a helipad. If we have to, we can get the Feds up here almost as fast as they could drive crosstown in Milwaukee or Chicago."

At this point, Kramer gives the reporter a sly grin and pats the police-issue revolver he wears on his hip. "Let me assure you, we are no longer looking to avoid trouble," he says.

Whatever Carelli's real motivations may be, he did not purchase Deep Spring Lake solely for recreation. He intends to live there. In the five months he has owned the property, he has rarely been away for more than a day or two at a time. He lives alone, and, for the most part, he keeps to himself. Mrs. Elva Johnson, whose home is located on Highway 51, directly opposite the dirt road that provides the only access to the Carelli home, says that there is very little traffic in and out. On the other hand, Tony Carelli is not a hermit.

"He does have visitors from time to time," says Mrs. Johnson. "People even come for the weekends sometimes." What kind of people, she is asked. "I saw two men drive in there once on a Saturday morning, then I saw them come out again Sunday afternoon."

Those area residents who have had personal contact with Tony Carelli speak surprisingly well of him. Mrs. Glenda Hartwig found herself stranded by a flat tire one night on County Trunk B, near Woodruff. Carelli was the sole driver to stop and offer her a hand. "I was very impressed, to tell you the truth," says Hartwig now. "I waved to flag him down, and he stopped right away. He was very respectful, and I really appreciated that he let me use his cell phone to call my husband before he got out of his car. It was dark out there on that highway, and I would have been really nervous if a big man like him had just gotten out, or even offered me a ride. But then, when I couldn't reach my husband, Tony pitched right in and changed my tire."

Carelli has become a semiregular at the White Tail Tavern in Minocqua, says Ray Galena, who is the weekend bartender there. "He comes in almost every Friday around supper time. He says we've got the best fish fry around, and I guess we do, too. Sometimes he comes alone, and sometimes he's got a young lady with him. They stop off in the bar for a drink before they eat. He seems like a good guy. He don't throw his weight around or nothing, and he tips better than most of the guys who come in here, too."

"I think he's cute," says Sandy Rorbach, a 19-year-old beautician at the Stylish Hair Salon in downtown Minocqua. "He looks like a football player with those big shoulders, but he's not really hulking or anything." Asked if she has ever met Tony Carelli personally, Ms. Rorbach giggles. "Oh no," she says. "I haven't actually *talked* to him or anything. I'd be just scared to death."

Tony Carelli's new neighbors have adjusted to the presence of a notorious stranger in their midst. Personally, they are more than willing to give him the benefit of the doubt. But can they really rest easy in the darkest hours of the northern night knowing that this man is among them? Or must they wonder whether his very presence, like Dillinger's before him, will someday bring violence and death to the Wisconsin northwoods?

Or to Pinery Falls?

Had Carelli somehow brought violence and death to Jack Drucker? I had no reason to think so. And yet—

I'd heard of Big Frank Carelli, of course. But I'd never heard of his son Tony. Maybe Tony was a violent man and maybe he wasn't, but he came from a violent milieu. When a mob guy's around, can anybody be really surprised if somebody winds up dead?

Before leaving the reading room, I photocopied Jack's stories, returned the papers to the stacks, and headed for the Wannigan.

11

NANCY WHISKEY

—The Hammer Singers

The *Torrent* is a rarity in this cable-news world. It's a true afternoon newspaper. People either pick it up on their way home from work or have it brought to their homes by one of the kids and retirees who deliver it after school. By the time I left the library it was after two o'clock. The *Torrent* had been put to bed, and from what Keith had said there was a good chance that Charlie Cleveland would be celebrating that fact at the Wannigan.

The Wannigan Club was founded by the local lumber barons over a hundred and twenty years ago. They were a collegial bunch who wanted a handy place to congregate and drink together. And to smoke cigars. And, most importantly, to engage in the favorite local sport of mutual back-scratching. Membership was never overly exclusive, though. It couldn't be. There weren't that many lumber barons.

Despite the fact that women had been admitted as guests since the early 1900s—and as members since 1948, when a strong-minded woman named Lanore Krushower inherited her husband's trucking business and claimed his membership along with it—the Wannigan still maintains the form, and some of the ethos, of a private businessmen's club.

The building is located on the edge of the downtown business district, two blocks from the *Torrent* in one direction and three blocks from City Hall in another. Its bars serve the cheapest drinks in town, if you don't count those places that serve only small-brewery Wisconsin beers and rotgut liquor. For that and other reasons, it's the traditional gathering place for people who work at the *Torrent,* as well as for local politicians and many of the town's leading businessmen. Some of the youngbloods who consider themselves too hip to wallow in such a hidebound atmosphere take their happy hours at McGruder's, but it's their loss. The Wannigan is still where a lot of the real business gets done. Pinery Falls is that kind of town.

I'm not a member of the Wannigan Club, but I occasionally meet clients there. The club has three bars, one on each floor. The upstairs bar is attached to the ballroom and used exclusively for banquets and other big events. The one on the ground floor is relatively upscale (it has a few tables and padded chairs with arms on them) and is used mostly by members entertaining guests. The downstairs bar is the one most members use for serious drinking, and it seemed the most likely spot to find Charlie Cleveland.

Counting the bartender, there were only five people in the room when I got there, all of them male. A trio of old men sat at one of the tables, and a slightly younger man sat alone at the glass-topped horseshoe bar that dominated the room. He was drinking something amber straight up.

"Hi, Charlie," I said, sliding onto the empty bar stool beside him.

He turned to look at me. His eyes told me the drink in his hand was not his first.

"Berlin, isn't it?"

"Hank."

"You're a detective," he told me, as if I might not know. "I met you once with Grabowski, right?"

"Right."

"Have a drink," he offered.

"I'm not a member."

"I am. You're my guest."

"Thanks."

He shrugged. "You can buy the round."

I grinned. "You got it," I said.

I summoned the bartender, a huge man the members call (what else?) Pee-Wee. The amber stuff turned out to be Jack Daniel's Green Label. The Wannigan didn't have Point Special, or any of the Canadian beers I'd gotten a taste for during my sojourn up there, so I ordered an MGD. That taken care of, I got down to the reason I was there.

"I'm investigating Jack's murder," I told Charlie. "Keith suggested I talk to you. He said you and Jack were drinking buddies and maybe he told you something that could shed light on his death."

"Oh yeah? Like what exactly?"

"You tell me. Did he ever talk about enemies? Journalists get all sorts of kill-the-messenger types, right?"

Charlie nodded. "You don't know the half of it. Every time I write anything negative about the Pack—you wouldn't believe the shit I get."

"Did Jack have any of that shit going on?"

He shrugged. "I suppose so. But he didn't talk about it. You get used to the cranks. They're mostly just blowing off steam. It's not the sort of thing you talk about a lot, except when you get a real funny one. Some real nutcake."

"Did Jack have any real 'nutcakes'? Maybe someone who scared him a little?"

Charlie shook his head. "Nah. Jack wasn't the kind to worry about something like that. Jack was a gutsy guy."

Cleveland downed the last of his old drink and picked up the one I'd paid for. He tilted it toward him and peered speculatively into the glass. He seemed to be sizing it up. Taking its measure. Then, he brought the glass to his lips and took a small, tentative sip. Something about the way he went about it reminded me of foreplay.

I tried a new tack. "Do you know what Jack was doing on Little River Road that night?"

"No idea," he said.

"Did he know anybody who lives out there?"

Charlie shrugged. "How should I know?"

"Do *you*?"

"Huh?"

"Do *you* know anybody who lives out there?"

He chuckled. "I know lots of people, but I don't know where they live. Hell, I've been in this town for ten years and I couldn't find Little River Road on a bet."

"Could Jack have dug up something that scared somebody? Or made somebody mad?"

"Hey, *anything* makes some people mad. Besides, Jack almost never talked about what he was working on."

"That's what his wife says, too. Why was that? I would've thought a reporter would want to put feelers out. Was he worried that somebody might beat him to his story?"

"Are you kidding? Who was going to scoop Jack Drucker around here? He had dibs on the *Torrent,* and the TV guys really suck. Hey, different guys work different ways. The way he did it worked for him."

Charlie turned his attention back to the contents of his glass, which he seemed to find intriguing. I thought of a song Wausau's Hammer Singers used to sing. *Whiskey, Whiskey, Nancy Whiskey. Whiskey, Whiskey, Nancy-O. I've got silver in my pocket. I'm going to follow wherever she goes.*

"You guys must've talked about work sometimes," I pressed.

He shook his head. "I'm on the sports side for a reason. Sports are what interest me. Jack was a sports fan, too. When we talked shop, we talked about *my* work, not his. Besides," he added, as if he'd suddenly remembered. "It's ixnay on the alktay boutahay Ackjay. Orders from on high." He peered at me suspiciously. "Didn't Keith tell you that?"

"As a matter of fact he did. But that applies to outside *journalists*, right? And to the public. It's all right to talk to the cops, isn't it? Well, I'm a cop, only private."

Charlie looked amused by my argument.

"I'm trying to find Jack's killer," I said. "Why would Keith tell me to talk to you if he didn't want *you* to talk to *me?*"

Charlie nodded, as if satisfied. I got the feeling he was glad to have a rationale for talking to me. Maybe for talking with anybody in the bar. After all, he'd recently lost his drinking buddy.

"Well, I've thought about it," he said. "Sure I have. I mean, how often does somebody you know get murdered and there's a mystery about who did it? You ask yourself: Do I know something? Do I have the clue that can help solve this thing?"

"And do you?"

He shrugged. "Who knows? All I've come up with is this one time a couple of weeks ago."

"Yeah?" I prompted.

"We were sitting right here at this bar, and Jack said, 'I'm gonna have to stop drinking here, Charlie.' So of course I asked why. And he said—now, how did it go exactly?" He shuffled around in the jumbled drawer of his memory. "Oh yeah. 'I'm not gonna be welcome here,' he said. 'Or you, either, if you're with me. This is *their* drinking grounds, too.' Well, naturally, I asked him what the hell he was talking about. He put his finger up to his mouth like he was shushing me. 'I'm gonna blow the lid off the whole damned thing, Charlie,' he said. 'You're gonna be surprised what's under there. Just you watch. This could bring it down—this town's whole power structure.'"

Charlie shook his head. "The 'power structure,' yet. We were back in the sixties again." The last seven words were half-sung to the tune of "Back in the Saddle."

"Gene Autry, right?" I asked.

"Or Roy Rogers," he said. "Somebody who was on TV when I was a kid."

This was interesting—no doubt about it—and well worth the price of a round. Even two. I summoned the bartender and made the universal circle with my forefinger.

"Tell me more," I urged.

Charlie shook his head. "Don't know any more. That's all he said. Then he clammed up. But I could tell he was really excited about something."

"What do you think he was getting at? Blow the lid off *what* 'whole thing'?"

Charlie frowned. "Tobacco Island, I suppose. I mean, that's the big thing around here, isn't it?"

"Well, Jack did a story about Councilman Sauerhagen's resignation. Could that have been what he was talking about?"

"No way." Charlie shook his head.

"How're you so sure?"

"Because the Sauerhagen story came out *before* Jack said what he said, that's how. He meant something else."

"So, you think Jack knew something fishy about Tobacco Island?"

"It's obvious, isn't it?" Charlie was grinning like a mischievous child. He may have been a sports guy, but he had a newsman's zest for chaos.

"What do you suppose Jack meant by the 'power structure'?" I asked him.

"There's only one power structure in Pinery Falls, isn't there? And they're all knee-deep in the Tobacco Island Development Project." He grinned, revealing surprisingly white teeth. "And most of them drink in here."

Pee-Wee arrived with the round and I settled the tab. It was a way of reminding myself that two drinks in the middle of the day were enough. Besides, school would be out soon and Harry would be waiting.

Expense-wise, the second round turned out to be a waste because I got no more information out of it. But the beer was cool going down.

I left Charlie gazing into his drink the way another man might gaze into a woman's eyes.

12

JUST LIKE A WOMAN

—Bob Dylan

My driveway is shaped like an upside-down L. The long end runs from the street alongside the house and past the backyard, where the short end branches right to the two-car garage behind the house. The Sentra is my only car, and, except in winter, I leave it outside. I use the extra half of the garage for storage all year round. Among the things I keep in there is an ancient Happy Cooker, on which I planned to grill hamburgers for supper.

Harry played in the maze of leaves while I rolled the grill out of the garage, poured charcoal into the bowl, and soaked it with a cancerous amount of starter fluid. Once the fluid had the time to soak in, I lit a match and flames shot up around the bowl. While they burned down, I sat back in a lawn chair and tried to think about something other than the case.

The first thing I thought about was the weather. It had been an unusually mild day, warming up from an overnight freeze to a high of nearly seventy, but now the temperature was dropping rapidly. It would probably freeze again tonight. There wouldn't be many more backyard barbecues this year.

My mind turned to Sarah. What time was it in Paris? Eleven

o'clock? Midnight? Would she be out on the town with some guy from the *Bureau de Fromage* or whatever it was called? Would they be going back to his place? Or to her hotel?

Well, that has nothing to do with me anymore.

Thinking of Sarah made me think of Rachel, which made me realize I hadn't thought about her all day. That was a surprise because I usually think about her a lot.

Rachel and I had been seeing each other for almost a year. We usually got together two or three times a week—sometimes less but rarely more than that. It was as if neither of us wanted to give the other a chance to get bored or to start taking *us* for granted.

Feeling guilty, I warned Harry to stay clear of the grill and went inside to give Rachel a call. I have a cell phone, but I refuse to use it when I have any sort of alternative.

"Hi, Rache. I'm just about to grill some burgers. Want to join us?"

"Sorry, Hank. I just finished an early supper."

"That's too bad. Harry was looking forward to seeing you," I added. It wasn't much of a lie. Harry liked Rachel, and he *would* have been looking forward to seeing her if he'd thought she was coming over. "How about stopping by later?"

"I wish I could, but I've got a mountain of papers to correct," she said. Rachel teaches English at John Marshall Junior High on the west side of the river.

"I guess it's not my night," I said.

The conversational ball was in her court, but she refused to return it.

After a few seconds, the silence began to sound like a comment.

Finally—"Hank?"

"Yeah?"

"What day is it?"

"Thursday."

"And what were you going to do on Wednesday night?"

"I was—oh shit."

"Exactly."

Rachel had an old edition of *Snakes and Ladders* and she'd invited us over to play the evening before. It was supposed to be a surprise for Harry, who was a big fan of the game. What could I say? "I'm sorry. I got a new case yesterday—the Drucker murder. It completely scrambled my brains."

A chuckle came over the line. "You don't have to sound so sad, Hank. You're forgiven."

Then, with what I hoped was mock severity, "Just don't ever do it again!"

Sleep is one of the great pleasures of life, and I don't like to have mine interrupted. Of course, what I like doesn't always matter. That night, for instance, my sleep was interrupted twice. The first time, it was by a tugging on the little finger of my right hand and a plaintive voice in my ear. "Can I come in with you, Daddy?"

My eyes blinked open, then squeezed closed against the light. I was lying on my side, with my head on the pillow facing the lamp on the bedside table. I'd turned that light off when I got in bed, so Harry must have flicked the wall switch on his way in. It's amazing how bright a 60-watt lightbulb can be. This one could have warned off ships at sea.

I faced away from the light and squinted my eyes back open. I checked my watch. It was 1:58.

"Can I *pleeeeaase*?"

"I don't know," I answered pathetically. It was a new question for me, and I was less than half-awake. What would Dr. Spock say—or whoever the expert was these days? "Does your mother still let you climb in with her?"

"Sure she does," he answered quickly. "Every night, she does."

I might be only a part-time father, but I had enough experience to recognize that as a lie.

"*Every* night, Harry?"

"Well, not *all* the time," he admitted sheepishly. "But she does sometimes. Honest!" His eyes were big and he was squeezing my finger very tight. "Please, Daddy. Can I—*please?*"

"OK, sport. Climb in. But I warn you, I snore."

He clambered onto the bed and happily snuggled up against me. When I reached over and turned off the bedside lamp, he protested.

"Does it have to be dark, Daddy?"

"Yes, it does," I answered. "I don't like sleeping with the light on, and if you sleep in my bed, you sleep by my rules. OK?"

There was a pause. Then, "OK, Daddy."

After a few minutes, a small voice came out of the darkness beside me.

"I like being next to you, Daddy. I like it a lot. 'Cause you wanna know why?"

"Why, Harry?"

" 'Cause I don't like it when I'm alone."

"Hey," I said. "Nobody likes being alone."

A minute later, a soft purring sound in the dark told me that he was asleep.

I wondered if what I'd told him was true. Didn't *I* like to be alone? Wasn't alone exactly the life I had made for myself, and wasn't I happy with it? For years now I'd assumed that I was. But at that particular moment—at two o'clock in the morning, with my son so temporarily beside me—I was no longer sure.

The second interruption to my sleep came about two hours later when the telephone rang.

On nights when Harry's staying with me and I don't have to worry about an emergency involving him, I usually let the machine pick up. This time, however, I knew who it must be. Sarah had been nervous about leaving Harry with me for so long, and she called every few nights (mornings in Paris) to check up on him. Or to check up on *me*. If I didn't answer, she'd worry, and that would make her even more reluctant to leave him with me in the future.

Besides, there was something I wanted to talk to her about.

I picked up the phone and whispered, "Hold on a minute," into the mouthpiece.

I scrambled groggily out of bed and headed downstairs. I didn't want to disturb Harry and I didn't want him to overhear what I planned to talk to his mother about.

By the time I got to the phone in my office, Sarah was grumbling her irritation across the Atlantic. "Jesus H. Christ, Hank. Pick up the phone, will you? The hotel charges a fortune for these calls."

"Better you than me," I greeted her. "You can afford it."

"Hello, Hank. It's good to hear your voice." She spoke with all the brightness of an ex-wife who knows she's just ruined your sleep.

"What time is it, for Christ's sake?"

"It's about nine thirty in the morning here," she answered innocently. "I don't know what it is in Wisconsin exactly, but I thought this would be a good time to catch you in."

She knew exactly what time it was in Wisconsin.

"I'm so glad you could take time out of your busy morning to give me a call," I said.

"No problem," she said, sailing above the sarcasm. "Things get started late over here. I'm just calling about Harry, to see if he's all right."

A small and totally irrational resentment flared up in me. "You mean, have I *misplaced* him or something? Left him behind in some bar?"

"Please, Hank," she said. "That was uncalled-for. I just want to know how he is, that's all."

"You're right," I admitted. "That was stupid. I don't even know where it came from. I guess I'm a little grumpy this time of the morning."

"And at other times," she agreed.

Enough of that.

"Harry's fine," I told her. "So am I, by the way. Thanks for asking."

She ignored it. "He's been eating well? He hasn't had trouble sleeping or anything?"

"Nothing like that. He's great." I took a deep breath. "There is one thing, though."

"What?" I could hear the quick alarm in her voice, the maternal antennae shooting out. "He's not sick?"

"Oh no. He's fine, just like I said. Only . . ." I was groping to think of how to put it. "He seems awfully demanding these days."

"Oh, *that*." There was relief in her voice. "Kids *are* demanding, you know. They need a lot of attention, and I suppose it's only natural, with his mother away—"

"Sure," I put in. "But this is more than that. He's really—I don't know, *huggy*."

There was a pause on the line. "I'm not sure what you mean."

"Huggy," I repeated. "I mean that he hugs a lot. Clings to me, you know?"

"Does he?" There was something new in her voice now, something thoughtful and reserved. "That's interesting," she said.

"You mean, he's not usually like that?"

"Oh, he is," she answered quickly. "He's like that with me sometimes. I just didn't realize that he'd be that way with you too. But, now that I think about it, I'm not surprised."

"You're not?"

"Not really. It makes sense, doesn't it? I mean, he clings to you because he feels so insecure."

"Insecure?"

"About *you*, of course," Sarah responded impatiently. "After all, you're his father and you left him when he was very young."

"Hey, wait a minute. I didn't leave him. Hell, I didn't even leave *you*. You left me, remember? And it wasn't my idea for you to have custody."

"You agreed to it."

I let that point go because she was right. I *had* agreed to it.

"I'm right here where I always was," I insisted. "I'm here for him any time he wants me. You're the one who says when he can see me and when he can't. You're the one who moved across town and took him with you. Now you're the one who's over there in Paris, living it up—"

"God *damn* you, Hank." Her voice didn't sound angry. It sounded hurt. "That's not fair, and you know it."

"Maybe not," I admitted irritably. "But I'm still half-asleep, you know. Besides, you started it."

How adult was that? And *had* she started it? I couldn't remember.

"I don't think I want to talk to you anymore right now, Hank." Her voice was cold and sad.

She'd stung me, so I'd turned around and stung her back. Or vice versa. Either way, the old connubial instincts were still functioning for both of us. Even years after the divorce. Even across an ocean and one-third of a continent. Even bouncing off communications satellites in space. *Jesus.*

"OK," I said. "I'm sorry."

"Tell Harry I miss him and I love him very much," she said quietly. "Give him a kiss for me, OK?"

"Sure."

It seemed that one of us should say something more.

But nobody did.

There was a distant—a very distant—click.

13

THE CANDY MAN

—Sammy Davis Jr.

I went back to the office after dropping Harry off at school the next morning. It's surprising how much paperwork a one-man detective operation generates. Ironically, most of that paperwork is done on a computer these days. When I first went to work for the Hanratty Agency, there wasn't a computer in the place. Now it's impossible to imagine doing my work without easy and constant access to the Internet.

Some things are still done the old-fashioned way, however. About nine o'clock, I sat down with the telephone, a phone book, and my calendar. It took me about forty-five minutes to make appointments to see all the members of the city council, as well as Anthony Mason, the lawyer who lived across the street from the murder site.

Sometimes it's better to drop in unannounced, but that wasn't the case with these people. I had no surprises to spring, and besides, there were too many of them. The problem with dropping in on people is that you waste a lot of time that way. Often they're not there or they're just too busy to see you.

I tried to set up a meeting with the owner of the third house on Little River Road as well. The name on the welcome mat was Holzmann, and the only Holzmann in the book was a James, with two numbers listed. When I called the *Res* on Little River Road, the phone rang eight times with no answer. The *Ofc* was listed at 1 Paper Lane, which I recognized as the headquarters of the Pinery Paper Company, the town's second-largest employer. This phone was answered on the third ring by a man who described himself as Mr. Holzmann's executive assistant. He informed me that the entire Holzmann family was in Florida on an extended vacation and had been there for the past three weeks. They were expected back this weekend, but they'd have to be clairvoyant to know what happened outside their home on the murder night.

I started to thank the guy when I remembered something.

"Just a minute," I said. "I was out at their house the other day. When I rang the bell, a dog started barking inside. They wouldn't leave a dog alone in the house for two weeks, would they?"

He chuckled. "Not Thumper," he said. "They love that dog. No, as a matter of fact, I stop by every day after work to feed him and take him out for his exercise."

The last person I called that morning was the one I wanted to talk to the most—the ex–city councilman, Derek Sauerhagen. He turned out to be an insurance agent with an office in the Chippewa State Bank building downtown. I punched in the number.

"Sauerhagen Insurance Agency." The voice was female and clear as the proverbial bell.

"I'd like to speak to Derek Sauerhagen please," I said. "My name is Hank Berlin."

"I'm so sorry, Mr. Berlin, Mr. Sauerhagen isn't here at the moment. Is there anything I can do for you?" she offered, as if she really wanted to make his absence up to me.

"Afraid not," I said. "I need to talk to Derek himself." I'd never met Sauerhagen, but when dealing with flak catchers it sometimes helps to refer to the boss by his first name. "Will he be in this morning?"

"Actually, I expect him any moment," she said, her voice brightening now that she had good news to convey. "May I have him call you?"

I thought about it.

"No thanks," I said. "I'll catch him later."

I had no problem finding a parking place across the street from the Chippewa State Bank building, which was just one more sign that the downtown business district was in trouble.

The board in the lobby of the Chippewa State Bank showed the Sauerhagen Insurance Agency in room 316. As I approached the bank of elevators, I recognized the lone man standing in front of them from the picture that accompanied Jack's article.

"Mr. Sauerhagen?"

"Yes?" He looked at me with a salesman's eager curiosity.

"My name is Hank Berlin. I'm a private investigator."

On TV, detectives often lie about who they are in order to trick information out of people. That's just bullshit. I won't say that I've never done it, but not very often. In the first place, I don't like to lie. In the second, you're bound to be caught at it a lot of the time. In a town the size of Pinery Falls, that kind of thing gets around and it's bad for business. Who wants to hire somebody with a reputation as a liar?

"I'd like to talk to you if you've got a minute."

"I've always got a minute," he answered amiably. "I'm just on my way to the office. Come on up."

This guy seemed so bright-eyed and cheerful that it was hard to envisage him as the angry crusader in Jack's story.

"Are you looking for insurance?" he asked me as we rode up in the elevator.

I shook my head. "Afraid not. I have all the insurance I can afford."

"All you can *afford*?" He chuckled. "A lot of people make that mistake. They think insurance is a possession. Something you collect like clothes or jewelry. It's not, you know. Insurance is an investment. Insurance is the future."

Ah, there it was. The glint of the true believer.

We exited on the third floor and turned left into a long corridor. Sauerhagen led the way to 316, opened the door, and conducted me in ahead of him. Inside was a standard-issue outer office, with a standard-issue secretary's desk, at which sat an extremely *nonstan*dard young woman. She was definitely top-of-the-line. She had green eyes and abundant red hair pulled up into an intriguingly asymmetrical arrangement on the top of her head. As we entered, she looked up and smiled at me. My day was made.

"Anything urgent?" Sauerhagen asked her.

"Nothing that won't keep," she answered cheerfully.

"Good," he said. "As you can see, I have company. Andrea, this is Mr. Berlin. Mr. Berlin, this is Andrea Havers—the finest private secretary in the state of Wisconsin."

I couldn't vouch for "finest," but I wouldn't argue with "prettiest."

"Mr. Berlin and I spoke on the phone," she acknowledged, smiling modestly.

Sauerhagen opened the door into his inner office and ushered me through. He hesitated a moment, then closed the door after us. Gesturing me to a chair in front of his desk, he walked around and took the chair behind it. He indicated a large glass bowl on the desk filled with jelly beans.

"Have some," he offered.

"Thanks." I took a handful and popped one in my mouth. "Hmmm," I said. "Tasty."

Sauerhagen took a handful himself. "These were Ronald Reagan's favorite candies, you know. Not that there's anything *political* about them," he added. "In fact, I understand he developed his taste for them while he was still a Democrat."

We sat there facing each other and munching our jelly beans. Sauerhagen finished his first and put on a salesman's smile. "So, Hank—I can call you Hank?"

"Sure."

"And you can call me Derek," he said happily, as though he'd just come up with a really terrific win-win deal for everybody concerned. "You're definitely not interested in insurance?"

"Not at the moment, Derek. I'm investigating the murder of Jack Drucker."

"That was just awful," he said, looking like he meant it. "I was sick when I heard."

"Yeah."

"Well, I'll be glad to help, of course. But what can I do?"

"It's possible that Jack was killed because of something he uncovered as a journalist."

He looked at me as if I'd been speaking Sanskrit.

"Well, Jack interviewed you for one of the last stories he wrote," I said.

"About my resignation, yes. But you don't think that has anything to do with the murder, do you?"

"Not your resignation itself, but maybe the reason for it."

"Oh, Lord! You don't think my—my *suspicions* about the council were responsible for Drucker's death?"

"I've no reason to think that," I assured him. "I'm just looking into everything Jack was working on at the time of his death. He was a journalist, and journalists stick their noses into things. Sometimes people don't like it."

Sauerhagen nodded thoughtfully. "I see your point."

"I've read Jack's article," I said. "But there's usually more to an interview than what ends up in the paper. I'd like you to tell me what you told him."

"All right," he said. "You have to understand that I was very upset at that time. Actually, I'm still upset. I told Jack I believed that somebody got to the council and greased the skids for Tobacco Island."

" 'Got to' "? I asked.

"Corrupted," he said. "That's not the word I used. But that's what I meant."

I nodded. Jack's story hadn't included that term, but it had implied it.

"You were opposed to the Tobacco Island development?"

He shook his head. "Not exactly. Developing the island may be a good idea. But I was—and am—very much opposed to the city taking financial responsibility for the risk."

"Well, I have to admit that it seems like a good idea to me." I said this partly because it was true and partly to see how he'd react. He rose to the bait.

"You really think it's a good idea to put the city on the hook just to protect a small number of private investors?"

"I don't know about that," I said. "But the downtown's been deteriorating for years. If Tobacco Island can bring more tax revenue back into the city, the whole city will benefit."

"Maybe," he admitted. "But we can't afford to lure it back with borrowed money."

"Why not?" I asked innocently.

"The city's credit rating is shaky as it is," he explained. "We're not a great risk, and that means we don't get great terms. The interest is killing us and the council keeps sinking us deeper into debt. They say they're trying to encourage business. But they're raising property taxes just to service this debt, and those higher property taxes *discourage* business. It's crazy!"

He didn't pound the desk, but his fists clenched as if he was thinking about it. I got the feeling that if the desk wasn't between us, he would have grabbed me by the lapels.

"Look," he said. "I want Pinery Falls to prosper more than anybody. Hell, I love this town. But if developing the island's a good idea, then it's a good idea for those guys. Why don't they put up their own money? Why do they need the taxpayers to pay for it? If this thing flops, the city'll be bankrupt. If it succeeds, we *might* break even."

It was an impassioned speech and he'd gotten a little red in the face delivering it. Catching himself, he grinned sheepishly. "I'm sorry, Hank. I get carried away on this subject."

"No problem," I assured him. "You said 'those guys.' Who are they anyway? Who's actually behind this thing?"

"Well, a lot of local names are on the project's incorporation papers—James Farminster from Pinery Paper, Rory McAllister from the Chippewa Bank, Wesley Drucker from the *Torrent* are some of them. But I suspect they're just window dressing. As for who's *really* behind it, I haven't been able to find out."

"Wesley Drucker is Jack Drucker's father," I said. "Did Wes's involvement in the development come up during your interview?"

"I think I mentioned it along with some others."

"Did Jack say anything about his father's connection to the project?"

"No," he said. "He didn't react at all. But there was nothing secret about the connection. I certainly didn't get the sense that it was any news to Jack."

So much for that.

"How did the city council get involved in the first place?" I asked.

"Mayor Duncan brought it to us about three years ago."

"OK. So, what happened when Duncan brought the idea to the council?"

"At first, we were split right down the middle. I mean, split on whether there should even *be* a project, much less whether the city should invest in it heavily. Half of us were for it from the start. Jim Ableman, Art Schultz, Ernie Kramer, Amanda Jackson, and Tim Trelawney didn't surprise me because they're free spenders. They love anything that sounds progressive. And Frank Bannister and Bill Freidman have business interests downtown, so they figured to benefit if the project brought business back there. Nothing underhanded, you understand, just legitimate business interests. So no alarms went off. The rest of us mostly voted against."

"The rest of you?"

"Yeah. The ones who actually care about fiscal responsibility. That would be me, Eugene Malik, Horace Breeder, Erin Hardecker, Ralph Beaman, Tom Ashton, and Dennis Dougherty." He rattled the names off easily, like a baseball manager announcing the day's line-up.

"Seven to seven," I said, proving I could count. "So, the council was deadlocked?"

Sauerhagen shook his head. "Not exactly. The mayor is usually a nonvoting member of the council, but he gets to break all the ties."

"And Duncan was in favor?"

"He was at first. But about eighteen months ago he started having second thoughts. If you ask me, he found out what was really going on. I can't prove it, but I'll bet that's why he didn't run for reelection last year. At the very least, the money guys let him know that they wouldn't support him anymore. That's why Ray Mulkowski's the mayor today."

"Just a minute, I'm confused here. How many different votes were there? On the council, I mean. About that development."

"Oh, lots of them," he answered. "There were financing measures, zoning matters, authorizations—maybe ten or twelve votes that related to the project in various ways."

"So, what was it that bothered you exactly?"

"Not much at first." he admitted. "But once Duncan started coming up with occasional 'no' votes, some of the others started shifting to the pro-project side. By the end, it didn't even matter that Duncan was gone. A majority of the regular council members were voting in favor. But the real turning point came on the final authorization for the bond issue. Jesus Christ! Seventy million dollars for a town this size. Just incredible."

"When was that?"

"About six months ago."

"And who cast the deciding vote on that one? Mulkowski?"

He shook his head. "That was the thing. There wasn't just one deciding vote. Bond issues require two-thirds of those present and voting. That meant that if everybody was there it would take ten yes votes. Up till then, the votes had always been close. Usually, the mayor would have to break a tie or the vote would be eight to six. That was mostly because Erin Hardecker voted for some measures that encouraged the project, but only the ones that wouldn't cost the city much money. Sometimes, Beaman would go along and the vote would be nine to five."

"A majority, but not two-thirds?"

"Right."

"So what happened on the big vote?"

Sauerhagen gave a sardonic laugh. "Funny thing," he said. "It came out eight to four."

"That adds up to twelve," I pointed out.

"That's right. But it was two-thirds that night. What are the odds on that?" he asked, sardonically. "The biggest vote in years and two council members don't bother to show up. And what are the odds that both of them would have voted no?"

"Who didn't show?"

"Erin Hardecker and Dennis Dougherty. Hardecker was out of town—on business, she said. Dougherty claimed his wife was sick that night and he had to stay home with her."

"I suppose Beaman was the eighth vote in favor."

Sauerhagen shook his head. "Oh no. Beaman stayed true to his principles. This measure costs the city a fortune in interest alone, so he voted against. It was Gene Malik who crossed over. That, along with the fact that we could only muster four votes against, gave the supporters their two-thirds."

"What are you saying exactly? That Malik, Hardecker, and Dougherty were all improperly influenced in some way?"

He winced. "I'd hate to say that. Two of those people are friends of mine. Or they were, anyway. But how else can you explain it? Particularly with Malik. He'd voted straight down the line against the project. Then, all of a sudden, on the most important vote—the most outrageous one—he turns in favor. And don't tell me the debate persuaded him either. Malik is stubborn as hell. He never got convinced by an argument in his life. If he switched his position, he must have gotten something out of it."

"You're talking about bribery?"

"I'm not *saying* that. I mean, I don't know how it was worked. Maybe nobody was passing out sacks of money. But somebody got to them. To *one* of them anyway."

"And you told all this to Jack?"

"Sure I did."

"But he didn't use it in his story," I pointed out. "There was nothing in the article about any vote but that last one."

Sauerhagen shrugged. "He wanted evidence. I didn't have any. All I had was some inference. And the feeling in my gut," he added.

"Have you got any evidence now?" I asked.

"No more than then."

"Did you tell Jack anything else? Steer him toward some other avenues of investigation maybe? Give him any other names to talk to?"

Sauerhagen took a minute to search his memory, then shook his head. "Not that I can remember. If I think of something, I'll let you know."

I stood up, and he did, too. He picked up the bowl of jelly beans and held it out to me. "Take some with you," he offered.

"Would you have an envelope I could use to carry some in?" I asked.

He raised his eyebrows.

"I've got a kid who loves jelly beans," I explained.

He laughed. Reaching into a desk drawer, he pulled out a 9½ by 12 inch manila envelope and proceeded to pour about half the bowl into it.

"There you go," he said, with a grin.

14

SWEET TALKING GUY

—The Chiffons

Anthony Mason's secretary was a trim young woman in a dark blue, smartly tailored suit. She was good looking, with perfectly coiffed blond hair and a really nice smile, but for my money she couldn't hold a candle to Andrea Havers.

She said my name into her phone, then told me to go on in.

Mason had one of those offices that exude prosperity and confidence. It was located on the southwest corner of the eleventh—and top—floor of the Chippewa State Bank building. Two large windows looked out on the city. The one on the south side of the building overlooked the city's decaying downtown: the one on the west gave an expansive view of the river. Tobacco Island figured prominently in the foreground, with the west side of town in the middle distance and the rising of wooded hills beyond. It occurred to me that sunsets must look really impressive from up here.

The gray carpet was thick and soft underfoot, the matching furniture elegant and expensive looking. Mason's desk was made out of some kind of dark wood, polished so that the surface reflected the sunlight coming in the south window the way a wet city street reflects neon at night.

Taken all together, the message the office sent was clear: Put your problems in the hands of the man who dwells here and you can relax.

Along with the great furniture, Mason had great teeth. I know that because he showed them repeatedly during my visit.

He not only stood up as I entered his office, but actually walked around the desk to shake hands. I felt dutifully privileged. He was several inches taller than I was and looked to be in much better shape. He smiled, giving me the first glimpse of those magnificent teeth.

"Mr. Hank Berlin?" he asked.

"That's right."

"Pleased to meet you."

He ushered me into a cushy armchair in front of his desk, then returned to sit in the black leather job behind it.

"I'm not sure I understand your business with me," he said.

I explained that I was a private investigator looking into the murder of Jack Drucker.

"Looking into? Like the police are doing?"

"Right. Only I'm working for Mrs. Drucker."

"She isn't satisfied with the police investigation?"

"She wants to be sure."

"So she came to you?" He looked a little amused by the notion.

I shrugged.

"And you come to me?"

"I'm talking to residents of Little River Road to see if they saw or heard anything that might help."

"This should be interesting," he said, giving me another look at those teeth. "In my profession, I'm usually the one asking the questions."

"You live alone?" I asked.

He shook his head.

"With my wife, Helen," he explained. "We have two children, but they're both grown and flown. My son is in his second year at Harvard Law School and my daughter's in her first at Stanford."

"Were you and your wife home that night?" I asked.

He looked both surprised and a little hurt that I hadn't congratulated him on his kids' prestigious matriculations. I suppose that
would have been polite, but he'd so obviously wanted me to be impressed that I'd decided not to be.

"I was," he said, getting over it. "Helen was visiting her sister in
Chicago."

"So, I guess the question is, did you see or hear anything?"

He shook his head. "I was sound asleep. I went to bed about
eleven or so."

"Nothing disturbed you?"

He grinned engagingly. "Not till the police came knocking around
dawn. I'm a sound sleeper. My wife says that if I can sleep through
my own snoring, I can sleep through anything."

This was interesting. Only four questions so far, and he'd lied to at
least two of them. Of course, people have lots of reasons to lie. Especially lawyers.

"How about earlier in the evening? Did you notice anything unusual in the neighborhood?"

"Afraid not," he said cheerfully. "It's pretty uneventful out there.
Most of the time," he added with a wry smile. He had quite a reper-
toire of smiles, and he was running through them fast.

I paused, trying hard to give the impression that I was struggling
to come up with something more to ask about.

After a while, Mason started to (what else?) smile again. Casually,
but obviously, he glanced at his watch. "Anything else, Mr. Berlin?"

"Not really. Except—what about the boy?"

It rocked him. He held his expression pretty well, but muscles
tensed all over his body. For a lawyer, he was surprisingly easy to
rock.

"The boy?" he asked.

I had chosen the term deliberately. It indicated that I knew something more about Mason's visitor than the mere fact that there had been
one, and it left open the possibility that I might even know who he was.

"Yeah," I said. "I'm wondering why you didn't mention him."

He thought things over before responding. He wasn't smiling now.

"If you'd told me that you knew about him in the first place, you would have saved me some embarrassment," he said.

"Why would I want to do that?" I asked, giving him a smile of my own.

He looked shocked. "As you may know . . ." He gave me a raised eyebrow, probably hoping I'd give him some clue whether I actually knew something more or not.

Fat chance.

"The young man is a client of mine," he finally went on. "He happened to find himself in trouble that night. The fact that it was the middle of the night may have made him even more frightened. He arrived around midnight and left well before one. The police feel that that removes him from any suspicion in the murder. That's all there is to it."

"Does the 'young man' have a name?"

"Of course he does, but if you don't know it already"—he raised the eyebrows again—"I'm not going to give it to you."

"Why not?"

"He's a client, Mr. Berlin. He was consulting me professionally."

"I have a client, too. I already told you who she is."

"Your ethical standards may be different from mine," he said drily. Then he pretended to take the edge off it: "That is not a criticism. I don't mean to imply anything denigratory about either you or your profession. I know nothing about a private detective's code of ethics. But I'm an attorney, and the matter the young man consulted me about has no connection with your investigation."

Was *denigratory* a real word? If it was, I planned to use it at my earliest opportunity.

"This kid has you on a retainer?" I asked.

Mason smiled, showing some of his earlier spirit. "Hardly," he

said. "I'm an old friend of his family, so he knew where I lived. Naturally, when he found himself in difficulty, he came to me."

"That's understandable," I said, as though any doubts I'd had had
been removed.

"Now, it's almost time for me to be in court," Mason said. "If
there's nothing else . . . ?"

"Oh, I think that's all," I said, rising from the chair. "Thanks for
seeing me."

"Of course," he said, coming around the desk and walking me to
the door. He gave me his biggest smile yet. This one was probably
sincere. He was sincerely glad that I was leaving.

"I'm sorry we got off to a bad start," he said. "You can understand
that I need to protect my clients' confidentiality. Since your investigation really has nothing to do with him . . ." He seemed to think there
was no need to finish the sentence.

"Sure," I said.

He shut the door behind me.

Passing through the outer office, I gave the secretary a friendly
nod. She was an attractive young woman and it wasn't her fault her
boss was a liar.

Back in the Sentra, I wondered why Mason had bothered lying to
me. It might be interesting to find out, but, whatever the reason, it
probably didn't have anything to do with the murder of Jack Drucker.

15

WITH A LITTLE HELP
FROM MY FRIENDS

—The Beatles

Pinery Falls Police Department."

"Augie Bendorf, please."

"Officer Bendorf is off today. I can put you through to his department."

"No thanks," I said.

This was what I'd been hoping for. It meant that I might catch him at home and away from the watchful eyes of George Carlson. With any luck, Augie might even be in an expansive mood.

Augie got his original idea of what a cop was like from watching Bull Connor on TV when he was just a little kid, and he still works hard to live up to that image. He even *looks* like a southern sheriff from the sixties. He stands at least half a foot taller than I do and outweighs me by at least sixty pounds. He's got a big belly that he wears hanging over his belt, and he sports the same crew cut he wore back in high school when it was already out of style. When he came to the door that day, he was wearing faded Wrangler jeans and a bulging T-shirt. There was a dollop of dried ketchup on his chin.

"Hi, Augie." I pointed at the dollop. "I'm not interrupting your lunch, am I?"

"Breakfast," he said, giving his chin a wipe with the back of a hand. "Bitsy's just cleaning up after. You wanna come in?"

The front door opened into his living room, which was straight out of the *Sears Big Book*, 1975. He plopped down in the huge La-Z-Boy that served as his official throne, and I sat on the nearby sofa.

"Want a beer?" he asked.

I looked at my watch. It was 11:15 in the morning, which was early even for me.

"Sure," I said.

"What kind you want?" he asked.

"Got any Guinness?" I asked, just for the fun of it.

He looked at me as if I'd asked for chocolate milk.

"Shit, no," he said. "I buy *American*. Got some Bud, though. And some Miller's and Point Special. I think Bitsy's even got some Lite. You want some of that?"

"No thanks," I said. "Any real beer'll do fine."

He laughed like a motorcycle backfiring. Augie liked jokes he could understand. Then he threw his head back and bellowed at the ceiling, "Sweetface! Bring us a couple Specials. Hank's over to see us."

"Hi, Hank!" called a cheery voice from the kitchen. "Be right there."

Back in my married days, Sarah would never have deigned to respond to such a summons, but Bitsy soon appeared with two beers.

"Thanks," I said as she handed me a cold can of Special. "I see you're looking as pretty as ever."

She grinned. "You're still pretty cute yourself."

She's a small woman, about five feet, one inch tall. Seeing her next to Augie, you had to wonder how they managed in bed. Specifically, how Bitsy managed to survive that experience. You also had to wonder what she ever saw in Augie in the first place. The two of them have been together since high school. It seems chemistry can be a terrible thing.

Bitsy handed the second can to Augie, then hesitated for a moment, uncertain whether to go or stay.

"You done with the dishes?" Augie asked.

She took the cue.

"Not quite, honey. I'll just finish up," she said. "Call me if you need anything."

Augie took a slug from his beer and then frowned at me—not unfriendly, just puzzled. "What ya doing here, Hank?"

Augie and I don't exactly chum around together. He considers me a little suspect, partly because of the Canada thing and partly because I don't scratch my balls in public the way he does. On the other hand, he's a jerk, and he's got a real mean streak in him. But we were neighbors when we were kids, so we still put up with each other.

"I'm investigating Jack's murder, and I'm hoping you can help me."

"Oh yeah? Who you working for?"

I shook my head. "No reason for you to know."

"Shit. No reason for me to help you either."

"Sure there is."

He frowned.

"Junior Girls," I said.

"Whatcha talking about?"

"I let you and Bitsy use my mom's car out in the parking lot," I pointed out.

A huge grin broke over his face.

"Jesus, Hank. You don't forget stuff, do you?"

"Not painful stuff," I said. "I had a hell of a time trying to explain the used rubber in the backseat to my mother. Not to mention the stink of booze. So you owe me one."

Augie chuckled. "OK. So, I owe you one. But maybe I don't know that much. It ain't my case."

"Come on, Augie. This is the biggest crime to hit Pinery Falls in years. Carlson's in charge, but everybody must be working on this thing. Besides, Jack was our classmate. You must at least be keeping tabs."

"Well, maybe," he said cagily. He took another slug of his beer.

Then, as if he'd decided something: "Tell you what, Hank. I'll talk to you, but you gotta promise not to tell Carlson."

"Promise," I agreed.

He nodded, then took another drink of his beer. "So, whad'ya wanna know?"

"Whatever you've got. What are you guys looking at? Any promising angles?"

"Hey, we're looking at everything. We've gone over the crime scene about a hundred times. We're combing Jack's records and his recent contacts. All that stuff."

"Liz says there was a phone call early that morning. Maybe before Jack went out. Have you found out who that call was from?"

"Nah. The phone company don't keep those records on local calls."

"Any ideas what Jack was doing out there that night?"

"Nope."

"What about the three houses across from where he was parked by the river?"

"We checked on the people there. Nobody saw or heard a thing. It figures, don't it? Everybody claims they were asleep at the time Jack was killed, and they probably were. Shit, I was."

"What about Anthony Mason? I understand he had a late visitor."

"Yeah, a teenage kid who's a client of his. We know the kid. He's a hard-ass who's always getting in trouble. But he was gone way before Jack even got out there."

"How do you know?"

"Mason says so and the kid says so. They got no reason to lie. Besides, we know where the kid was at the time of the murder."

"Where was he?"

"In the police station," Augie said, grinning broadly. "He went to a party after he left Mason's. It was a noisy teenage thing. The neighbors complained and some uniforms checked it out. They smelled weed and hauled the kids in. They found some joints but couldn't stick them on anybody. We ticketed the kids and let them go the next morning."

"What about the Druckers' home life?" I asked. "Anything there?"

"Nothing much. The kid Tommy's had some problems at school."

"Problems?"

"The usual stuff. Cutting classes and a few fights. That kind of thing's a big deal these days. Not like when we were kids."

"Any trouble between Jack and Liz?" I asked.

Augie shook his massive head. "The people who know them say they got along fine."

"What about their finances? How were they doing?" I felt uncomfortable talking about these things, but Liz had asked for it.

"They both made pretty good money. Of course, they had some credit card debts, just like everybody else. Nothing they couldn't handle. No new insurance policies or anything like that. And they must have had some great prospects. Old Wesley Drucker's getting on, and Jack stood to inherit the paper."

All in all, it seemed that Liz's impression was accurate. The cops really weren't getting anywhere.

"Exactly who found the body?" I asked.

"Billy Freeman."

I'd seen Freeman around. Except for the fact that he was younger than most of the other cops, the only thing that set him apart from them was a face full of pimples.

"He was doing his regular run," Augie explained. "The folks out on Little River Road got clout, so we show the flag a few times every night. It makes them feel protected. We swing by before one, then again around three or three thirty. I mean, the times ain't set in stone, but around there. Anyway, it was on this second run—three thirty-six, he clocked it—he saw Drucker's car."

"It definitely wasn't there the first time? Around one o'clock or whenever?"

"Nope. And there weren't any strange cars in the driveways, either.

The patrol's supposed to make a note of things like that, in case there's a home invasion or something."

"But why did Freeman stop? There are no parking restrictions on Little River Road, are there? Was there anything suspicious about the car?"

"He saw this guy bent over in the front of it. He thought it was a drunk sleeping it off, or some kid getting a blow job. He figured he'd roust whoever it was and have some fun. When he got close enough to see what it really was, he puked all over the side of Drucker's car. Talk about contaminating a crime scene!" He snorted. "Can't blame him, though. You ever see what a dum-dum bullet can do to a head? Jesus!"

Bitsy came in with two more beers and handed them to us. "I finished the dishes," she announced. "What are you guys talking about out here?"

"Jack Drucker's murder," Augie answered slyly, watching for her reaction. When she gave a start, he grinned.

"That was terrible," she said, addressing me. Bitsy's eyes were soft with immediate sympathy. "I feel so bad for Liz. Jack was a friend of yours, wasn't he?"

"Once," I said.

She looked at me curiously, obviously puzzled by my tone.

"Well," she said, "I don't think that is something I really want to talk about, if it's all the same to you two."

"You can go and get the bedroom warmed up for us," Augie suggested, giving her a lingering pat on the rear. Bitsy smiled embarrassedly.

"I'll be there in just a little bit," he told her, winking broadly at me.

On the way out of the room, she stopped by the couch to lean over and kiss me on the cheek. "By, Hank. It was really great seeing you."

"You, too," I said.

"*Women*," Augie pronounced, looking after her. "They're so fuckin' *squeamish*."

I felt like telling him that any woman who stomached being called Sweetface and having her rear fondled in front of company couldn't be all *that* squeamish. I didn't, though. Augie can be touchy sometimes and I wanted information.

"What about the Stingray?" I asked. "Do you know what the crime scene guys found in it?"

"Sure. I saw that stuff myself. I was there when they went over it." That was luck.

"What'd they find?" I asked.

"Not a lot. Jack must have loved that old car. He kept that car so *tidy,*" he said with distaste. "The big thing was the gun. It was down by his feet—by the brake pedal."

"What kind of gun was it?"

He grinned just thinking about it. "Man, that was some gun. A Python .357 Mag. with a *combat* stock. A real serious piece."

"What's a combat stock?" I asked.

"And you call yourself a detective," he said snortingly. "It's a stock with grooves in it. For the fingers, you know? To get a better grip. And this one was custom fitted too."

"You mean shaped to a particular hand?"

"Right. Hand-worked walnut. It didn't come that way from no factory. It had to be made special."

"What else?"

"Well, there was the slug. We found it in the passenger door. It went right through Jack's head. It spread on impact, though, so the exit wound was bigger than the entrance wound. Lots bigger. There was all this glop from inside his head all over the passenger side. Man, you *did not* want to see that. It was like somebody'd barfed up blood and oatmeal in there."

"For Christ's sake, Augie."

He laughed. "Feeling a little squeamish yourself, Hank?"

"What else was in the car?" I asked coolly. Then I took a slug out of my glass.

"There was some loose change stuck down in the seat, and some hairs."

"What kind of hairs?"

"Human hairs. People shed, you know. Just like dogs."

"Jack's hair?"

"Some. And some from Tommy. *Aaand*"—he drew it out suggestively—"*aaand* there was some other hairs, too."

"Whose?" I asked.

"I don't know. And nobody else does, neither. Not even Carlson, and he thinks he knows everything. It was brown, but dyed black— that real flat kind of black a lot of the young girls have now. They make their hair look like a gook's for some reason. It was long and straight, like more than a foot. Sounds like a woman, don't it? But these days, who knows? Anyways, the lab couldn't come up with a match, but it definitely don't belong to anybody in the Drucker family."

Augie was grinning at me, like he'd just sprung a big surprise.

"It might not mean much," I pointed out. "Maybe Jack picked up a hitchhiker, or gave some woman a ride to work."

He looked hurt. "Hey, there was a lot of hair in that car."

"She might have brushed her hair while she was in there. A lot of hair comes out when you brush it."

"Oh, sure," Augie agreed mockingly. "I'll just bet."

I shrugged. "Anything else?"

"The usual stuff. A tire gauge, road maps—Wisconsin and Illinois, and one that had all the interstates. Let's see. There were some butts in the ashtray. No matches. He must've used a lighter. There was one in his pocket."

"How do you know the butts were from Jack's cigarettes?"

"Well, there was no lipstick on 'em. And they were Camels, which was Jack's brand. He had half a pack in his pocket."

So Jack had kept on smoking. Nonfilters, yet. We both had smoked back in high school and college. Everybody did in those days. When the Surgeon General's report came out, we were just getting started. Most of us put off thinking about it until we matured enough to realize that we were actually going to die someday. Then some quit. I didn't get to that stage until 1985, when my doctor told me that the leg pain I was feeling on exertion was the result of a clogging leg artery and that my four-packs-a-day habit must be causing it. Apparently, Jack never got to that stage at all. It figured. Jack had always scoffed at the idea that little things like cigarettes would vanquish him. Well, he turned out to be right about that.

"That's it?" I asked.

Augie concentrated. "Jesus, man, I don't remember for sure. Some dinky stuff, I guess. Oh, there was a pen with his fingerprints on it down by the driver's seat. And there was a button from one of Liz's winter coats on the floor over on the passenger side. There might a been a couple other things. Nothing that didn't belong to one of the family. Nothing except that black hair. Like I said, the car was pretty clean. You want another beer?"

My can was still almost full. I shook my head, feeling virtuous.

"One thing really puzzles me," I said. "Why are you guys so convinced that this was murder?"

He looked at me like I was crazy. "What else would it be?"

"A man's found shot once through the head, with the gun right there. The first thought is usually suicide. But, right from the start, everybody's been assuming it was murder. Why? What's the evidence that Jack was killed by somebody else?"

"There's all sorts a stuff. Leastways, according to Carlson, and he ought to know."

"Such as?"

"Like Jack was right-handed, for one thing. The bullet hit him in the left temple. That figures if someone shot him from outside the car, but not if he did it himself."

That was logical but hardly conclusive.

"Besides, there's the gun," he added.

"What about the gun?"

"It wasn't his, for one thing. Jack was a gun guy. He had a mess of guns—rifles and handguns both—but not this one. Why would a guy with lots of guns need to off himself with somebody else's gun?"

"How do you know the gun wasn't his?"

"Liz couldn't ID it, for one thing. Besides, Jack had a display case for his gun collection and there's no place for it. A man who liked to show off his guns would have a special piece like that out front. Besides, Jack registered his handguns, and this one ain't registered."

"Not to anyone?"

Augie grinned. He obviously had another surprise to spring. "Hard to tell. Everything that could identify it's been filed off."

"You're kidding me."

Augie shook his head. "Carlson figures it's a real pro's piece. And that means"—he positively leered—"Jack's murder was a professional hit."

As Augie's surprises go, that one was pretty good.

"A professional hit? In Pinery Falls?"

"That's what Carlson says, and like I said, he ought to know. He worked in Chicago for a while, so he's seen the signs before." Augie spoke of working in Chicago the way a parish priest might speak of working at the Vatican.

"Signs?" I asked.

"The stock was wrapped up in a tape that don't take fingerprints. That's an old pro trick. And then there's the way the bullet spread like that. The rounds you get at Gander Mountain don't do that kind of damage."

"When you say 'pro,' you don't just mean somebody who was hired to kill Jack. You mean somebody who's done this before?"

"That's what Carlson thinks."

"Because it was a pro's gun, and because the stock was wrapped?"

"Yeah. That, and because it was *there*. Only a pro, or somebody fuckin' careless, leaves the weapon at the scene. An amateur can panic and drop it, but then the gun turns out to be registered to him, and it's got his fingerprints all over it. But a pro goes out on a hit, he takes along a clean gun. He uses it, then he drops it."

"Why?" I asked.

"Hey, shit happens. Killers know that better than anybody. They get pulled over for speeding, or for a little accident or something. The cop checks the car and—bingo! There's the gun. They're fucked. So what do they do? They leave the gun there. That way, nobody finds it on them. Nobody can connect them with it. I mean, this was a pretty good piece just to throw it away. But I guess if you can get away clean, it's worth it."

"Makes sense," I said.

"Fuckin'-A."

I spotted Harry's green-and-gold Packer jacket in the middle of the horde of kids pouring out the front doors of the school. When he saw the Sentra, he separated from the crowd and came running.

Climbing into the backseat, he leaned forward and gave me a big hug. Then he pinched his nose.

"Jeepers, Dad. You smell like beer."

"Do I?" I said, feigning surprise.

"Come on, Dad. It's the middle of the *afternoon*."

"Is it?" I asked wide-eyed. "So *that's* why it's so bright outside. And here I was thinking it was night already."

Harry giggled, attaching his seatbelt.

I reached down beside my seat and picked up the manila envelope I'd put there.

"These are for you," I said, handing it back to him.

He opened the flap and looked inside.

"Oh, wow!" he exclaimed, pulling out a handful of jelly beans. "Thank you, Daddy. Jelly beans are my favorite *favorites*!"

"I know, *I know*," I said with a grin.

16

LITTLE CHILDREN

—Billy J. Kramer and the Dakotas

When I'm around the house on Saturday mornings, I usually tune the radio in my "entertainment center" to Wisconsin Public Radio *Zorba Paster on Your Health,* and *Car Talk,* and *Whad'Ya Know?* That Saturday, Zorba's recipe for tofu chili was interrupted by the ringing of my doorbell. I turned off the radio without regret. I love chili, but I've never eaten tofu and never will.

My front door has three glass panels that let me see what's on the porch before opening the door. This comes in handy in my work and even more when Seventh-day Adventists come to call. (Why do some religions think that they can save your soul by pissing you off?) That Saturday morning, what I saw through the panels was Tommy Drucker. He was standing on the front porch. His hands were stuffed in his pockets and he was shifting restlessly from one foot to the other, like a child who needs to piss.

"Hello, Mr. Berlin," he muttered when I opened the door. "Is the kid around?"

"He sure is."

"I thought maybe he'd want to play or something."

"I'll bet he would," I said. "Come on in."

Tommy shuffled into the hall, shutting the door behind him.

"Harry!" I called from the bottom of the stairs. "You've got company!"

Harry came running out of his room. Company was an unusual event for him.

"Hey, Tommy!" he shouted excitedly when he saw who was standing beside me.

"Hi, kid."

Harry bounded down the stairs in a kind of controlled fall. Once at the bottom, though, he pulled up shy. He looked from Tommy to me as though searching for a clue on how to behave in this unusual circumstance.

"Tommy came by to see you," I explained.

"I thought maybe we could play for a while," Tommy offered.

"Sure," Harry said. "I got a Xbox!" When Sarah had told me how long she might be gone, I'd bought Harry the game. It was up in his room.

"That'd be great," Tommy said.

"I'm learning how it works," Harry said. "Maybe you can help me."

"Sure I can," Tommy said. "I know all about that stuff."

Harry grabbed one of Tommy's hands. "Come on, let's go!" he urged.

Grinning, Tommy let himself be pulled up the stairs.

Looking after them, I wondered how common it was for an adolescent to volunteer to spend Saturday morning with a six-year-old. I didn't know, but my impression was not very. Particularly an adolescent like Tommy, who seemed to be somewhat withdrawn and even sullen. Of course, a lot of adolescents act that way around adults.

While the kids were upstairs, I called Rachel. I'd invited her for supper on Friday, hoping to make up for my gaffe, but she'd had chaperone duty at a school dance. Now I told her I had to be out on a job that afternoon, and asked her if she could look after Harry. This wasn't an unusual request. As I said, she *likes* Harry and genuinely seems to enjoy spending time with him. Even so, I explained that my errand wasn't urgent. If she passed on my request, it wouldn't be a problem.

But she said, Sure. Her place or mine?

"That depends," I said. "Your place if you just want to play with Harry for a while. My place if you want to stay and play around with me after that. It's a beautiful day out, and I could grill some steaks for supper."

"Your place," she chose.

Wednesday was forgiven.

About an hour later, I heard footsteps coming down the stairs. Tommy appeared in the doorway of my office.

"Hi," I said. "Where's Harry?"

"He just started a video game. I told him I had to get going."

But Tommy didn't go. He stayed in the doorway as if he was waiting for something there.

"Yes?" I prompted.

"Can I ask you something?"

"Sure. Come on in and sit down."

He slouched across the room and plopped into one of the client chairs in front of the desk.

"Mom says you used to know my dad," he said. "Back when you were kids."

He wasn't looking directly at me. Instead, he kept his eyes lowered as if he was examining something on the surface of the desk.

"That's right. We were the same age, you know. How old are you, Tommy?"

"Twelve."

"Then your dad and I met when we were around your age."

He nodded. "Yeah, that's what Mom said."

He had something on his mind, and I waited for him to come out with it.

"You must've really liked my dad, right?"

"Yes, I did. We were best friends in school," he said.

He took a deep breath. I had the sense he was about to get down to whatever it was. "Uh—Could you maybe tell me about him?" he asked.

"What do you want to know?"

"What was he like? I mean, was he a nice guy, or was he . . ." Tommy seemed to be searching for the opposite of "nice." "Or was he *mean* or something?"

It was an odd question to ask about your own father, but Tommy was obviously in earnest about it.

"Your father was a good guy," I assured him, changing Tommy's wording. I'd never thought of Jack Drucker as nice—or as not nice, for that matter.

"He was fun to be around," I added. "He was always into something interesting."

"Yeah? Like what was he really interested in?" Tommy asked.

"Like books and music. Like sports. He was the one who turned me on to the Packers."

Tommy grinned. "Oh yeah? I like the Packers too."

"You think they'll take the division this year?" I asked.

"You bet," he said. "I don't know about the Super Bowl, though."

I thought the story of how Jack and I had met might impress him. It did.

"Dad was really scrappy, huh?" he asked.

"You bet he was."

"He liked to hit people?"

"Oh, I don't know about *that*," I said.

The truth was, I did think that Jack liked to hit people. He enjoyed the physicality of a fight and the challenge of it. But that's not the sort of thing you tell a kid Tommy's age. I could see him clocking some schoolmate, then explaining to Liz that he was just following in his father's footsteps, 'Mr. Berlin told me that Dad really got off on hitting people.'

"The thing was, your father didn't believe in backing down," I told him. "He believed in standing up for himself. And for what he thought was right."

"He always told me I should do that."

"Well, that's what he did himself."

Tommy nodded thoughtfully. When he stayed quiet for a while, I took the opportunity to change the subject.

"Tommy, do you know why your mother came to see me the other day?"

"Yeah. She hired you to figure out who killed him."

"That's right. So, it might help if *you* could tell *me* some things. Would that be OK with you?"

He nodded. "Yeah, sure," he said.

"I understand that you were at a friend's house that night?"

"Sort of," he said. "I was at Andy Keeler's house. He's not my friend exactly, but we're on the same basketball team."

"You play basketball?" That surprised me. Tommy seemed so lethargic, he didn't strike me as the athletic type.

He made a little ducking motion with his head that reminded me of his mother.

"It's just this Y team," he explained. "I'm not very good."

"So Andy had a sleepover for the team?"

"There are only six of us. His parents have this huge house with a big rec area in the basement. We all had sleeping bags."

"Had you noticed anything different about your father that day?"

"Different?" The question seemed to puzzle him.

"I mean, did it seem like there was something going on with him? Did he act worried about anything? Or excited maybe?"

Tommy thought for a moment but shook his head. "Naw, he just seemed like—like Dad, you know."

"And how was that?" I asked him.

"What do you mean?"

"Tell me something about him. What he was like."

Tommy looked confused. "But you knew him. You knew him lots longer than I did."

"I knew him when we were kids," I told him. "I don't know anything about the man he turned out to be. Can you fill me in a little?"

"I don't know," he said, frowning. "Like how exactly?"

This was tricky. The boy had just lost his father and I didn't want to rub any salt in that wound. I didn't want to scare him off, either. I knew the young Jack Drucker as well as I've ever known anybody in my life, but I needed to find out about a different Jack Drucker. Jack Drucker the middle-aged family man. Jack Drucker the reporter. Jack Drucker the guy who got himself murdered.

"Look, Tommy. My own dad died when I was just a little kid, so I don't really know what it's like to *have* a father. I was thinking that maybe you could tell me what it was like to have Jack for a father."

Tommy's frown disappeared.

"Well, yeah, I can do that," he said. "He was—I don't know exactly. He was a really *powerful* guy, you know? I mean, he didn't take shit from anybody."

Then he grimaced.

"Sorry about that," he said. "It kinda slipped out."

"Don't worry about it," I told him. "I've been known to use the word myself."

He grinned. "Well, Dad was pretty strict. Most of the time, I mean. But sometimes he really loosened up."

"Oh yeah?" I prompted him.

"Yeah. It was just like you said. He could be a lot of fun sometimes. Like, sometimes he'd take me for a ride in the 'Vette. We'd go out on one of those twisty little roads, the ones out past the school. Then he'd just open it up. Man, that's a kick-ass car! We'd just *fly!* Over these little hills, you know, and around the corners. It was like a roller coaster." Tommy was beaming now, jacked with the memory. "I really don't know what would of happened if somebody had come in the other direction though," he admitted.

"That sounds like the Jack I used to know," I said.

"And once, he . . . If I tell you something, you won't tell my mom?"

I had a minor ethical dilemma here. His mother was my client and entitled to all the information I collected working for her. Of course, I could always get around that by not charging her for this discussion.

"Of course not," I said. "This is just between us."

"Well, one time when she was out of town, he let me drink *beer* with him."

I looked appropriately shocked.

"Budweiser!" he exclaimed. "I had three cans!"

Tommy was leaning forward in the chair now, alive and eager. This was a different Tommy from the kid who had slouched up my walk a few days before.

"Did you like it?" I asked him.

"Huh?"

"The beer. Was it good?"

He looked sheepish. "Not really," he admitted. "It tasted sort of funny."

"But it was cool—drinking with your dad?"

"Yeah! I mean, how many kids my age get to do that?" he asked.

"Not many." I smiled.

"I really got the feeling that maybe he liked me after all," Tommy said.

After all. The words hung out there in the air between us, heavy with implications. I didn't know quite what to do with them. I waited to see if Tommy would go on, but he just waited too. In the end, I dodged it.

"Your dad doesn't sound very strict to me."

"Oh, he *was*," Tommy quickly assured me. "He had his rules, and if I broke them he could be really tough. I mean, if I didn't get home when I was supposed to. Or didn't get my homework done or something. He could really blow, you know?"

"Blow?" I asked.

"You know," Tommy said, pulling back a little as if he was afraid he'd opened up too much. "Get really mad sometimes."

"Oh yeah? What did he do when he got mad?"

"Nothing much," he said evasively. "Besides, what does it matter now anyway? He's dead."

What do you say to that?

Tommy's eyes were moist. I thought he was going to cry, but he didn't. He didn't say anything more either. Instead, he suddenly pulled himself to his feet. "Look, I've got to get going, Mr. Berlin. Like I told Harry."

"Sure," I said.

I stood up and followed him to the front door. "Come by again sometime. Harry would really enjoy that."

"You bet," he said.

17

DAYTRIPPER

—The Beatles

About half of the cars and at least two-thirds of the SUVs that crowded the northbound lanes of Interstate 39 that afternoon had Illinois plates. They were the late starters, desperate for one more weekend at the cottage before winter really closed in. Even with all the traffic, it was a great day for a drive, cool and clear and cloudless.

For the first ten miles or so, the view out the Sentra's windshield alternated between farmland and forests. The fall colors were close to their peak and some of the vistas were spectacular. Just north of Wausau, the interstate skirts a ridge high above the Wisconsin River and the picturesque village of Brokaw appears like Brigadoon in the wooded valley down below. The little company town snuggles up against the massive Wausau-Mosinee Paper Mill like some medieval hamlet huddled beneath the protective walls of a lord's castle. On that Saturday, a plume of white smoke rose from the mill and hung over the village like a battle pennant. It was a form of pollution, I suppose, but if an artist had painted the scene and the smoke hadn't been there, he would have added it.

It was pretty much all forest after that, except for the occasional billboards that touted north-woods living. One of them advertised a hotel in St. Germaine called the Rustic Manor. It pictured an attractive young couple in swimsuits dangling their toes in the bubbling waters of an in-room spa. I guess that's what *rustic* means these days.

Outside of Tomahawk, the interstate shed its four-lane persona and reverted to its original identity as Highway 51. Up here, the forests consisted heavily of pines and other evergreens, and the remaining deciduous trees had long since lost their leaves. The calendar might have jumped ahead a month or two. There was a winter chill in the air and patches of snow were visible under some of the trees. It looked like a lot of those late starters were going to be disappointed.

Approaching Minocqua, I mentally rehashed Jack's piece on Tony Carelli. It contained several quotes, but none of them were from Carelli himself. That probably meant that he hadn't been cooperative, which probably meant that he didn't appreciate having a reporter nosing around. That, in turn, probably meant that he *really* wouldn't appreciate having a private detective nosing around either.

I almost wished I'd brought my gun.

My *Wisconsin Atlas and Gazetteer* showed Deep Spring Lake as a little blue spot west of the highway a few miles south of Minocqua. As I got closer, I studied the ladders of white sword-blade-shaped shingles that marked many of the side roads. Each shingle carried the names—or, more often, the nicknames—of some of the lakes, businesses, cabins, or property owners that could be found down that road.

Some of the nicknames people gave their vacation homes were clever, others were just cloying. "Trail's End," "Bugler's Retreat," "Alan's Aerie," and even "Fernando's Hideaway" are a few that I remember. But I found myself entering Minocqua without having spotted any that read "Deep Spring Lake," "Carelli's Castle," "Gangster's Hideout," or anything remotely similar.

I stopped at the first combination gas station, convenience store, and bait shop that I came to. The middle-aged woman behind the counter welcomed me with a cheerful but tooth-challenged smile.

Asked for directions, she told me to keep going south for about half a mile, then turn right on the first unmarked dirt road past Kulwicki's Bar and Grill. There was no sign for Deep Spring Lake, she said, but I'd know the road by the cream-colored house just opposite. That house, I assumed, would be where Elva Johnson lived.

"Know anybody with a cottage on that lake?" I asked innocently.

"Used to," she answered. "They sold out, though. Some new guy bought up all the properties around the lake."

"Oh yeah?"

"A guy named Carelli, I think I heard." She was watching me closely to see if I recognized the name.

I looked completely vacant. "Carelli, huh?"

"So I heard. My understanding is, he likes his privacy."

"I'll keep that in mind."

I bought a bag of mixed nuts and a Diet Pepsi in return for the information, then boarded my trusty Sentra and headed back down Highway 51. The turnoff was right where she said it would be, although it was more like a rutted trail than my idea of a dirt road. I ignored the NO ENTRY sign and drove on in.

Even denuded of their leaves, the branches that converged overhead shut out most of the sunlight. The farther I went, the thicker the forest seemed to get and the darker it became.

About a quarter of a mile in, the road forked. A faded sword blade pointed to the right read, Norton's Nook. No sign at all pointed left, so that was the direction I took.

About fifty yards later, I came to a pair of black-on-yellow WARNING! NO TRESPASSING! signs, nailed to trees on each side of the trail. I kept going, but the farther I went the more uncomfortable I got. I'm not a woodsy sort of guy. I hate mosquitoes and all little things that fly up your nose, and whenever I'm in the woods for very long I start picking at my scalp for ticks.

After a while, I saw a big slice of sunlight up ahead. Almost immediately the trail opened into a large clearing. It was like walking out of a dark room into bright sunlight. A black Grand Cherokee was parked off to one side. I idly wondered how it could possibly have traversed that narrow trail. In the distance beyond the clearing I could see the still blue waters of what must have been Deep Spring Lake.

The clearing itself was roughly a hundred feet across. Sitting in the middle of it was an authentic hand-hewn log cabin. For the second time that day, I was reminded of a medieval castle. This one was sitting in defensive isolation in the middle of a plain, and there in the forecourt stood a large man with an ax in his hands.

That man was shirtless and, despite the cold, his well-developed upper body was running with sweat. He was standing over a tree stump that he was using as a chopping block. Put a hood on him and he could be an executioner waiting to behead a traitorous knight.

What he was actually doing, of course, was chopping firewood. He walked over to what looked like a pile of two-foot sections cut from the trunk of a good-sized tree. Picking one up, he returned and set it down on the stump. Using both hands, he lifted the ax up over his head and brought it down with a *thwunk* that resounded through the closed windows of the Sentra. The log split cleanly into two pieces that flew off the stump in opposite directions. Moving slowly, he set the ax down on the stump, walked over and picked up each of the cleft pieces in turn, and carried them to a waist-high woodpile near the cabin.

He must have seen me, but he gave no sign.

I did a tight Y-turn, pointing the Sentra toward the entrance to the trail down which I'd come. Before getting out of the car, I checked in the rearview mirror and saw the axman place another section of tree on the block.

I got out of the car.

"Mr. Carelli?" I started walking toward him, smiling in what I hoped was a friendly sort of way.

Instead of responding, he hoisted the ax up high over his shoulder and swung it down in a strong, sweeping arc.

Thwunk!

I tried not to wince.

"My name is Hank Berlin," I said, extending my right hand to show him there was no sword in it. "I'd like to talk to you a minute."

He ignored me.

I put his age at thirty-five, maybe a little older. His body was tanned, thickset, and built for power. His head was large and his features broad. His longish hair was black and straight and combed back off his forehead. He looked more like an Indian than my idea of a wiseguy. A very big Indian.

"I'm a private detective from Pinery Falls," I continued. "I'm investigating—"

He turned and walked away. Just like that. Slow and easy. He took the ax with him. I watched him cover the twenty yards or so to the cabin, then start up the steps to the unrailed porch. About halfway up, he turned and looked back over the clearing.

I was still there.

He considered me for a moment. Then he slowly lowered his rear end until he was sitting on the surface of the porch, his feet on the third step down. He laid the ax across his knees and rested his arms on the handle. From that position, he watched me in silence.

His face had no expression at all.

I thought of getting back in the car and returning to Pinery Falls, but instead I followed the route he had taken to the cabin. His eyes remained fixed on me, the way they might on a rabid dog that had wandered into his clearing.

I stopped at the foot of the porch steps. It meant surrendering the high ground to him, but what the hell? It was his porch.

I was about to reintroduce myself when he broke the silence.

"What do you want to talk to me about?" he asked. His voice was higher pitched than you'd expect it to be and much, much smaller than he was. It was a shock, like the first time you heard Mike Tyson speak on television.

"I'm investigating the death of a man named Jack Drucker," I explained.

The muscles in his massive neck tightened at the mention of Jack's name. A lot of people are like that. They remember to control their faces, but they forget about their necks.

"Jack was murdered," I continued. "He was a reporter for the *Pinery Falls Torrent,* and he wrote a story about you a few weeks before he died. I wondered if there was a connection."

He seemed to think that over. Then, very slowly, he stood up again. He was taller than I was to begin with, and, with the added height the porch gave him, he towered over me.

"Get the fuck out of here," he said, speaking very quietly, but also very distinctly in that funny little voice of his.

I didn't move.

"You didn't hear me?" He hefted the ax in both hands as if testing its balance. There was nothing overtly threatening in the movement, but it felt threatening to me.

Now it was my turn to think things over. If the man didn't want to talk, he didn't want to talk. Besides, he had an ax.

"I'll leave if you want me to," I told him. "But you should know that Jack Drucker used to be a friend of mine and I'm a stubborn man. There's no way I'm just going to drop this."

When he didn't respond, I shrugged and turned away, walking back across the clearing. I had almost reached the Sentra when he spoke.

"Mr. Berlin."

It was a summons.

I turned and walked back toward the cabin. He waited until I'd resumed my place at the foot of the steps, then he took a deep breath in through his nose and let it out through his mouth.

"I'm sorry to hear about your friend," he said then. "But I told him, and I'll tell you—just once I'll tell you. I'm not in the business you think I am. I never was. It may be true that some of my relatives are in that business, but I am not. In any case, that business does not operate within a hundred miles of this lake." His tone was precise, flat, and emotionless. He might have been reading from a legal document.

"I used to sell cars and distribute beer," he said. "But I don't even do that anymore. I'm retired now. This cabin is my retirement home. I own it, and I own the land around it. As a matter of fact, I own this whole lake. Maybe you saw the No Trespassing signs on the trail," he added, with a real hostility returning to his voice. "But then again, maybe you didn't, since you ignored them."

He stood there, breathing deeply, as if the talking had winded him. At first, I thought he was just pausing. But he wasn't. He was done.

"You say that you told this to Jack," I began. "When was that? Did he come up here, or did you—"

I was wasting my breath.

Tony Carelli had turned and gone into his cabin, slamming the door behind him.

18

FOOL ON THE HILL

—*The Beatles*

Rachel cooked us an early supper of chicken Portuguese—skinless chicken breasts, sautéed, then stewed with paprika, oregano, thyme, and garlic in an onion and tomato sauce, served over rice. It was a real treat. Even Harry loved it.

After we ate, I asked if she could watch Harry again if I had to go somewhere.

"Well," she said, "if you *have* to go somewhere, I suppose I *could* watch him."

She smiled to take the edge off it.

"You got me," I said. She keeps teaching me these things I should already know.

Once she'd agreed, I made a telephone call.

I hadn't used Wes Drucker's unlisted number since I called Jack when we were in college, but it came right back to me. Back then, Drucker kept his home number unlisted and only allowed Jack to give it to two friends, and those two were Liz and me. I had used it so often in those days that the number got permanently burned into my memory bank. Not sure it would still be good, I punched it in.

A phone rang on the other end of the line. It rang again. And again. *Two more rings,* I told myself. *Then I'll give up.*

It rang again.

There was a click on the line.

"Hullo." A man's voice. Was it Wes Drucker's?

"Hullo," it said again, irritably and a little slurred. "Who the hell is this?"

It was Wes, all right.

I hung up.

The Drucker house is roughly a mile away from Red Maple Street on the top of the hill—or The Hill, as the town's natives think of it. A number of small hills flank the river in and around Pinery Falls, but only one gets the mental capitals. That's because it's the one where the town's old money built their houses a century and a half ago and where a lot of the town's current money, both old and new, still lives.

When I was a kid, I used to enjoy walking up to Jack's house. It was a journey out of my own world where houses were serviceable rectangles, and into a world where houses were icons of fantasy and imagination. The difference between the houses in my neighborhood and those on The Hill was much greater than money. The lumber barons, the bankers, and the merchants who had built up there might have been showing off their wealth, but they were doing more than that too. They were expressing their vision of themselves. Like medieval lords, they built on the highest ground available. And, also like medieval lords, they went in for gables and garrets, widow's walks, turrets, and even mock battlements. As a result, some of the houses on The Hill resembled medieval *châteaux* and others the gloomy mansions in the Hammer Films movies, but not one of them resembled, either in shape or in spirit, the middle-class dwellings on Red Maple Street.

The late afternoon sky had turned cloudy, but the setting sun was still visible as a white-gold ball behind the overcast. Leaving the Sentra parked in the drive, I climbed the six steps to the large wooden porch.

It felt strange to be standing on that porch again. The two arched mahogany doors were of a size and quality you'd expect to find gracing a small Catholic church. Each of them had its own brass knocker, shaped like a lion. I'd never felt comfortable using those things, so I knocked with my knuckles, the way I always had.

Hi, Mrs. Drucker. Can Jack come out and play?

Except that Jack was dead.

And so was Jack's mother.

After a long wait, I knocked again. There was no point listening to hear if anyone was coming. The doors were too thick and well fitted for any sound from inside to penetrate.

I knocked one more time.

Suddenly one of the big doors swung inward, and there, in the opening, was Wes Drucker. That surprised me a little. In all the years I'd been a regular visitor to the house, he'd never answered the door himself.

The impressions you get in childhood stay with you, and I had always thought of him as very tall. Now I saw that he wasn't really tall at all. Stooped with age, he was actually shorter than I was. The change was shocking. When I was young, he had seemed ancient but ageless, like an indestructible monument carved out of stone. Now, more than thirty years later, he just looked incredibly old.

He must have been in his eighties, and he looked every bit of it. His complexion, which had always been ruddy, now looked unhealthily splotched. His hands and face were covered with liver spots and his nose was a jumble of burst capillaries.

He wore the same kind of snow-white, loose-cut trousers he'd always affected. His hair was the same color and so were his eyebrows, which resembled nests of tiny and malevolent snakes.

Above the white trousers, he wore a white shirt and a red cardigan sweater. Only one button of the sweater was buttoned, and that one in the wrong buttonhole. In his right hand, he held a glass containing two fingers of some kind of clear hard liquor.

He scowled at me.

"I know you," he said suspiciously, his voice slurring a little. "I know that face, anyway."

He thought for another moment, then took a swallow from the glass. "So, who the hell are you?" he demanded.

"Henry Berlin, sir," I said using my rarely used formal name. The "sir" came out automatically. It was an old habit around him.

"Shit!"

The single syllable was so explosive that I almost jumped, but his face broke into what he probably thought was a smile.

"I remember you," he said with a kind of grim delight. "You and Jack. Two little monkeys, always together. Sweet Jesus Christ, just to think of it, after all these years. Come on in!"

He made a gathering gesture with his right arm, splashing a small amount of the contents of his glass onto the plush hall carpet. Reaching out with his left hand, he flicked a wall switch that bathed the hallway with light.

He led me through the dim house, flicking switches as we went. We ended up in his study. It was a good-sized room. Two of the walls were taken up by built-in bookcases, every shelf of which was crammed with books; the others were lined with the kind of wood that the most expensive paneling sold at Home Depot pretends to be. The oriel window in the far wall was concealed by thick red drapes, so that the room was in almost total darkness. A huge Oriental rug covered most of the floor.

He crossed to a sideboard against one wall and picked up a half-full bottle of Bombay Sapphire gin. "Care to join me?" he asked.

"No, thank you." If he'd offered me a cold beer, I would have accepted gladly, but I didn't see any ice in the room and warm gin isn't my style.

There was a small bowl filled with cut limes on the table. After refreshing his glass, he squeezed a half section of lime into his drink. Then he licked juice off his fingers and took a sip from the glass. Satisfied, he crossed to a large oxblood leather armchair near the junction of the two bookcased walls.

"Sit down," he ordered, gesturing toward a similar but smaller leather-covered chair near his own. It made a crunching sound as I sat down. I wondered how many other people had ever been invited to sit in it. Not many, I guessed.

The light from the shaded lamp surrounded his chair and reached out just far enough to encompass mine as well. Beyond that circle of illumination, the room was masked in shadow. I imagined the old man sitting here in this wet dream of a study, drinking Bombay Sapphire while the world went dark around him.

The lamp cast shadows over his face, sharpening and exaggerating his features. He licked his upper lip with a long and almost equine tongue. That was a habit of his, I remembered, as if he were preparing to bite into something delicious. In a sense, he was. He was about to launch into speech, and Wesley Drucker loved to talk. Like an actor, he didn't just love to hear himself—in his mind's eye, he loved *to watch* himself talk as well.

"So, Harry boy. What do you want with me?"

The "Harry" threw me. Harry was my son. Then I remembered that Harry was the nickname Wes had used to call me back in the early years when I'd first started visiting this house on The Hill. The memory shook me. I'd completely forgotten that anyone—much less Wes Drucker—had ever called me that.

"Haven't seen you in years," he muttered. "Damn near a lifetime. So, why are you here now?"

"It's about Jack, sir." That "*sir*" just wouldn't stay down. "I'm trying to find out who killed him."

"Son of a bitch!" he exclaimed. "You're a *detective* now, aren't you?"

"That's right," I said.

"Well, I'm afraid you're shit out of luck, Harry boy."

"What?" The anger I heard in his voice puzzled me.

"I mean that you get no money," he explained. "Not from me you don't."

"But I don't want any money," I protested.

"Well, that's a lucky thing, because you're not getting any. I'm not about to pay some goddamned *private investigator* to snoop into Jack's death. And, if I was, I sure wouldn't pick an opportunist looking to cash in on a childhood friendship."

The charge stung me. "That's not what I'm doing," I said.

Wes picked up his glass and gulped down at least half its contents. That amount would have made a lesser man puke, but it only seemed to calm him a little.

"Don't misunderstand me, Harry. It's not the money. I don't give a damn about that. If Jack was alive, I'd pay anything to keep him that way. Anything at all. But he isn't, is he? Jack is dead."

It was hard to tell exactly how drunk the old man was, but if he'd been drinking at the rate he was going for any length of time, he must be very drunk indeed.

"All the money in the world isn't going to bring him back, is it?" he said. There might have been tears in his eyes, but with the shadows cast by those writhing eyebrows I couldn't be sure. "So, there's no way I'm going to pay—not you nor anyone else either. That's all there is to it. That's it. Thirty."

"That's fine, Mr. Drucker," I said. "I wouldn't expect you to pay me anything. Besides, I've already got a client."

"You do?" It seemed to surprise him. "And who would that be?"

"Liz," I answered.

"Ah. *Eee*-liz-a-beth." He drew the name out, and not lovingly, either. That was a vocal trick he had, rolling a name around in his mouth as if he were chewing on it, tasting it, deciding whether to swallow it or spit it out whole.

He took a moment to digest the news. "So why are you here?" he asked shrewdly. "You think maybe *I* killed him? My own son?"

"I'm here for information," I explained, ignoring his suggestion. "Whatever you can tell me that might help me find Jack's killer."

"You think I have information like that?"

"I don't know. You might. You were his father."

"And you think that means I know anything about him?" He made a sound that was somewhere between a snort and a chuckle. "You remember that term people used to use when you and Jack were young—'the generation gap'?"

"I remember," I said.

"You don't hear it anymore, but you should. It was a good term. It applied. And in this case, it still does."

He started to reach over to the table for his glass. When he realized it was still in his hand, he lifted it and took a swallow. He set the almost empty glass down and slumped in his chair.

I waited in case he had more to say. A minute went by.

"Did Jack have any enemies?" I prompted him.

He made that snorting sound again. "Anybody who's worth a shit's got enemies. You must have learned that by your age."

Resting his elbows on his knees, he leaned toward me. "What about you, Harry boy? Have you got any enemies?"

"I've got an ex-wife," I said.

He laughed—a startling horselike sound that ended in a kind of dying whinny. "Then I guess you do, Harry boy. I guess that you do."

He was still chuckling as he took another swallow from his glass. Some of the liquid dribbled down his chin and dripped off onto his cardigan. "I've never had one of those myself. An ex-wife, I mean. But I've had plenty of enemies."

"What about debts?" I asked. "Big ones, I mean. Was Jack into anyone for serious money? Maybe money he couldn't pay?"

The old man shook his head, but not in answer to my question.

"You think I know these things?" he asked morosely, staring at his nearly empty glass as if wondering where his drink had gone. "You think he came to me with his problems? That I gave him advice?" His mouth curved into what might have been a bitter smile. "How sad."

Once again, he fell into silence. The conversation was clearly on its last legs, but I still hadn't gotten to the thing I told myself I'd come there for.

"You weren't just his father," I pointed out. "He worked for you. Could some story he was working on have led to his death?"

He didn't answer right away. His head was down, and his eyes were in deep shadow. It occurred to me that he might be asleep. But then he spoke. "I wouldn't know," he said. "You want to know what Jack was working on, ask Keith Grabowski. He's the managing editor. I'm just the publisher. I don't know what the reporters are working on anymore, not till the results come out in the paper."

"Not even your star reporter, who was also your son?"

"Especially not my son."

He sounded even older all of a sudden, and very tired.

"Look, Mr. Drucker. I did ask Keith about Jack's work, but he wouldn't talk to me about it. He says you don't want him to. Is that true?"

He didn't answer. I wasn't even sure he'd heard. After a moment, he heaved himself up from the chair and took his glass to the sideboard, where he poured himself another gin.

"One for the road?" he asked.

"No, sir. I've got to get going." Like the "*sir*," that declaration just slipped out. I didn't have what I came for, but I didn't want to be there anymore. Wesley Drucker had been a giant in my life, or at least in my imagination. Now he was just a caricature of himself. And a drunken caricature at that. It was depressing.

He didn't offer to walk me to the front door, but, just as I reached it, he called out from behind me, "Hold on a minute!"

I turned to see him standing at the far end of the front hall. He was bracing himself against the wall with one hand.

"Listen, Harry boy. I don't want you to misunderstand."

"Misunderstand what?" I asked.

"About Jack and me. There was a—there was real feeling between us."

I waited, but he didn't continue.

"Yes?" I prompted.

"Respect," he said finally. "We respected each other, Jack and I. He was a good reporter and I respected that. And he respected his father. Always did." He nodded as if in agreement with himself.

There didn't seem to be anything more for me to say.

Outside, I was surprised to see that some sunset light remained in the autumn sky. The setting sun had broken through the clouds, giving what had been a gray dusk an orange-tinted glow. I must have been inside for half an hour at the most, but it had felt much longer. It had felt like night.

I backed the Sentra out of the long driveway and pointed it down The Hill toward home. Pinery Falls lay stretched out along the banks of the river below like a reclining woman posing for a camera.

Seen from up here, the town appeared deceptively luxuriant. Relics of the sylvan past were everywhere. Evergreens, maples, and basswoods graced the lawns, and the city parks were lush with similar trees, their rich fall colors muted in the failing light. The houses down below looked picturesque and comfortable, as cushioned in the soft, protective foliage as the eggs in an Easter basket.

To the people living up here, secure in their money and their petty authorities, Pinery Falls must look like a feast spread out on a table.

Spots of light were already visible in the windows of some houses. Soon, a real darkness would envelop the valley and the lights of the city would mirror the stars. Then the town would become a second sky—one that you descended into, instead of rose toward.

Not exactly Paris, the City of Light, I thought. *But it'll do.*

. . .

After I left Drucker sloshing around in the big house on The Hill, I drove around for a while before heading back home. Night fell for real while I was driving, and it was completely dark by the time I pulled into the parking lot next to the Wautauqua County Public Library downtown.

Leaving the Sentra unlocked, I walked the block and a half to the Williams Street Bridge, which is the largest of the three bridges that connect the east side of Pinery Falls with the west side. It's also the longest, arching up and over not only Tobacco Island but the two channels of the Wisconsin River that flank it as well.

Zipping my jacket against the cold, I walked out along the sidewalk on the south side of the bridge. At the highest point, I leaned on the metal railing and looked down on the island. Immediately below me, the detritus of the Tobacco Island Development Project was barely discernible in the dark. Off to the south, I could just make out the tops of the two dams that control the falls. A distant roar told me that they were at least partly open.

I wasn't sure exactly why I was there. I just had an urge to take a look at the site of the historical genesis of Pinery Falls—and, just maybe, the genesis of Jack Drucker's murder as well.

If the loggers who founded Pinery Falls had been superstitious, they would have built their town somewhere else. But then, they probably didn't know the history of the place. The Tabac Indians had built a village on this island just before the brutal winter of 1660 killed about five hundred of them. The first French missionary to try to minister to Indians in Wisconsin, Père Réné Ménard, disappeared into the wilderness trying to reach that devastated village—on this very island—the next spring.

If Tobacco Island's past was unhappy, its present didn't look much better. Viewed from the bridge at night, the construction site looked like the ruins of a bombed-out city. Great holes scarred the earth. Skeletal walls reached up out of the rubble of building materials and construction equipment. The inchoate shells marked not where buildings had once stood and been destroyed but where they would stand in the future. For now, however, the visual effect was much the same.

The stark illumination from the street lamps on the bridge cast blacker shadows into the general darkness down below. The only visible light source on the island itself, a yellow glow in the window of a watchman's shack, shone like the signal light of some mad survivor of the war that had devastated the place.

In the daylight the construction site might seem ordered and purposeful, but at night it looked like a massive sculpture representing Havoc Wreaked. The impenetrable shadow cast by the bridge slashed through the site like a line of absolute destruction. On one side, chaos. On the other, the void.

A wind had come up, and the cold air nipped at my face. I walked back to the car and headed for home. I didn't know what I'd expected to find out on that bridge, but whatever it was, it wasn't there.

19

I THINK WE'RE ALONE NOW

—Tommy James and the Shondells

A few hours later, Rachel and I were on the couch in the living room basking in a postcoital glow. When I'd suggested that we might go to bed together, I hadn't meant it literally. We'd always agreed that she would never sleep over at my place when Harry was there. Now, since Harry had climbed in with me the other night, Rachel and I couldn't risk being in the same bed together, even temporarily. But there were other venues.

Because Harry might have come downstairs at any moment, we'd kept most of our clothes on, a fact that added a zest of adolescent furtiveness to our activities. We were a little rumpled—and, I'm pleased to say, more than a little worn-out—from our exertions. I was lying on my back with my feet over one end of the sofa and my head in her lap. It was a very comfortable lap. In fact, it was an excellent lap in every respect.

"What are you thinking about?" she asked me.

It was a classic question people asked when they really wanted to know something else. I thought about how to answer it.

"The truth?" I asked.

"Of course," she said, sounding a little amused.

"This case I'm working on," I answered.

"Can you tell me about it?"

So I did. She'd heard about the Drucker murder, of course, so there was no need to describe it to her. Instead, I explained that Liz had hired me, and filled Rachel in on where the investigation stood at the moment.

Rachel, who is incredibly sensitive to subtexts, went straight to the essential point. "You knew both these people in high school?" she asked.

"He was my best friend."

She was quiet for what seemed a long time. Then, perceptively, "She was your girlfriend, wasn't she?"

"Things were pretty hot and heavy between us for a while," I admitted. "Hotter and heavier for me, it turned out, than for her."

"In the end, she chose him?"

"Yep."

"Back then?" she asked. "Or when you were in Canada?"

Before I could respond, she hurried to add, "I know it's none of my business. Don't answer unless you really want to."

Surprisingly, I found that I *did* want to. Rachel was good to talk to, and we'd discussed all sorts of things since we'd come together—my job, her job, books, movies, ideas, politics, and even religion—but we hadn't talked much about either of our pasts. Hers or mine. Maybe it was time to start.

"In high school," I said. "Just before our senior year. I think it was one of those things that just had to happen."

Rachel looked down into my eyes. "It must have been hard for you."

"It was," I said. "I took it like a man, though. Or like an adolescent boy's *idea* of a man anyway. What could I do? I loved her and Jack was my best friend. I buried my feelings as deep as I could and stepped aside. It was a pretty good act, but I don't think it fooled anybody. It sure as hell didn't fool me."

"So you all stayed friends?"

"Oh yes. She needed me, I think. At least a little. Her parents drank a lot, and they were pretty mean-spirited people. Really pathological, I thought. They took it out on each other, and when they got bored with that, they took it out on her.

"Not that they ever beat her," I added. "Or even denied her things they knew how to give. But they were relentlessly critical. They weren't naturally loving people."

"They sound pretty awful, all right," she agreed.

"She and Jack and I all moved down to Madison after the senior year," I told her. "Freshmen had to live in one-sex dorms in those days. She lived in Langdon Hall the first year. Then, sophomore year, I got a one-and-a-half-room walk-up off campus and they got an apartment together. Once they had their place, the two of them would invite me over for dinner. That was pretty uncomfortable, though, and after a while the invitations stopped. Mostly I'd hang out with Jack."

I swung my feet to the floor and hauled myself up so I was sitting beside Rachel. I put my arm around her shoulder and she snuggled up against me. I was strongly conscious of her warmth and softness—and, most of all, of her listening intelligence. Her presence was both comfortable and comforting as I talked about things I hadn't talked about with anyone for more than thirty years.

"Every now and then, Liz showed up at my place," I said. "Usually late at night, and usually crying. She'd had a fight with Jack, or she was worried about an exam or something. And she needed to talk. There'd be no warning, no call first. Just knock-knock-knock, and there she'd be. 'I have to talk,' she'd say. 'You're the only one I can talk to.'"

"And you always let her in?"

"You're really good at this, aren't you? Yeah, I'd let her in. Once, about one o'clock in the morning, a girl and I had just gotten back to my place after a date. Liz showed up, and I made the girl leave. She'd never go out with me again."

"Gee, I wonder why."

I grinned. "My job was to reassure Liz," I said. "To remind her that she was beautiful, and smart, and competent, and lovable—all of which she really was. She was never totally convinced, of course. But eventually she got so she'd stick up for herself a little. Even then, she kept coming to me. I'd do my thing and she'd go away feeling better."

"And you? How did you feel?"

"I felt glad because she came to me. But when she left, I felt frustrated and very, very tired."

Rachel seemed to think that over.

"How do you feel about her coming to you now?" she asked.

"I don't know," I answered honestly. "Some old feelings got stirred up when I saw her, but I'm not sure what they amount to. Whatever it is," I assured her, "I've decided it's not love."

Rachel smiled. She reached out and took my hand. Our fingers intertwined.

"In all the years I've been back from Canada, I never talked to either one of them," I said. "If we saw each other on the street or somewhere, we'd just look the other way. Or if we couldn't avoid it, we'd nod or wave. That was all. It wasn't very grown-up, but that was how we handled it."

She looked puzzled. "Handled what exactly? Did something else happen between you?"

"Oh yeah," I said. "Vietnam happened."

"Vietnam? You're losing me here, Hank. How did that affect you with them?"

"Well, Vietnam affected everything in those days. You were probably too young to realize how much."

"A wee slip of a girl," she agreed, in an Irish burr. "Why sure, my grandparents were just off the boat."

"Did you ever see that documentary *The War at Home*?" I asked. "It was on public TV a few years ago."

She shook her head no.

"Well, that was about Madison in those days. The campus was a kind of battlefield. There were demonstrations. We occupied Bascom Hall, and the National Guard moved in on campus. Things were really electric."

"It sounds like fun," she said lightly.

"It was. In a way. It made us feel important. But emotions got pretty high sometimes. Everybody took sides. You wouldn't believe how *political* kids were in those days. The SDS guys, the Maoists, the Trotskyites, the pacifists, and the antidraft crowd were all against the war. But each for their own reasons. A lot of guys just didn't want to go, and a lot of the girls just didn't want their boyfriends to go either."

She gave me a little pop of a fist. I grinned at her.

"Meanwhile, the flag-wavers and the anti-Communists and even some liberal types were all for it. Stop the Commies, you know. The sheep were too—the ones who just believed in following orders, no matter what. Well, Jack and I were on different sides."

"You were against it, of course, or you wouldn't have gone up to Canada."

"Right. My slant wasn't really political. It was more of a moral thing. I'd stopped going to church by then, but I still took what I'd been taught there pretty seriously. It was hard for me to square it with what was going on in Vietnam. Maybe you could justify killing someone, but you'd better have a damned good reason to do it. And you'd better be sure you were killing the right person. I didn't see how any of that applied to Vietnam."

"But Jack was in favor of the war," she commented.

"You bet," I answered. "Jack was gung ho from the start. Machismo was like a religion with him."

I was suddenly remembering scenes I hadn't thought of for decades.

"We used to drink beer at this place called Glenn 'n' Ann's near the campus," I said. "Over our first pitcher, Jack would ramble on and on about the domino theory—how if North Vietnam won, the yellow *tide* would *flood* the Philippines and *engulf* Hawaii!"

Rachel grinned.

"I'm not kidding," I told her. "That's exactly how he talked. 'Vietnam's our *destiny*,' he'd say. 'It's where we face our ultimate reality. Where we experience life and death.'

" 'Dying isn't going to help us much,' I told him once.

" 'I'm not talking about dying!' he protested. 'There are two ways to experience death. You can die or you can kill. And believe me, killing's better!' One night, he insisted that we had to go to Vietnam to become men. 'No boy becomes a man until he gets his first kill!' he said."

Rachel seemed to be looking a little uncomfortable.

"All that was just crap," I assured her. "The real reason he loved that war—loved the *idea* of it—was his ideal of manhood."

"*Man*hood?" she asked, with a look of mock puzzlement. "Most of this country's hoods are men, aren't they? At least they are on TV."

I grinned, and she grinned back at me.

"So Jack went over to Vietnam?" she asked.

I nodded. "He must have been pretty good at the war, too. He won a few medals, and some were the kind that meant more than just you were there or got shot at. I heard about the medals from one of our classmates. I never talked to Jack about his war experiences, or about anything else, either."

She looked a little surprised at that.

"In all those years, you never spoke to him?" she asked.

"Or him to me," I added.

A memory was flooding my mind. The last time I'd ever talked to Jack had been on a Friday in September 1971. I had received my draft notice a few weeks before and spent a lot of time deciding where to go—to jail or to Canada. I sure wasn't going to Vietnam. In the end, I couldn't see the point of going to jail either. I'd do everything I could to avoid imposing an injustice on the Vietnamese, but I didn't feel any need to impose one on myself.

I hadn't told Jack about my draft notice yet. But now that my decision to go to Canada was made, I wanted to tell him as soon as possible. We might not be as close as we used to be, but he was still the best friend I'd ever had.

We ran into each other in the hall outside the Rathskeller that served cheap food and tap beer for UW students in the Memorial Union. It was the most popular meeting spot on campus, and the hallway was crowded with people moving in both directions.

When Jack and I greeted each other, I suggested that we go inside and get a beer, but he was too excited to wait. "I'm going to Vietnam," he announced proudly. "I signed up, man! I'm going to do it. One week from now, I go."

He was so pleased with himself, I didn't have the heart to tell him how depressing that news was to me.

"I've got some news, too," I said. And then told him I was going to Canada instead of Vietnam.

Jack stared at me as if my face had just broken out in oozing sores. His body tensed, and his face turned red as if he was holding his breath. I was about to say something more when he whacked me across the face. It was an open-handed blow, but as hard as he could swing. I was so unprepared for it that it nearly knocked me down.

That blow startled a girl who was just passing by us and she dropped an armload of books on the floor. She hesitated as if she might bend down to pick them up, then thought better of it and hurried into the Rathskeller.

Some of the other passing students scurried away with their heads down. Others stopped to watch.

"You miserable coward," Jack snarled with contempt.

His anger astonished me. I hadn't expected him to *like* my decision any more than I liked his, but I'd thought that he'd respect it.

"This war—," I began.

He spit on me. Most of it hit my cheeks, but a few flecks landed in my eyes.

I kicked him in the groin. I'm not exactly proud of that, but something triggered in me and I put all my strength behind it.

He let out a scream and clutched at himself in agony. At the same time, his knees buckled under him and he fell down to the floor. A crowd of students began to form around us now, eager to get a better view of Jack writhing in pain in the hallway. After no more than a moment, I pushed through them and walked away.

"We had a fight down in Madison," I explained to Rachel, who had been watching me very curiously as the memory flooded my mind. "A week later, I went to Canada. A few months after that, Jack went to Vietnam."

She was about to say something when a sudden thump came from upstairs. We reacted like criminals surprised, then grinned at our own embarrassment. "Harry's up," I explained unnecessarily.

Rachel scrambled to her feet. She gave herself a quick once-over to be sure that all her buttons were buttoned. "I'd better get going," she said.

I got up and took her in my arms. We kissed. It wasn't a deep kiss, but it wasn't a peck, either.

"I really enjoyed tonight," I told her.

"Isn't that funny? I really did too," she said.

We stood there, beaming at each other like teenagers.

"Daddy?" The tentative voice came from the hallway upstairs. Harry had gone to my bedroom and discovered that I wasn't there.

"Be right up!" I yelled to him.

Rachel grabbed her jacket from a hook in the hall and hurried to the front door.

"I'll call you tomorrow," I promised.

She blew me a kiss as she slipped out, closing the door behind her.

I headed upstairs.

20

THE GAMES PEOPLE PLAY

—Joe South

I've got a pair of season tickets to six of the Green Bay Packer games at Lambeau Field every year. One of them that year was a game against the Bears that Harry and I went to that Sunday.

Since Green Bay is roughly a hundred miles east of Pinery Falls and the kickoff would be just after noon, I seat-belted Harry into the Sentra around eight thirty that morning and we headed east out of town. Harry looked puzzled when he saw that we were turning right on Menard Avenue instead of left toward St. Mary's.

"What about church?" he asked.

Before Harry was born, Sarah and I had agreed to raise our kid a Catholic. Sarah had been brought up in an indistinguishable Protestant sect and rarely went to church at all. As for me, I had long since "fallen away" from the practice of Catholicism, but I still felt an odd connection to it. A kind of haunting.

The agreement on Catholicism meant at least one of us would have to practice that religion ourself. At first, that one was me. By the time Harry got old enough to know the difference, the primary responsibility had fallen on Sarah as the custodial parent. She accepted it grudgingly at first, but nowadays she took up Catholicism with all of a convert's zeal.

Meanwhile, I had become a card-carrying hypocrite, miming Catholicism when Harry was around and ignoring it when he wasn't. On the weekends he was with me, we usually went to Mass together.

"Are we gonna go to a church in Green Bay?" he asked.

"We haven't got time," I told him. "We'll have to skip Mass this week."

"But I gotta go *every* Sunday," he protested.

"God's a Packer fan, Harry. He'll understand."

The Packers and the Bears are in the same division, and, except for the one year the players were on strike, they have played each other twice every season forever. For the fans of both teams, the games between them are always special, no matter what kind of season each team is having. Being at Lambeau when the Bears come in is like being in a forest in the middle of an electrical storm.

It was a terrific game. That is to say, it was close and the Packers won it on the most beautiful play in football—a high arcing pass down the sideline late in the game. Everyone in the stadium came to their feet as the receiver strode untouched into the endzone. Harry was jumping up and down with glee and so was I. We high-fived each other. Everybody was high-fiving everybody.

It was a great day to be a Packer fan!

The University of Wisconsin marching band put on a "Fifth Quarter" show after the game, and, together with several thousand other people, Harry and I hung around to watch. It was the first time Harry had experienced the controlled anarchy that is that band's special art form, and the little guy got a big kick out of it.

On the way out of the stadium, we ran into Keith Grabowski and Charlie Cleveland coming out of the Players Entrance. Charlie had been attending postgame interviews and Keith had taken advantage of the *Torrent's* second press pass to tag along. I introduced them to Harry, and we walked together toward our cars.

The parking lot was still crowded, and still ringing with the whoops and cheers of happy Packer fans celebrating the victory over their ancient rivals.

"Great game today!" "Man, I wasn't sure they'd pull it off." "Did you see that hit on Brett? Holy shit!" "I don't know how he got up." "How about the one Butler laid on Kramer?"

With Harry's attention fixed on the crowd, I turned to the journalists.

"You guys worked with Jack," I said. "You saw a lot of him, so maybe you can tell me. Was he fooling around on his wife? Did he have a girlfriend?"

Charlie shook his head and Keith snorted, "Jack? I don't think so. If he did, he never let on to me." He looked at me shrewdly. "You think he did?"

"No reason to think so," I said. "I'm just trying to account for something. Maybe there was some woman he worked with? Straight, raven black hair, dyed from brown."

Keith and Charlie looked questioningly at each other. Both of them shrugged.

"Doesn't sound like anybody at the paper," Charlie said.

"Does anybody with hair like that hang around the Wannigan?" I asked Keith. "A waitress maybe? Not necessarily a girlfriend. Just somebody he might have given a ride to on some nights?"

"Doesn't sound like anybody I've seen around there, either," Charlie said.

"Well, if you remember seeing Jack with somebody who has long black hair, let me know. OK?"

When we got to Charlie's SUV, he climbed right in. I grabbed Keith's arm before he could join him.

"You thought of it, yet?" I asked.

"Thought of what?"

"The good reason to bury an important story."

"Who says I've got an *important* story to bury?"

"If it's not important, you might as well tell me about it."

"Look, Hank," he said. "If I was going to talk to you about that—which I have no intention of doing—I sure as hell wouldn't do it out here."

"Will you just tell me this? Is there anything there? Don't tell me what it is if you don't want to. Just tell me if something Jack was working on might be related to his murder."

"Who knows what might be related?" he asked.

"So just tell me *anything*. Whatever you can."

"My lips are sealed." He grinned. "In fact, they're Super-Glued."

He opened the passenger door of the SUV.

"Come on, Keith. Talk to me," I pleaded. I just couldn't believe that my friend would keep stonewalling me forever.

"Mmmph-hmmmm-mmummph," he noised with his lips pressed shut. Then grinning, he climbed into the SUV and slammed the door behind him.

"He was really *funny!*" Harry giggled as we walked on to where the Sentra was parked.

"Yeah. He's a real laugh riot." I muttered.

Sarah called to talk to Harry that night. The phone rang at 7:20, which was just before his bedtime.

It was a joy to hear him telling his mother about the Packer game. He was so excited that he kept forgetting to hold the phone up to his mouth. She must have missed a lot of what he said, but that didn't matter. She wasn't a football fan anyway, and she couldn't have missed his enthusiasm.

"When will you come home?" he asked finally.

The answer seemed to disappoint him. "Oh, I miss you so much, Mommy," he crooned into the mouthpiece.

She must have said she missed him too, because he responded, "I miss you more. I miss you *double*."

Then, after she said something else, "I miss you *dozens*."

"I *love* you, Mommy," he said at last. He gave the phone a big, loud kiss, listened for another moment, and then hung up.

"She didn't want to talk to me?" I asked.

"Oh, gee!" He looked guilt stricken.

"What's the matter, sport?"

"I'm sorry, Daddy." He came over and gave me a big comforting hug. "I forgot to ask her."

"That's OK," I assured him. "If she needed to talk to me, *she* would have asked *you*."

That cheered him up. In fact, he was beaming. The call from his mother had topped what was for him a perfect day—a day he was still talking about when I tucked him in.

"Mommy says that France is really cool," he said. "She wants me to come with her next time."

"That's great," I said.

"She says she's having lots of fun. I told her we were too."

I could feel a big grin spread across my face.

21

BAD MOON RISING

—Credence Clearwater Revival

Once the nightly ritual was over and Harry was actually asleep, I called Rachel and we talked for a while. I heard myself telling her about the day with an only slightly more restrained version of Harry's enthusiasm.

After we hung up, I went to the refrigerator, got a beer, and settled down on the living room sofa with the TV remote. I fully expected to stay there, with occasional visits to the refrigerator, until I felt dozy enough to go to bed. So much for expectations. My great day was about to turn sour.

Flipping channels, I saw a familiar landmark—the CN Tower in Toronto, the city I first lived in when I went to Canada. It turned out to be a scene from a made-for-cable thriller and I decided to watch it for old times' sake. It was just mindless enough to let me concentrate on how many of the outdoor locations I could recognize.

It wasn't long before I was distracted by two brief bursts of sound. They came from outside, and they sounded suspiciously like the self-effacing bleats made by the horn in the Sentra. With the noise from the TV, however, I couldn't be sure.

One of the great advantages of owning an aging econocar is that you never worry about it being stolen. Because of this, I rarely lock my car, and never when it's in my own driveway. Sometimes I even leave the key under the driver's seat. Even now, I wasn't concerned. If someone *had* blown the horn, he obviously wasn't planning to steal the car or he wouldn't have advertised his presence.

Some kid, I thought. *He's probably run away by now.*

About a minute later the sound was repeated. This time in the rhythm of the old *Dragnet* theme: Dum de-dum dum. Dum de-dum dum—DUM.

I considered ignoring it. The beer was still cold, the sofa was comfortable, and the street scene on TV looked tantalizingly familiar. Whoever was out there would probably get bored soon enough. But it occurred to me that the noise might be annoying the neighbors. I decided I'd better go and check.

The temperature had dropped below freezing and a sharp wind had blown up since we got back from Green Bay. I considered going back in to get my jacket but decided that I wouldn't be out there long enough to need it. The night was overcast, but my eyes were adjusting quickly and the light spilling from the windows was helping me out.

Once I got past the rear corner of the house, I had an unobstructed view, both of the Sentra and of a large man in a dark overcoat standing on the far side of it. The driver's side door was open and the man was bent down with his arm inside the car. When he saw me, he straightened up and walked around the back of the car. There he stopped, folded his arms across his chest, and leaned back against the fender watching me.

More curious than angry, I cut across the backyard toward him. I could see that he was wearing a tailored overcoat of the kind a lawyer or corporate executive might wear. He was too far from any good light source to make out his features, but the closer I got, the surer I was that I'd never seen him before.

"What the hell are you doing?" I demanded.

"You're Henry Berlin?" he asked. His voice was calm and quiet, his accent midwestern.

"Yes, I am," I told him. "And that's my car you've been playing with."

As I got closer, he pushed his rear end off the car and straightened up to his full height. He had at least six inches on me.

"Sorry I took liberties with your car," he said. "I just wanted to talk to you."

"I do have a doorbell," I responded.

"You also have a son, right?"

I stopped cold. I was still about ten feet away from him, but I wanted to think over what he'd just said. *Who does this stranger think he is, leaning against my car and talking about my kid?*

"Am I right?" he asked again. When I didn't answer, he just shrugged.

"Well, I just happen to know that you do," he said.

"What the hell is this all about?" I demanded.

"I wanted to get you out here so your son wouldn't have to hear this," he said.

"*This?*" I asked.

I never heard the guy coming up behind me. He must have been standing right up against the back of the house. With my eyes fixed on the man standing by my car, I'd walked right past him. The first I knew of his existence was when his shoulder slammed into my back. At the same time, his foot must have hooked in front of my legs, because when the blow hit, I found myself pitching forward. The next thing I knew I was face down on the grass with some guy's knee planted between my shoulder blades. The guy who owned the knee needed to go on a diet.

If I'd been on my back, I could have put up some kind of fight, but pinned down on my stomach, I was helpless. My arms were spread out along the ground to either side of my body, and my assailant was shoving my head into the freezing turf. With my range of vision severely limited, the first I saw of the man in the overcoat's approach was his shoes. They were good shoes, but they'd seen some wear. I hoped he wasn't planning to use them to kick me with.

He squatted down beside me, leaning forward so that his mouth was only about a foot above my left ear. I could smell Binaca on his breath. Apparently he'd taken precautions so as not to offend. It was almost funny. Endearing even. Of course, he might have a date lined up for later.

He had a boyish face and looked a little like Audie Murphy. Seeing him close up, I was surprised by how young he was. He couldn't have been more than about twenty-four or -five. It occurred to me that he couldn't have heard the original *Dragnet* on the radio and, if he'd ever seen the show on TV, it must have been on the TV Land cable channel.

"You recently visited a man by a lake," he said, his voice as calm and reasonable as before. "That man doesn't want to see you again. Do you understand?"

I assumed that the question was rhetorical, but apparently it wasn't. One of the two hands holding my head raised up and came down hard on my exposed ear. It hurt like hell.

"Do? You? Understand?" he repeated.

"I understand," I said. My voice sounded odd because my mouth was half-full of dirt and grass and my jaw had a limited range of motion.

Some small crawling insect marched into my right nostril and began to root around in there. I exhaled abruptly through my nose, trying to blow it out. Whatever it was crawled even deeper inside. I snorted frantically. A gob of slimy snot came out of the other nostril. The man with his knee on my back chuckled. The man in the overcoat looked mildly alarmed.

Feeling increasingly absurd, I kept trying to dislodge the creature with a series of desperate snorts. Eventually, the thing was ejected.

Or else it died in there. Or maybe it moved somewhere deeper inside where I couldn't feel it anymore.

"Are you done?" the squatting man asked. "OK then. Like I said, the man doesn't want to be bothered. We're going to assume that you will respect his wishes."

"Why should I?" I asked defiantly. I braced myself for another blow, but it didn't come. Instead, the squatting man simply answered my question.

"It's the golden rule," he declared. "Tit for tat."

"What do you mean?"

He sighed, as if saddened by the need to explain such an elemental courtesy. "Reciprocal consideration, Mr. Berlin. We've been considerate of you, haven't we? We're even taking the trouble of meeting you out here in the cold. You know why we did that, Mr. Berlin? We did it so we wouldn't involve your little boy in our business. It would be a shame if we came to regret that decision."

"You bastards!"

"You do understand me then. Good."

He rose to his feet and backed away a few steps. "Now just stay where you are until we leave, all right?"

He nodded, and the man who was holding me down released my head and removed his weight from my back.

I pulled my hands under me and scrambled to my feet. The man in the overcoat looked at me in astonishment as I came hurtling toward him.

Something exploded against the back of my head.

When I came to, I felt so stiff and cold that at first I was afraid that I couldn't move. The only reason I knew that I wasn't dead was because I hurt all over and it doesn't hurt to be dead. At least, we all hope that it doesn't.

I discovered through experimentation that I could move after all, although moving hurt more than just lying still. In time, the pain took on a specific modality inside my head. My body felt cold and foreign. The ground underneath me was rough and hard, and the air above it was lashed by a wind that cut through my clothes like a cat-o'-nine-tails tipped with icicles. Even so, I had to think before deciding that moving might actually improve my situation.

The first time I got to my feet, I felt so light-headed and nauseous that I dropped back down—first onto my knees and then onto all fours. I stayed there until my head regained some of its normal mass, then tried again to rise. This time I managed to stay on my feet, although I staggered and almost fell more than once on my way to the porch.

Once inside the house, I struggled up the stairs, which seemed steeper and more numerous than they ever had been before. I felt as though I'd been through some immense physical ordeal, which, in fact, I had. Feeling incredibly tired, I longed to lie down and slip into unconsciousness. Before I could do that, however, I had to check on Harry. The man in the overcoat had threatened him. Even though that threat had been indirect and contingent on my own future actions, I couldn't be sure that he had left it at that. Besides, Harry might have woken up and been frightened when he discovered that he was alone.

I needn't have worried. Harry was right where he should have been, sleeping soundly and looking blissfully peaceful. His blanket wasn't even tangled.

I felt immensely grateful, but I also felt faint. The prospect of walking down the hall to my bedroom seemed impossibly daunting. It was all I could do to stop myself from collapsing onto the bed beside Harry, but I fought the impulse. Just a few days ago, I'd been worried about letting him climb in with me. To climb in with him now would be just too fucking ironic.

I staggered down the hallway and fell face down on my own bed.

My head still hurt like hell, but there was nothing I could do about that. The possibility of a concussion occurred to me, but there wasn't anything I could do about that either.

Rolling onto my back, I watched a familiar crack drifting lazily around the familiar ceiling. My stomach felt like it was drifting right along with it. I thought that I might feel better if I threw up, but before I found out, I fell asleep.

22

MONDAY, MONDAY

—The Mamas and the Papas

D addy, wake up! *Daaadyyyyy!*"
A frantic Harry was pulling, poking, and shaking me into
wakefulness. It felt like I was being pummeled by an angry mob.

"It's OK., Harry," I assured him, although I didn't feel OK at all.

"But it's been light out *forever*. I should be at *school!*"

"You don't *like* school," I protested reasonably. "Let Daddy sleep."

Harry had hold of my arm and was yanking on it with all his
might. I gently disengaged his grip so I could look at my watch. My
eyes burned when I opened them, and my head hurt like hell. Altogether, I felt like I had the worst hangover of my life. The thought
was encouraging. I'd always survived my hangovers.

"Shit," I said. Harry was right. He was already half an hour late for
school.

"*Daddy!*"

"Sorry, Harry." Along with my general misery, I now felt mildly
ashamed of myself.

"You win," I told him. "I'm getting up. You go and brush your
teeth, all right?"

He pulled his lips back and showed me his teeth. "I already did. See?"

I nodded but then regretted it. I wondered what that guy had hit me with.

"Get your books and wait downstairs, OK?"

Once he left, I had to work hard to muster the will to get out of bed. Eventually, I managed to swing my feet to the floor and sit up. It took me at least another minute to pull myself to my feet. My whole body felt *wrong,* the way it does when you've got a bad case of the flu.

I shuffled to the bathroom. By the time I got there, my stomach was swimming on the edge of nausea. Looking in the mirror, I discovered that I looked exactly the way I felt. My clothes were dirty from my time on the ground and even more rumpled since I had slept in them. I emptied my insides out, brushed my teeth, and washed down three aspirin with a handful of tap water. By that time, Harry was yelling, "Come on, Dad!" outside the bathroom door.

I stopped in my office just long enough to write Harry an excuse. It explained that he was late because his father had had an unavoidable emergency. It said nothing about the nature of that emergency. The less the school knew about that, the better.

After I watched Harry safely inside the school building, I drove back home to shower, shave, and change my clothes. By the time I was done with all that, the pain in my head had eased to a steady throb. I was beginning to think that I was going to recover.

I needed to get my mind around last night's events. What had happened exactly? Two members of the Carelli crime family (I assumed) had warned me off the Drucker case. No, that wasn't right. They hadn't warned me off the *case*, they'd warned me off Tony Carelli. So what did their warning mean for the case? After talking to Carelli on Saturday, I'd thought it unlikely that he had anything to do with Jack's murder. This changed the odds. Or did it?

Last night seemed to prove that Tony Carelli liked his privacy enough to protect it with violence. But Jack's piece had already been published. Whatever its publication meant for Carelli had already happened. What could he have accomplished by killing Jack except bringing more unwanted attention to himself? Attention like mine, for instance.

All of that was more or less academic right now. The more immediate problem was that two goons had made an implied threat against my son. Was that threat real? It was hard to say. There were no Mafiosi in Pinery Falls, so I had very little to base an opinion on. But, from what I'd heard, hurting children wasn't their style. But what if I'd heard wrong? And what was I going to do about it?

I could think of only four possible courses of action. My gut wanted me to drive up north and have it out with Tony Carelli right then. Maybe he wouldn't have an ax in his hands this time. But even if I did that and lived to tell the tale, which was hardly a sure thing, would that really protect Harry from Carelli's goons? I didn't see how.

Another alternative was to go to the police. But what good would that do? The thought of Augie Bendorf going up against the men who'd visited me last night was ludicrous. Besides, those guys weren't local, and I had no way of identifying them. They were only surrogates anyway. There were probably plenty more where they came from.

My third option was to drop the case. I wasn't about to do that for a lot of reasons, only some of which I fully understood.

The fourth option—and the one I decided to adopt—was to carry on as though Tony Carelli didn't exist. I'd pursue other lines of investigation for a while and hope that one of them led me to the killer. If not, I'd have to revisit the Carelli connection somewhere down the road.

Councilman Eugene Malik taught biology at Pinery Falls West High School. He first ran for the city council when a school bond issue was up for consideration and the teachers union needed someone to make a case for it. He won, and the bond issue got approved. That had been two election cycles ago and Malik was still on the council. He apparently really liked the job.

He saw himself as the voice of both local education and fiscal responsibility. No education-related expenditure was too large for him to champion. No ordinary expenditure was too small for him to oppose. Not until Tobacco Island came along anyway.

When I'd called him on Friday, he'd agreed to meet with me on Monday but told me that West frowned on teachers conducting outside business on school property. He had a free period at 10:50, and we arranged to meet at 11 o'clock Monday morning at a Burger King near the school.

The place was almost empty when I got there. The only other customer was a little woman with a deeply wrinkled face and scraggly gray hair, who looked much older than she probably was. She was sitting at a table in the corner, wearing a long, ratty overcoat and a pillbox hat. Nursing a huge paper cup of coffee and chain-smoking cigarettes, she looked like she'd been there for years.

I bought a large soft-drink cup, filled it with Diet Pepsi, and sat down on a molded plastic chair attached to a table right between the two entrances to the restaurant. While I waited, I tried not to think about my head. It actually hurt more when I thought about it.

I'd never met Malik, but tapes of the council meetings are played on the public access channel and I've occasionally been bored enough to watch them. I figured I'd recognize him easily enough. As it turned out, however, I almost didn't.

Seated alongside his fellow council members on my TV screen, Malik came across as an average-sized guy—a little overweight, which was nothing out of the ordinary in central Wisconsin. But the Malik who walked into Burger King that morning was a lumpy little potato of a man with unnaturally short legs. Give him a mustache, a top hat, and a monocle, and he could have passed for a chubby descendant of Toulouse-Lautrec.

Stopping just inside the door, he looked around. As I was the only man present, his eyes settled on me. I stood up and raised my hand in greeting.

"Mr. Berlin?" He greeted me with a friendly smile.

"Call me Hank," I said.

"Gene," he reciprocated.

We shook hands. His were small, but he had a good grip.

"Thanks for making time to see me."

He waved a hand in front of his face, as if shooing away a fly. "No, no. I'm always glad for an excuse to get away from the building during the day." He smiled, revealing rabbity front teeth. "It's kind of fun. Lets me know how the kids feel cutting classes."

"Can I order you anything?" I offered.

"No, no. Nothing for me." He patted the bulging stomach under his Pacific Trail jacket. "I'm skipping lunches these days," he said.

"Coffee then?"

He shook his head.

I sat down and he took the chair across from mine.

"So, what are your concerns?" he asked.

Setting up the appointment, I hadn't said why I wanted it. Apparently, Malik had assumed I was a constituent. Now I told him that I was investigating Jack Drucker's murder and that one of Drucker's last stories had been about Derek Sauerhagen's resignation. I told Malik I was looking into whether that story had any connection to Drucker's death.

"My God!" Malik exclaimed. "Why would you ever think such a thing?"

"I don't really," I said. "But in my business, you have to walk down a lot of blind alleys, just in case."

"How can I help you?" he asked.

"Sauerhagen told Drucker that he thought there was something suspicious about the council's support for the Tobacco Island project."

Malik nodded. "Derek has a bee in his bonnet about the project."

"According to Sauerhagen, you opposed it too. Then you did a sudden one-eighty on the most important vote."

Malik scowled. "There was nothing sudden about it," he said. "Derek is right when he says that I was against the project at first. I considered it grandiose and far too expensive. But the more I looked into it—the more I learned about the quality of the people behind it—the more I was attracted to the idea. I finally concluded that the benefits to the city would be worth the financial risks."

"Did Drucker interview you for his story?"

He shook his head. "No, no. And I don't know why he would have."

I might have thought that the double "no" was a case of protesting too much, except that Malik had used it before. It was probably just a conversational tic.

"Did he ever talk to you privately about Tobacco Island?"

Malik looked puzzled. "I just told you no," he said.

"That was for the article. I mean anytime after that."

"*After* the story appeared? Why would he do that?"

"Sauerhagen had suggested that there was something funny about the council's support for the project. I wondered if Jack was interested enough to investigate that charge."

"Nooo," he said, drawing out the word. "Drucker never talked to me. I don't know that I ever saw the man." His pudgy hands were resting on the edge of the table in front of him, the way a pianist's rest on a keyboard. His index fingers tapped on the table's surface. "You don't think somebody on the council might have killed him, do you?"

"Could be," I said. "The fear of scandal is a powerful motive for some people."

I found myself staring at his fat little index fingers, which were tapping to two different rhythms. When I looked up, Malik had the look of a man in the throes of a shocking epiphany.

"Wait a minute here," he said. "Are you accusing me of something, Mr. Berlin?"

I could have said, *No, but Sauerhagen is.* Or I could have asked, *Why would anybody do that?* I could even have reassured him. But I didn't. Instead, I waited to see what he would do.

What he did was almost have a heart attack. His face flushed red and his neck muscles tightened so much that his head began to vibrate. When he tried to speak, the words came out in a kind of blubber. "Wh-what are you imp-p-plying?"

It might have been funny if I hadn't been a little worried about him. The man was clenched so tight, I was afraid that he might keel over in front of me.

"I'm not really implying anything, Mr. Malik," I told him.

"B-but I'm a teacher, Mr. Berlin. Any accusation is a serious ma-matter to me."

"Please understand me, Mr. Malik—Gene. I have no reason to think you've done anything wrong. I'm not accusing you of anything. It's just that Sauerhagen's raised certain questions and I'm investigating them."

Malik was breathing deeply and deliberately, making an obvious effort to calm himself. "I th-think I'd better leave," he said.

He slid clumsily off his chair. His mouth was open as if he was going to say something more, but he didn't. After a moment, he just turned around and waddled rapidly out of the restaurant on his stubby little legs.

After he left, I sat there sipping my Diet Pepsi and waiting for the throbbing in my head to go away. While I waited, I thought about Eugene Malik. His reaction had been obviously real but way off center. It was almost as if he had reacted not to me, and to what I was saying, but to something shocking that he had seen just over my shoulder.

The suggestion of wrongdoing obviously scared the hell out of him. That would ordinarily suggest some degree of culpability, but in his case, maybe not. It might not be the *content* of the accusation that frightened him but the simple *existence* of it. As he said, for a teacher any accusation can be serious.

In his favor was the fact that he seemed genuinely shocked that anyone could suspect him of corruption, much less of murder. On the whole, I decided that his reaction was at least as compatible with innocence as it was with guilt.

And vice versa.

23

I GET AROUND

—The Beach Boys

Hank! How you doin'?"
I'd known Gus Duncan in high school. We weren't exactly friends, but we were friendly. A decade after graduation, he inherited two corner grocery stores from his father, sold them, and then parlayed the money into a down payment on the biggest supermarket in town. Now he had eleven of them. Three in Pinery Falls, two in Wausau, one each in Stevens Point and Wisconsin Rapids, and four in smaller towns around Wautauqua and Marathon counties—making Duncan's Save 'n' Smiles the largest local chain in the area.

Gus and I got reacquainted more than a decade after high school when his burgeoning supermarket chain hired the Hanratty Agency to set up their security system. After Pat Hanratty retired and I went on my own, Gus hired me to deal with a serious pilferage problem at one of his stores. He suspected that his own son, who was the store's manager, might be involved in the thefts. As it turned out, his kid was innocent and Gus seemed to think that I deserved some of the credit for that. When he'd been elected mayor in 1989, I attended his victory party.

"Doin' well," I answered. "You?"

"Just great."

We were meeting in the room that served as his office at the back of his McClaren Street store. The Spartan cubbyhole was lined with cheap paneling that pretended it was oak. Gus's desk was a pale green metal box that his father had probably bought back in the 1970s. It matched the four-door filing cabinet that sat in one corner of the room. The only objects in the place that were unquestionably post-1970 were the Apple PC that sat in the middle of the desk and the inkjet printer that sat on the small table beside it.

There were two chairs in the room, neither of which was ergonomic. That was fine by me. I have never gotten up out of an ergonomic chair without a backache.

"You've been listening to that asshole Sauerhagen," Gus said after I explained the purpose of my visit. He had an energetic and humorous way of speaking, like a comedian who is always "on." You kept expecting him to wink at you.

"Derek doesn't know shit about what was going on with the council. He never did. He's one of those conspiracy nuts. You want to know how paranoid he is? A bunch of us went over to the Wannigan one night after a council meeting. He gets a few drinks in him and he starts telling me this theory he has. Seems the guy who shot Kennedy—not Oswald, mind you, the *other* guy—was an assassin for the Trilateral Commission. You may not be aware of this, Hank, but the Trilateral Commission kidnaps promising children around the globe and raises them in the Himalayas. That's so they can totally indoctrinate them. When they're done, they've got agents who'll do anything they're told."

He laughed out loud. "Honest to God, it was something like that."

"Why did you bring the Tobacco Island project to the council in the first place?"

"Are you kidding me? By the time it came to me, it already had the backing of almost every power center in Pinery Falls. It was the Patterson Foundation that came up with the idea to begin with. Half the town's banks were prepared to invest if the city got behind it, and the *Torrent* was prepared to back it editorially. Hell, the committee that pitched the idea to me had representatives from the Pinery Falls Business Association, the chamber of commerce, *and* both the MacAllister and Grandeboise Foundations. Even the local historical society was for it. They saw it as a means of highlighting the island's role in the town's history."

"Is that all?" I asked wryly.

"Not quite. There's one other thing. It was a damned good idea for the city."

"Sauerhagen thinks that you uncovered something rotten on the council, but you couldn't deal with it. That's why you didn't run for reelection."

"That's complete and total bullshit," he declared. "First of all, I didn't uncover anything. And second of all, the only reason I didn't run for reelection was because the job was taking too much time away from my business."

"So, you don't think there's anything to his suspicions?"

"Of course not. Derek's talking out his ass. The surprise wasn't that the council went along with the project. Given the forces behind it, the surprise was that there was any resistance at all. Local government's pretty clean in this town. Chummy, sure, but clean. And if it wasn't"—he paused for a drumroll—"would I tell you about it?"

He chuckled. "Look, to be honest, there's always a chance that somebody's doing somebody a favor. People scratch each other's backs. Big hairy deal. There's no real corruption going on. No *bribery*, for Christ's sake. Nobody's betraying the public interest, which, by the way, is always debatable. People make judgments, and they change their minds. Stubborn bastards like Derek don't understand that, because *they* never do."

His definition of clean government sounded different from mine, but I took his point. He was convinced that there was nothing sinister about the council's support of the Tobacco Island project. Of course, the fact that he believed it didn't make it so.

On my way out, I hesitated at the door.

"Say, Gus—do you know a lawyer named Mason? Anthony Mason?"

I'm not sure why I even asked about him. As far as I knew, Mason had nothing to do with the case. But something about the man and his routine had bothered me.

"Sure I do," Gus answered. "Mason did some negotiating with the city during my term."

"Anything to do with Tobacco Island?"

"Nope. He represented the Hardwick Corporation when it sold that land to the city for the new high school."

"What do you know about him?" I asked.

"His firm specializes in contracts and real estate law, but mostly he's a fixer. He does a lot of legal consulting for some of the bigger companies in this part of the state. Of course, 'consulting' covers a multitude of sins, right? I don't know about his lawyering, but he's a damned good negotiator. He picked our pockets on that land deal."

"Does he do criminal work?" I asked.

Gus frowned and shook his head. "Don't think so. Wait a minute—I take that back. I might have heard that he started out in criminal law. But that would have been a long time ago," he added.

I was now more interested in Mason than ever. The lawyer Gus was describing wasn't the kind a kid in trouble would seek out in the middle of the night. Of course, if Mason was a friend of his family, the kid might not know what kind of a lawyer he was.

I thanked Gus for his time and opened the office door. Then I turned back again.

"Hey, Gus," I said. "What do you call an honest lawyer?"

He grinned expectantly, always up for a joke. At that moment I saw not a balding middle-aged entrepreneur and ex-mayor but the prankster who'd snuck into Mr. Aden's room one morning before first period and Super-Glued everything he found on Aden's desk to the surface. He glued Aden's chair, too, but the glue dried before Aden sat on it.

"I give up," Gus said. "What do you call an honest lawyer?"

"A contradiction in terms," I said.

He laughed.

"Hey, I got one for you," he said. "What do you call a boatload of lawyers at the bottom of the ocean?"

"What?"

"A good start."

He laughed at his own joke even harder than he'd laughed at mine. "One more—what do you call a fireman who rushes into a burning building to save a lawyer's life?"

"I think I know this one," I said. "A real asshole, right?"

That afternoon, I met with four more of the city council members— Ableman and Schultz, both of whom had supported the project from the beginning, and Beaman and Breeder, who had started out opposing it. To a man, they agreed with Gus Duncan that the Pinery Falls city council was a model of propriety (wink, wink) and that Sauerhagen was a well-meaning crank.

Breeder turned out to be a close friend of Dougherty's and he told me that Dougherty's wife had been rushed to the hospital with an attack of appendicitis the day of the big vote on the Tobacco Island project.

It was clear that if Jack had spent the days before his death investigating Sauerhagen's charges he hadn't gotten very far. Only one of the council members acknowledged that Jack had even interviewed him. That was Ralph Beaman, and even Sauerhagen said that he had "stayed true to his principles." Beaman told me he got the impression Jack was only going through the motions and didn't take Sauerhagen's accusations very seriously.

I was about ready to give up on them myself.

24

A WORRIED MAN

—The Kingston Trio

As soon as I brought Harry home that afternoon, he scampered upstairs to play his kid's video games while I went into the office to do some work. I was just getting started when the doorbell rang.

Through the glass panels on the front door, I saw the hulking form of Tony Carelli standing on the porch. He was wearing an unbuttoned lumberjack shirt hanging open over a black turtleneck sweater. Behind him, a black Grand Cherokee was parked at the curb. As far as I could see, there was no one in it.

I called up to Harry and he came running to the head of the stairs. I told him that I was about to have some company and he should promise to stay upstairs and not to bother us at all. When he crossed his heart and rushed back to the video games, I proceeded to the front door.

"What the hell are you doing here?" I demanded, opening the door part of the way.

"I drove down as soon as I heard," Tony said assuringly. "I've been here twice already. You weren't home."

"That's no answer, Carelli. What the hell do you think you're do-ing here?"

His eyes narrowed. I got the sense that a part of him was getting angry. Fortunately, another part won out.

"I owe you an apology," he said.

"An apology? Jesus Christ! You send those goons to threaten my son, and you fucking *apologize*?"

"Your child's not in any danger," he promised earnestly. "Not from me, and not from the men who came here last night either. I swear this to you."

My anger deflated. *Whoosh*. Just like that. I'd been telling myself that there was no real threat to Harry, but the overwhelming relief I felt at that moment proved that I'd been kidding myself. Inside I must have been worried as hell.

"I didn't send those men last night," Carelli was saying. "They thought they were doing me a favor, but they weren't. I've explained that to them. More important, I've explained that to their employer."

I assumed that meant his father. If what he was saying was true, he must have a twenty-four-hour hotline to Oxford Penitentiary.

"They won't bother you again," he assured me.

I believed him. Why would he send people to threaten me and then *pretend* to cancel that threat? That would make no sense.

"Come inside," I said, opening the door.

I led him to my office. He didn't look around the way most people do when they come into a house for the first time. What did he care what kind of house I lived in?

I took my chair behind the desk and he took the bigger of the client's chairs in front of it. He sat straight up with his eyes fixed on my face, waiting for me to speak.

"OK, Carelli. Why are you here?"

"I told you, I came to apologize."

"Your apology's not accepted," I said.

He looked alarmed.

"Besides, if that's all you wanted to do, you could have phoned."

He shook his head. "I thought you'd be more likely to believe me if I came in person."

"What do you care if I believe you or not?" I asked curiously.

He didn't answer right away. I got the feeling he was thinking about how to proceed. When he finally spoke, it wasn't to give an answer but to ask a question.

"Have you gone to the police, Mr. Berlin?"

"Not *yet*," I said pointedly.

He nodded, showing that he understood my threat.

"I thought there was a chance that you'd believe me," he explained. "But I didn't—I *don't* think that the police would though. It's hard for me to convince them that I'm a law-abiding citizen. I moved up to Deep Spring Lake to make a new life for myself. Organized crime has no part in that life, and neither do the police. So far, I'm succeeding. But if the police hear about this there'll be no end to it. I won't have a new life, only the old one in another place. That's why I'm really hoping you'll drop this."

I felt the back of my head. It was still tender.

"Why should I?" I asked.

He looked uncomfortable.

"Look, Mr. Berlin. I'm not the kind of man who apologizes. But here I am. I never wanted what happened last night. Nothing like that will ever happen again. I swear to you, the men responsible will be punished."

If he was telling the truth, I didn't like to think what the "punishment" might be.

"They won't be harmed physically," he assured me. "But they've been dismissed from their employment, and in their line of work that's a serious penalty."

"Am I supposed to be grateful?" I said.

"Of course not," he admitted. He closed his eyes for a moment and then opened them again. "Listen, Mr. Berlin, this is very important to me. How can I persuade you to drop the matter?"

"What matter are we talking about? Last night or the Drucker murder?"

"The matter of *me,*" he said. "I swear that I wasn't involved with either one of those things."

I thought about it. What did I have to gain by causing trouble for Tony Carelli? Nothing. On the other hand, I might have something to gain from *not* causing trouble for him.

"All right, Tony. Answer my questions. If you're being straight, I'll forget about last night. I can't forget about the murder, but unless I become convinced that you or your 'family' were involved in it, I won't sic the police on you either."

Now it was his turn to think about it. He took more than a minute before he responded.

"All right," he said. "But understand something. I have no relationship with my father's organization, except for a few people who were good to me when I was growing up. Those men last night were just jerk-offs who thought they could ingratiate themselves with my father by helping me." He took a deep breath, as if he needed it. "That being said, you also have to understand that I love my father. I'm not going to say anything that would implicate him, or give you anything that you might hold over him."

"OK," I said. "That's fair enough."

"So what do you want to know?"

"Up at your cabin, you said you'd told Jack exactly what you were telling me. When was that? When did he interview you?"

"He didn't. He called me on the phone to arrange a meeting. I told him no. I didn't want anything to draw attention to me."

"When was that?"

Carelli shrugged. "Maybe a week, ten days before he was killed."

"And that's the only time you talked to him?"

It seemed like an easy enough question, but he took a while to answer it. I had the feeling that this was getting into something he didn't want to talk about. Then he decided to come clean.

"No," he said, finally. "I'd met Drucker before."

"Before?" I was puzzled. "Before what?"

"It was years ago," he said. "Drucker was in Milwaukee, working on a series of stories about my father's organization."

"Yes," I said. "I know about that series."

"He talked to a lot of people. One of them was me."

I'd had no idea that Jack and Carelli had been acquainted. There had been no hint of it in the story Jack wrote about him.

"I was very rebellious at that time," Carelli went on. "I was angry at my father and alienated from my family. When Drucker came to me, I told him things."

"Things?"

"Things I'd seen. Things I'd heard about."

"You were a source for Jack's exposé on the Carelli family?"

"My impression was, I was his main source."

"Wow," I breathed. "What did your father think about that?"

For the first time in my experience, Tony Carelli smiled. Sort of. He had very even teeth.

"He didn't know," Carelli said.

"And you're telling me this?" I asked suspiciously. "You said you wouldn't give me anything I could hold over your father. But couldn't I hold this over *you*? What's to stop me from telling your father that you betrayed the family to Jack Drucker?"

He shook his head. "Oh, he knows all about it *now*. That's ancient history. My father and I have reached an understanding. We've accepted the fact that we're different people, with different lives. He even wishes me well. That's why he was willing to intervene with the men from last night."

"Even so, he couldn't have been happy when Drucker's series came out."

Carelli shrugged. "He got over it."

"Maybe he did," I said doubtfully. "But what if somebody else didn't? What if somebody nursed a grudge and decided it was time to get even?"

He shook his head. "That's not how it works. They know better than to go after a reporter doing his job. That's as stupid as going after an honest cop. Besides, in a funny way, the guys *liked* Jack Drucker. They admired his balls."

I must have looked surprised.

"Oh yeah," Carelli said. "Drucker was nosing around for weeks. He got to know a lot of the guys. My father has a soldier named Al Mattiacci. He's a real badass. Well, Drucker was snooping around something Mattiacci was into and Al decided to run him off. So Al pulled a gun. Now Al with a gun would panic a rabid dog, but the way the guys tell it, Drucker didn't even blink. He just took Al's gun away and clocked him with it. Two seconds and Al was out cold, just like you were last night."

Good for Jack, I thought. *The Army must have taught him well.*

"Drucker earned a lot of respect with that," Carelli said.

"And this Al Mattiacci?" I asked.

Carelli shrugged again. "He took some shit for a while."

"Maybe he decided to get revenge," I suggested.

"Five, six years later? No way."

Despite what Carelli said, this raised an interesting possibility. Suppose my visitors hadn't been trying to help Carelli at all. Suppose their real purpose had been to cover Mattiacci's ass. Suppose—

"So Mattiacci wasn't one of the men who was here last night?" I asked.

"No way. He's a capo now. He doesn't lower himself to do muscle work anymore. I don't think those guys belonged to his crew, either."

"I've got two more questions for you," I said.

He nodded.

"Where were you on the night that Jack was killed?"

He smiled again. "And the second question is, Can I prove it, right?"

"Exactly," I said.

"No, I can't. I was at my cabin that night. Alone."

Before he left, Carelli asked for a piece of paper and wrote down a phone number.

"Here," he said, handing it to me. "If there's anything reasonable I can do, I swear I will."

That night I received a cryptic telephone call.

"Hank, this is Keith."

"I recognize your voice. What's up?"

"Do you understand what 'on background' means?"

"Yeah, I think so. That's when a reporter gets some information on condition he doesn't say where he got it."

"Right."

I waited.

The line went dead.

Like I said, cryptic.

25

WHITE BOOTS MARCHING
IN A YELLOW LAND

—Phil Ochs

When Harry and I climbed into the Sentra on Tuesday morning, there was a sealed 9 by 11½ inch manila envelope lying on the driver's seat. The words "Hank Berlin" were scrawled on the back. We were running late, so as Harry strapped himself into the back, I tossed the envelope over to the front passenger side. Then I drove straight to the school. Once Harry was safely inside, I returned home, retrieved the envelope, and took it to my office, where I ripped it open and removed five double-spaced pages printed off a word processor. The title was set in caps across the top of the first page, and just beneath it was the author's name:

WISCONSIN'S WAR CRIMINAL
by Jack Drucker

Now I knew what that brief telephone call had been about. I read the pages with a growing sense of excitement.

On the afternoon of September 6, 1972, a rump squad of a Baker Company, consisting of 22 American soldiers, entered the tiny South Vietnamese village of An Doc. The exact location of the village, which no longer exists, is unimportant now. What is important is that, at that time, An Doc was in an area controlled by the South Vietnamese and their American allies during the day but infested with the enemy Vietcong by night. The village was disputed territory, and its residents had divided loyalties. They were caught between contesting military forces and also between conflicting imperatives in their own desperate struggle to survive.

In theory, the Baker Company, along with the entire American military force of which it was a very small part, was there to protect South Vietnam from invasion by the Communist North. In reality, however, the men of the Baker Company had not come to protect An Doc. Instead, according to information developed by a secret Army investigation of what took place on that September day, the Americans had come to the village to wreak a merciless revenge.

Only the day before, the entire company had been ambushed by the Vietcong in the dense jungle near An Doc. Two of their number had been killed in the ensuing firefight, and three more had been seriously injured. The survivors were convinced that the villagers had betrayed Baker Company to the enemy, and they held the villagers responsible for the deaths of their comrades.

The soldiers summoned the residents of An Doc together and herded them into a clearing, just outside the clump of huts that constituted the village. To this day, no one knows exactly how many villagers were present (estimates range from "about a hundred and fifty" to "over two hundred"), but it is certain that most of the Vietnamese were women and children, and the rest were elderly men. Mysteriously, and, in the eyes of the embittered soldiers suspiciously, almost all the young men had disappeared from the village before the Americans arrived.

Once the frightened villagers had been gathered together in the center of the clearing, the American soldiers proceeded to torch all the huts of the village. Some of the adults protested, but the soldiers ignored them. A young boy, perhaps ten years old, broke and ran toward one of the huts, presumably to rescue something precious to him that remained inside. One of the American soldiers stepped forward and struck him on the head with the butt of his rifle. The child dropped in his tracks and lay motionless on the ground, his blood pouring into the dark soil around his head.

The accounts of the soldiers present in the village that day differ in many respects over exactly what happened next. One, questioned by Army investigators, stated that several of the village women threw rocks at the Americans and that at least one rock struck a soldier in the face, breaking his nose. Another swore that a grenade came flying out of the crowd of villagers, although if such a grenade was thrown, it failed to go off. Others deny seeing any missiles at all. Despite such differences, the essential fact is clear. At some point, several of the soldiers opened fire on the huddled villagers. More joined in, until soon the jungle roared with the sound of automatic weapons fire. That roar continued for at least two minutes before coming to a ragged end, which one of the participants described as "like what you hear when all the popcorn is just about popped."

By that time, there were no Vietnamese left standing; the bodies of villagers littered the clearing. Some had fallen on top of others, making small piles of corpses. Dead mothers still clutched squalling babies in their arms. The jungle was eerily quiet now, except for the isolated cries of a few surviving children and the incoherent moaning of the wounded.

There was movement among the bodies. Some of the children tried to crawl away into the undergrowth. Old men and women clutched at their wounds, as though they might hold in the life's blood that was seeping out of them. A few arms extended upwards out of the carnage, like those of drowning men hoping against all hope that a rescuer will arrive and save them. The squirming mass of bodies reminded one soldier, whose father ran a bait shop in Minnesota, of night crawlers writhing in turned-up earth.

Calmly, two of the Americans walked among the bodies with pistols drawn, firing *coups de grâce* into any who showed signs of life. This time, the gunfire was measured, slow, and methodical, and it didn't stop until all movement had ended and all sounds of agony had ceased.

The highest-ranking American in An Doc that day, and, indeed, the only officer present, was 2nd Lt. Andrew Mulroney. Although only 21 years old at the time, Mulroney was already a seasoned combat veteran. He had been in the Army for three years and in Vietnam for two. It was Mulroney who ordered the villagers to be brought to the clearing, and it was he who gave the order to fire.

Andrew Mulroney grew up on a farm about thirty miles southwest of Pinery Falls in the town of Dunoon. He received an honorable discharge two months after the massacre at An Doc, which was several months before the Army launched its investigation into the incident. At the time of his discharge from the service, he returned to Wautauqua County to live with his parents on the farm where he was raised. His mother died in 1985. Times have been hard for family farms, and most of the Mulroney farmland has been sold in pieces over the years.

Today, Andrew Mulroney supports both himself and his aged father by work at a Wisconsin Rapids paper mill. He is uncomfortable discussing the events of September 6, 1972, in any de-tail. Surprisingly, however, he is willing to acknowledge his part in them, even though he knows that many people who learn about An Doc will regard him as a war criminal. Does he regard himself in that light? "I didn't think of it that way then, but I guess I do now," he says.

How did he think about it then? "We were tired, and angry, and just sick to death of the whole Vietnam thing," he says. "Those people got our buddies killed. I guess if we thought anything, we thought that we were doing justice."

Unlike the notorious massacre at My Lai, which had taken place almost exactly four years earlier, the slaughter at An Doc has never become public knowledge. The incident did not go unreported, however. Following a spate of rumors, the Army conducted an extensive investigation in 1975. That investigation included interviews with all of the then surviving members of Baker Company, including those who were not present on September 6, as well as several other American and Vietnamese witnesses. Until now, however, even the fact that an investigation was conducted has been kept secret, perhaps because it was thought, at the time, that one My Lai was all that the nation's troubled psyche could take. For whatever reason, a decision was reached, somewhere inside the U.S. government, that the American people should be protected from what their sons, husbands, and brothers had done at An Doc.

This is the first mention of the incident ever to appear in print. The occurrence is only being revealed now because information from the files of the Army investigation, including photocopies of key interviews with members of Baker Company, found their way into the hands of this newspaper.

Contacted by the *Torrent,* both the U.S. Army and the Department of Defense acknowledged that there had indeed been an investigation of a "firefight" that took place in the village of An Doc on September 6, 1972. Both, however, claimed that the investigation proved inconclusive as to whether or not the actions of the American soldiers had been justified. So far as the American government is concerned, there is no proof of a massacre. Officially, therefore, nothing untoward happened at An Doc that day.

My mind was racing. This was definitely the kind of thing that someone might kill to prevent being revealed. Who? The most obvious answer was Andrew Mulroney. As the man who had given the orders, he was both the most culpable and the one who had the most to fear.

Judging from the quotes in the story, Jack had actually talked to Mulroney. Unless Jack had conned him, that meant Mulroney had known Jack was writing about An Doc, and so he knew the threat that Jack represented to him. What's more, Mulroney lived just down the road from Pinery Falls in the Town of Dunoon. Virtually in the neighborhood.

The story provided a motive to several others as well. Theoretically, any of the twenty-two men who took part in the massacre might have killed Jack to keep him from revealing it. At least any of them who knew that he was planning to do it.

Another possibility occurred to me—one that could explain why Wes Drucker had spiked the story. The Army had investigated the incident at An Doc and considered the matter closed. In fact, this story strongly suggested that the Army had successfully covered up the massacre. How embarrassing would it be for the Army if the story came out now? How high would that embarrassment go?

Was Wes Drucker afraid of the U.S. Army? Did he suspect that the Army, or some element of it, had killed Jack to keep the massacre quiet? Or—my mind was flying in all directions—to protect someone who had taken part in it? Someone who had become too important to be tarred with what had happened at An Doc? Was Wes afraid that if he published Jack's story they'd come after him too?

That explanation was tempting until I thought about where it led. If it was true, it put me on a collision course with the U.S. Army.

Stop it! I told myself. *You're having a seventies-paranoia flashback. The Army doesn't operate that way.*

The hell it doesn't, myself answered back.

26

STAND BY YOUR MAN

—Tammy Wynette

Shortly after noon I called the mill in Rapids and asked to speak to Andrew Mulroney, thinking I might catch him on his lunch hour. The company operator put me through to "the floor." There was a tremendous racket going on in the background and I could hardly make out the voice of the man who answered. *"Andy ain't here,"* it said. *"He works nights and he won't be in till Thursday."*

I made myself a couple of pressed-turkey sandwiches with white bread, a few leaves of lettuce, Heinz ketchup, and the Benecol Light spread my doctor recommends. Then I got a small jar of sweet gherkins and a cold can of Diet Pepsi out of the fridge and sat down at the kitchen table. Munching on the sandwiches, I thought about the case.

Tobacco Island looked like a dead end. Of course, in my business, dead ends sometimes opened out into sweeping boulevards.

The Carelli angle still had some promise, particularly in light of Carlson's theory about a professional hit. But while I could just about imagine Tony Carelli ordering that Jack be killed to spike the story about him, why would he bother once the story had already come out? Besides, I had this annoying feeling that Tony was telling the truth.

Al Mattiacci was a dark horse at best. Resentment over an humiliation that took place several years ago seemed like a pretty thin motive to me. But then, I wasn't Italian.

One possibility I hadn't really considered yet was Big Frank Carelli himself. He might have ordered the hit from his cell down at Oxford. But why? Because of Jack's series about the Carelli family? That had been years ago. If Big Frank was going to have somebody killed over it, why would he wait so long?

Besides, did mobsters really kill reporters?

All things considered, if it wasn't for the envelope I'd found in the Sentra I'd be feeling pretty depressed at the moment. As it was, I felt better about the case than at any time since I took it on. As a possible motive for murder, the An Doc story felt real to me. But one question nagged at me. Would a trained soldier—one who'd taken part in a bloody massacre—hire the professional hit man who probably used that gun to do his killing for him?

The phone rang late that afternoon.

"Berlin Investigations."

"Hank? It's Liz."

"Hi, Liz. It's good to hear from you."

"I know you told me you'd call when you had something to report, but I thought maybe you could fill me in on what's happening."

"Sure," I said. "But not on the phone."

"I can come to your office," she offered. "Or you could come to the house."

"Here is better for me," I said quickly. If she asked me why, I could plead Harry, who was playing upstairs. But the truth was, I'd answered instinctively. I felt uncomfortable at the prospect of entering the house that Liz and Jack had shared. Having that instinct was one thing. Giving in to it was another.

"No, wait a minute," I said. "Is Tommy around?"

"He's doing his chores."

"He actually does chores? I didn't think kids did those anymore."

She chuckled. "Well, his allowance depends on getting them done."

"Hey, whatever works," I said. "Do you think he'd be willing to keep an eye on Harry while we talk?"

"I'm sure he would."

"Then I'll come over there," I said, thus proving that I was a man and not a mouse. "Is now OK?"

"If you're free."

"Nothing *free* about it," I said. "After all, you're paying me."

I meant it to be funny and she laughed.

"Then you hop to it," she ordered.

Come on in," Liz said, stepping back into the foyer.

A small but unnerving sense of dread hovered over me, the kind you can feel entering a hospital, even when you're not a patient. By the time I shut the front door behind us, however, the dread was gone. The house was just a house. There were no ghosts there for me.

"Tommy's in the den," she told Harry, pointing down a hallway off to the left. "It's right through there."

Harry ran off to find his new friend, while Liz led me into the living room.

"Would you like a drink?" she asked me.

"Beer, if you've got it," I said.

"Sure I do. I'm afraid I don't have any Point Special," she said with a smile. "Will a Beck's do?"

"Beck's is great," I said.

While she was off getting the beer, I took the opportunity to look around. Thanks to a large bay window the room was bright. The carpeting was plush and the furniture was near the top of a good manufacturer's line. Everything was done in light, undramatic colors that seemed to blend without effort. Altogether, it was a comfort-

able, soothing sort of room—one I thought had more of Liz than of
Jack in it.

I sat down on one end of a soft-looking off-white sofa. It was even
more comfortable than it looked.

Liz returned with two pub glasses filled with beer. Handing one to
me, she joined me on the sofa. There were three seat cushions. The
one in the middle remained empty between us. We were close, but
not too close.

"Why not on the phone?" she asked, after taking a sip of her beer.
"I'm glad you came over, but why didn't you want to talk on the
phone?"

"I like my conversations with clients to be private," I said.

She frowned. "You think your phone is tapped?"

"No," I said. "But yours might be."

She looked shocked.

"You're the widow," I pointed out. "And these guys don't have a lot
of imagination."

"You really think the police are listening to my phone calls?"

"Not *really*. But I have to consider the possibility. This obviates
that concern."

"Obviates." She smiled, and the skin at the edges of those magnificent eyes crinkled becomingly. "I used to love it when you talked
dirty," she said.

It didn't take me long to fill her in on the developments, which
were, of course, mostly negative.

"In the last few weeks, did Jack ever mention anything to you
about a man named Mulroney?" I asked her.

She shook her head. "I told you, he didn't confide in me. Not
about his work."

I gave her thumbnails of my interviews with Sauerhagen and the
others involved with the Tobacco Island project, none of which
seemed to lead anywhere. Then I told her about Carelli. When I got

to the part about the two goons from Milwaukee, she reacted with real shock.

"My God, Hank! Did they hurt you?"

"Mostly my pride," I said. "It's a little embarrassing, being felled like a tree in your own backyard."

She reached across the space between us and squeezed one of my hands in hers. "I never imagined that this could be dangerous for you," she said.

I returned the squeeze, then withdrew my hand.

"It's not," I assured her, dismissing the subject.

I could still feel the phantom of her hand on mine. I took a big drink from my glass. Then another one. Then—

"The police found some hairs in Jack's car," I said.

"Hairs?"

I nodded.

"Human hairs. A woman's. They're very long and straight, and they're dyed black. Do you have any idea whose they might be?"

She thought it over.

"I know a few women with black hair," she said. "But most of them style it, or wear it short. In the Corvette?" she asked, as though that fact really puzzled her.

I nodded. "Look, I'm sorry about this, but the police think the hairs might have come from someone Jack might have been romancing. For what it's worth, I've asked people at the *Torrent* and they don't believe Jack was fooling around." This was a little more than Keith and Charlie had actually said, but it was close. "The thing is, someone with long black hair was in the car recently. Maybe that night. It would be good to find out who it was."

She thought some more, then shook her head again firmly. "I'm afraid I can't help with that," she said. "And I really don't believe that Jack was 'romancing' anyone."

"Would you have known?" I asked as gently as I could.

She took a deep breath before answering, steeling herself.

"Jack had two affairs that I know of," she said. "The last one was a few years ago. Yes, I think I would have known."

She reached over and picked up her glass from the end table, took a swallow from it, then set it back down.

"That damned car," she muttered.

"What?" I asked.

"He bought the Corvette Stingray last summer. It was his pride and joy, but I just hated that car. After the first few weeks, I wouldn't even ride in it."

"Why not?"

"It was *hostile*," she said. "A sign of hostility, I mean."

"Whose hostility?" I asked, puzzled by the turn the conversation had taken.

"Jack's of course. He used it as an excuse to escape from Tommy and me. He spent most of his spare time working on the thing in the garage. It needed a lot of work, too, because it was so old."

"I'll bet," I said, knowing something about keeping up old cars.

"And have you ever actually *seen* the thing?" she asked.

I nodded.

"It's a two-seater," she said. "What kind of car is that for a man with a wife and child? We couldn't even all fit in it together. Whenever we went somewhere as a family, we had to take the Sable."

"You think Jack was going through some kind of midlife crisis?" I asked.

"More like adolescence," she said somewhat ruefully. Then she didn't seem to have any more to say on the subject.

"How is Tommy taking all this?" I asked.

"As well as you can expect," she said. "He misses his father, of course. But, in a way . . ." Her voice drifted off.

"He seems like a great kid," I volunteered.

"Oh, he *is*, Hank," she said, brightening at the praise for her son. "He really is."

"We had a talk," I told her.

She looked surprised.

"On Saturday, when he came over to play with Harry," I explained.

She looked bemused. "He went out with his bike in the morning. I had no idea he'd gone to see you."

"He wanted to talk about his father," I explained. "About what Jack was like when he was young. He asked me if Jack was a 'nice guy' or if he was 'mean.'"

She bit her lower lip, a mannerism I remembered from the old days.

"I told him about a fight Jack got into when were kids," I said. "He asked me if his father liked to hit people."

"Oh dear," she said, seeming concerned but not surprised.

My glass was still half-full and I took a slow drink from it, just to give her some time. Then I put the glass down on a small table at my end of the sofa. Her eyes followed my movements with a fierce concentration.

"Was Jack in the habit of hitting Tommy?" I asked her.

She stared at a spot on the sofa cushion between us.

"Not in the habit, no," she said after a moment.

"But he did sometimes?"

I waited.

When she spoke, it came out in a low, tight voice, as though the words were hurting her. "Jack and Tommy had a troubled relationship. At least Jack did. Tommy adored him, I believe. But Tommy was a spirited kid and he would only be pushed so far. Jack just couldn't take anything he saw as defiance from his son. Sometimes, physical"—she seemed to be searching for an acceptable term for it—"a physical *domination* was the only way he knew how to stop it."

"When he was drunk?" I asked. In the old days, Jack sometimes got belligerent when he drank. I'd seen him get into two bar fights in Madison, both of which he'd started. One was with a trio of fraternity morons. The other was with a guy who was twice as big, and only half as drunk, as Jack was.

"No," she said firmly. "Never when he was drinking. He seemed to know that if he did that, he might not know how to stop."

"Was there much damage?" I asked, thinking of the smooth-faced, earnest kid who'd sat across the desk from me in my office. *Dad was pretty strict. . . . He could be really tough.*

She shook her head vehemently.

"Oh no," she said. "It wasn't like that. There was never any serious physical harm. Jack was very controlled. But he was almost . . ." Again she searched for a word. I thought she was going to say "sadistic," but she didn't.

"Cold," she said finally, plucking at no-see-ums on her slacks. "Jack would be angry, but he'd be very calm and deliberate. He seemed to know just how hard to hit so there wouldn't be any serious harm." *Or any visible evidence?* "When I'd protest, he'd say that a spanking never hurt anyone. He called it spanking, but sometimes he'd actually cuff Tommy on the head, and sometimes he'd use a book."

"Jesus," I said. "How did Tommy react?"

"He'd look at his father as if he couldn't understand why he was doing this. Sometimes, he'd cry. I'd comfort him and tell him everything was going to be OK."

"How did Jack feel about that?" I asked, thinking he might have regarded it as interference.

"Oh, he didn't mind," she said. "He'd comfort Tommy, too. Once it was over, it was over. He'd give Tommy a hug and tell him that his dad loved him very much. Then he'd expect Tommy to go on as if nothing had happened. Jack saw himself administering discipline, you see. He said that discipline was how boys learn to be men. I was a woman, so naturally I couldn't understand."

"What about you?" I asked quietly. "Did he hit you too?"

"Only that one time back in college," she said shaking her head. "Do you remember that?"

"Oh yes," I said. "I remember."

She'd come to my place in Madison one night and told me that she and Jack had had a quarrel. She made me swear to keep it secret, but he'd been so annoyed with her he'd smacked her across the face. She'd gotten a kind of revenge on him by having sex with another man a few nights later. Now she felt guilty.

"Should I tell him what happened, Hank? What I did, I mean," she added, correcting herself sternly. "I think maybe that was why I did it, so that I could tell him afterwards. But now, it seems that would be cruel."

Tears came into her eyes.

"Do I even love him, Hank?" she asked. "Would I have ever done that if I really loved him?"

"Oh shit, Liz," I said, embracing her. "I'm in a tough position here. Jack's my best friend, and you—I'm in love with you. You know that."

"Please, Hank. You know me better than I know myself. So tell me. What do I really feel?"

"Well, I told him what I'd done," she said. "I think he was afraid I might react that same way if he ever hit me again."

It was painful, but far too easy, to reconcile the Jack she was talking about with the Jack I'd known—the fifth grader who took on seventh graders to protect a stranger, the college kid who picked up fights with guys who were bigger than he was.

"Don't think of him too harshly," she said. "I'm afraid that he really didn't know any better. I think it went back to his own relationship with his father."

"I'm sure it did," I said, thinking about Wes Drucker. "I didn't realize it back then, but I think their relationship must have been all fucked up."

"Jack tried hard to be a good father himself," she insisted sadly. "He just didn't know how."

Who does? I thought. But at least some of us don't knock our kids around.

Was I being unfair to Jack? A lot of people do get physical with their kids. I even slapped Harry once when he'd tried to cut a plugged-in electrical cord with a scissors. I'd done it to teach him an important lesson and I told myself it wouldn't've really hurt. But Harry had cried with the shock of it and how could I be sure?

Harry was only six years old now, and kids get harder to deal with when they get older. Maybe I should wait a few years before judging Jack too harshly.

While I was there, I took a look at Jack's gun collection. As a boy, Jack had been fascinated by guns, and as a man they had apparently become a minor obsession. He kept the collection in two locked cases in a rec room in the basement. A standing case held eight long guns. I'm no gun expert, but the two deer rifles and a shotgun looked like modern hunting weapons and the others seemed to be antiques. One looked like something from the First World War and another looked like the title weapon of the classic Jimmy Stewart Western *Winchester '73*.

The second case, which was hanging nearby on the wall, had obviously been made specially for Jack's handgun collection, as it had seven sized spaces for the precisely seven guns it contained. Three were revolvers and the other four were automatics.

Liz gave me free rein to go through Jack's personal things, including the papers he kept in the house. The police had already done that, of course, and hadn't found anything that interested them enough to take away with them. There were no personal letters that I could find, and Jack apparently kept his work-related papers at the *Torrent*. I wasn't going to get access to them unless old Wes had a change of heart. Nothing I found in the house suggested any new motives for Jack's murder that I could see.

27

SYMPATHY FOR THE DEVIL

—The Rolling Stones

After lunch that Wednesday, I went to the safe in my office and took out the pistol Pat had given me when I set up on my own in the detective business. I'd never carried a gun when I worked for him, partly because I didn't want to and partly because he told me I didn't need one. Any job that required a gun he did himself.

"Now you might need it," he told me. "At least once every five or six years."

The gun was a six-shooter—a .22-caliber Sturm, Ruger Bearcat revolver—and handling it made me feel like a kid playing cowboy. It was smaller than the pistols you see in old Western movies but still too big to be comfortable in a shoulder holster.

"That's not a bad thing," Pat advised me. "A gun shouldn't feel comfortable, and it shouldn't be an everyday accessory in a place like Pinery Falls. It's strictly for special occasions."

In my opinion, going to an isolated farmhouse to meet an alleged mass murderer who might have killed to cover up his crime qualified as a special occasion.

My pacifism had never been the absolute kind that rejected legitimate self-defense. Even so, I'd never actually carried the gun on a job before. There'd never been a situation that seemed to call for it. Except for the lessons that Pat had given me, and the one time a few years ago when I took the Bearcat out in the woods for some target practice, I'd never even fired the thing.

Pat himself rarely carried a gun in Pinery Falls, but when he did, it was the same Colt Officers .45 he'd used as a plainclothes policeman in Milwaukee. It had a lot more stopping power than the Bearcat. I asked him once why he carried such a powerful weapon, while I got a .22.

"Sentiment and swagger," he'd answered. "That's all there is to it. If you're a good shot, a .22'll kill a person just as dead as a .45. If you're not, you shouldn't be shooting a gun at any villain in the first place."

Well, I had no desire to kill anybody, and I felt a little absurd slipping the gun into the inside pocket of my bulkiest winter jacket. There had been a lot of freezing nights already, but this day was actually pretty mild and a windbreaker would have been more appropriate for the weather. But a windbreaker wouldn't have had room for the gun.

If you want to see somebody, it generally saves both time and aggravation to call ahead and make sure they'll be around. But after the abortive attempt to call Mulroney at the mill the day before, I'd decided it would be better to confront him unannounced. That meant I'd have to find his farm without directions from the man himself, and that might take some time to do.

In the event, it took almost half an hour to drive out to the town of Dunoon and another half hour to find Mulroney's place. It was located off County U on a mile-long gravel road that zigged its way through rich-looking Wisconsin farmland. The fields on either side of the road were empty now, stripped of their harvest and waiting patiently for the winter to set in. I wondered if this was the land the Mulroneys had been forced to sell.

At the end of the road was a two-story house, a barn, and a double silo. An aging piece of farm machinery (a thresher, I thought it was) stood next to the barn. A scattering of raggedy-looking chickens pecked about the yard. The gray-white paint on the farmhouse was flaking badly, and the railed wooden porch that ran across the front was sagging in the middle.

I parked the Sentra next to a Ford pickup truck in front of the house. Three of the wooden steps to the porch creaked and the other one cracked ominously when I stepped on it. The front and screen doors were both closed. I didn't really expect the doorbell to work, but it did.

The man who came to the door was roughly my age but half a foot taller. He had reddish hair and a matching mustache. He was thin and wiry, and, from the way he carried himself, I got the feeling he might be a lot stronger than he looked. Dressed in a sweatshirt, jeans, and heavy work shoes, he looked like what he was: a guy who worked in a factory.

"Mr. Mulroney?"

"One of them," he said. "My dad's inside."

"My name's Henry Berlin." I held out my hand and he shook it. He had a strong, workingman's handshake. "I'm a private detective from Pinery Falls."

It's like saying you're a policeman—sometimes people look guilty when you spring it on them. Andrew Mulroney didn't look guilty. He didn't even look distressed. He just looked puzzled.

I decided to try another tack.

"I know about An Doc," I said.

Now he looked distressed.

"But that's not what I want to talk about," I added. "Not directly anyway."

"No?"

"No," I said. "Would you mind if I ask a few questions about something else?"

"Probably," he said. Then, suddenly and unexpectedly, he grinned. "But what the hell? I don't get many visitors. Come on in."

I stepped through the doorway and into the past. The room I entered was a large, overheated farmhouse kitchen from at least fifty years earlier. The only light came from two small windows above the sink and three 60-watt bulbs hanging in a ceiling fixture.

The sink itself had two faucets, one for the hot water and one for the cold. The ancient gas stove had the kind of big high-rise burners that were starting to come back in fashion, although these had obviously never been away. The wallpaper was peeling at the seams. Its flowered design had once been bright and cheerful but now was dimmed by layers of grease and dust. The linoleum that covered the floor was yellowed and stained. A half century of cooking smells lurked in the hot, stuffy air.

A sturdy-looking rectangular wooden table stood in the center of the room with two equally sturdy chairs on opposite sides of it. Mulroney and his father must not get much company. Not for meals anyway.

"Have a seat," he offered. "We could sit in the parlor, but Dad's taking a nap in there." *The parlor?* My great-grandmother had a parlor, but I'd never known anyone else with one.

"This is fine," I said, sitting in the nearest of the two chairs.

"Let me take your coat," he offered.

I shook my head. There was no way I was handing him my gun.

He dropped into the chair on the opposite side of the table, then immediately jumped up again as if struck by a sudden idea.

"Let's have a beer," he suggested. "You want one?"

"Sure," I said, eager to encourage him. Some people open up when they drink.

He got two bottles of MGD out of the refrigerator, uncapped them, and handed one to me before plopping back in his chair. He took a long swallow.

"Oh shit!" he exclaimed, suddenly remembering his manners. "You want a glass?"

"No thanks," I said.

He made a toasting gesture with his bottle and took another swallow.

I matched his gesture and took a companionable swig.

"So, what you want to ask me about?" he asked.

"Did you ever talk to a newspaper reporter named Jack Drucker?"

"I thought you weren't going to talk about An Doc," he said.

"This isn't about An Doc. This is about Drucker."

"What about him?"

"Did you talk to him?" I repeated.

"Yeah, I talked to him," he admitted. "So, what about him?"

"He's dead."

"Oh shit," he said.

"You hadn't heard?"

"What about Drucker's story about An Doc?" he asked. "Has it been published?"

"Don't you know?" I asked.

He shook his head.

"We don't get the *Torrent* out here," he said. "But I've been figuring it hasn't come out. I mean, I ain't heard about it, and it seems like I would have."

"You're right," I told him. "It hasn't been published. I've read it, though."

He puffed out his cheeks and released the air in a slow, almost silent whistle.

"So, are they gonna print it?" he asked.

"I don't know," I said.

"That figures, man." He shook his head. "That fucking figures."

"What do you mean?"

Instead of answering, he took another swallow from his bottle.

"Does it worry you?" I asked.

"Does what worry me?"

"What happens if the story comes out. What the authorities might do."

He shrugged. "The authorities already know about An Doc. Why should they do something about it now? Even the Vietnamese don't give a shit anymore. I guess those people don't matter to them either."

This conversation wasn't going the way I'd expected. I'd come to see a man with a guilty secret. A man so afraid of exposure that he'd killed to keep it from being revealed. The last thing I'd expected was openness, much less a friendly manner and a cold beer.

"Aren't you—"

"Andy!" An anxious male voice sounded from a nearby room. "Are you there, Andy?"

Mulroney gave me an apologetic shrug. Then he called over his shoulder, "I'm here, Dad. Don't worry. Just go back to sleep."

When no further sound came from the other room, he turned his attention back to me. "Sorry about that. He gets insecure sometimes, you know?"

"No problem," I said. The interruption had actually suggested another question.

"What about your father?" I asked. "Does he know what happened at An Doc?"

"Dad? Most of the time he don't even know where he is anymore. Why should he care about something that happened a long time ago in Vietnam?"

"Your friends? Your neighbors?"

He grinned sardonically. "I don't have much of a social life, to tell the truth."

"What about work? What would your coworkers say if they found out?"

"I work next to a wood chipper, man. It's like *Norma Rae* in there. I can't even *hear* what my 'coworkers' say, much less give a shit about it."

"What about your boss?"

"Hey, I'm union. Why should I worry? And what do you care anyhow?"

"It just seems that, if it was me, I'd be worried as hell that people might find out."

He drained his bottle and stood up

"How about another one?" he asked.

My bottle was still half-full. "I'm good," I said.

On the way to the refrigerator, he tossed his empty in a wastebasket. He was obviously not a recycler.

"Why are you here, man?" he asked, returning with a new bottle of MGD.

"Jack Drucker was murdered," I said.

"Jesus!" He looked genuinely stunned.

I shook my head.

"Who the hell killed him?"

"That's just the question, isn't it?" I asked.

"So what do you want from *me*?"

"For starters, I'd like to know where you were at the time he was killed."

"When was that?"

"Night of the fifteenth, morning of the sixteenth. Say, midnight till three."

He thought about it. "That was a Thursday night?"

I nodded.

"Easy. I was working third shift at the mill. If you need proof, there'll be lots of witnesses."

He could have been lying, but it didn't seem likely. There was no point lying about something so easily checked. My new theory of the case seemed to be slipping away from me. I took a healthy swig of my beer, then washed it down with what was left.

"I'll take another beer now," I said. "If the offer's still open."

Before he got up from his chair, he chugged the remains of his own bottle. He was a man after my own heart—or he would have been, except for the little matter of all those corpses at An Doc.

"Mind if I use your bathroom?" I asked him.

"It's right through there," he said, pointing to the doorway through which his father's voice had come. I followed his gesture into an overfurnished room that looked like a cluttered living room to me, but that I recognized as the "parlor" by the elderly man sleeping fitfully on a frayed sofa.

The room was dark and ugly, but there was something homey about it, too. None of the furniture in it matched. The shades were drawn on all the windows, but there was still enough light to make out a door on the far side of the room. Opening it, I found a small but surprisingly clean bathroom. A sink, a toilet, and a tub-and-shower combination were packed into just about enough space to hold a pinball machine. They all looked old, but they seemed free of stains of any kind—that was a rare fact in an old house like this. One that suggested obsessive scrubbing. But by the ex–military man Andrew Mulroney or by his "insecure" father? Or maybe by both of them?

I didn't need to piss as much as I needed time to think, but I used the toilet for verisimilitude. If Andrew Mulroney really had been at the mill that night, he couldn't have killed Jack himself, but he could have gotten someone else to do it. And didn't the gun *imply* a hired killer? Except, unless Mulroney was an incredibly good actor, he didn't seem worried about the story coming out.

Of course, he'd been only one of a lot of soldiers at An Doc that day. What if he had told others that a reporter was snooping around? What if one of them hadn't shared Mulroney's equanimity? For that matter, what if Jack himself had found and questioned other members of Baker Company? Mulroney's was the only name in Jack's story, but there must have been other names in the files.

Before I left the bathroom, I took the Bearcat out of the inside pocket of my jacket and checked that the safety was off. Maybe Mulroney really *was* an incredibly good actor.

The old man was still asleep on the sofa. When I returned to the kitchen, there was a freshly opened bottle of beer waiting for me on the table. The new bottle in front of Mulroney was already half-empty. Even before I'd left the room he'd shown signs that the beer was affecting him. A little fuzziness in his speech and the slightest deterioration in his physical coordination. In the short time I'd been gone, those signs had accelerated. I wondered if he'd chugged an extra bottle or two while I was gone. He took another swig while I resumed my chair. His movements when he put the bottle down were strangely precise, as if he was taking care to place it on an exact spot on the surface of the table.

"How'd it happen?" he asked me. "The murder, I mean."

"Drucker was parked in his car. Someone came up alongside and shot him. In the head," I added, tapping my temple to show where the bullet had probably hit.

"What kind of a gun?"

"A Python .357 Mag. with a combat stock. I suppose you've got a few guns yourself, living out here?" It wasn't exactly subtle, but then it wasn't meant to be.

"You suppose wrong," he said. "I used to have some hunting rifles, but I got rid of them when I got back from Nam. I made Dad get rid of his, too."

I didn't ask why. I was pretty sure I already knew.

"Did Drucker mention anyone else who was at An Doc? Was he talking to any of the others?"

"Not that he mentioned to me," Mulroney answered. "I don't know who he might've talked to after that."

"And when did you talk to him?" I asked.

He thought about it. "The thirteenth it was."

"The thirteenth of this month?" I asked, surprised.

"That's right, yeah."

Jack had died just two nights later. That hadn't left much time, either for Jack to write his story or for a hit man to come to Pinery Falls and find the opportunity to murder him. Now that I thought about it, how would a stranger have lured Jack out to Little River Road at that hour? How would this hypothetical out-of-towner even *know* about Little River Road? A city map would show its existence but not its suitability for an early morning ambush.

"I'm afraid I lied," I said to him.

"Oh?" He didn't seem exactly shocked.

"I do want to talk about An Doc."

"That's what I figured," he said, giving me a sour grin.

"You willing?"

He took a drink. It emptied the bottle.

"Why not?" he said.

"I want to know who was there."

He frowned. "That's a matter of record," he said.

"Maybe. But I haven't got the record and I'm not sure how I'd get it. Besides," I added, "you guys were all from Baker Company, but just some of Baker Company went to An Doc that day, right?"

"That's right."

"So, what record could I depend on to tell me everybody who was there?"

"I see what you mean."

"So?"

He thought about it but shook his head. "I don't think so, man. Those guys were my buddies. I'm not going to sit here and name them for you. You can probably get the names if you want. But not from me."

"OK," I agreed. "How about this? Will you tell me—no names—if anybody there is important now?"

"What do you mean, 'important'?"

"Prominent," I said. "Anybody who's any kind of big wheel now. Maybe in business or in the Army. Maybe in politics. Anything like that."

He actually laughed. "Are you kidding? We were grunts, man. You never saw a more pathetic bunch a bastards in your life. I was the fucking *officer*, for Christ's sake. Just think about that."

There went another theory.

Mulroney lifted his bottle to take a drink and realized that it was empty. He went to get another.

"Did Jack say how he found out about An Doc in the first place?" I asked him. "Or where he got the material from the Army files?"

"He didn't have to say. He got them from me."

"*What?*"

He enunciated carefully, as though speaking to someone unfamiliar with the English language. "He. Got. Them. From. Me."

"How the hell did *you* get them?" I asked.

He shrugged. "I was a civilian by the time the Army started investigating. My lawyer got a court to make them show us what they had that incriminated me. We made copies and I kept them." He was speaking in an odd, flat tone and almost as if by rote.

"And you gave them to Jack?"

"Yeah."

"Why did you do that?"

"Why?" He looked at me like I was really slow. "It was proof, man. It showed the paper that I wasn't just some nut."

I finally got it.

Up until that moment, my assumption that Jack had been killed to keep the lid on An Doc had given me tunnel vision. I hadn't even considered that Jack might not have sought out Mulroney, but Mulroney might have sought out Jack. Mulroney hadn't tried to *stop* Jack from exposing the massacre. He'd been trying to expose it himself.

"Why did you do it?" I asked him.

I meant, why did he tell a reporter? But he took me to mean something else entirely. He held up his beer bottle.

"I was drunk," he said. "*And* I was high. Most of us were. Shit, we'd been awake for nearly two days. I was hallucinating most of the time. It didn't seem real anymore. Actually, it never seemed real over there. I mean, that war was freaky, man. It messed with your head. That whole country seemed like, I don't know, one fucking bad trip. It was hot as hell, and everything was different from here. The trees, the smells, even the dirt felt wrong. The whole place was like a movie. You know what I mean? One a those old movies where the outside scenes are really shot inside and nothing looks quite real. Them people—were you over there, man?"

I shook my head.

"Then I can't explain it to you." he said. "Them people were just *different*. They weren't like you and me. We called them 'gooks' and 'slants,' and that ain't 'politically correct' these days. But it was because of that *difference,* you know."

He had entered into the drunk's confessional. I recognized the signs. Purely by listening, I had assumed the role of father confessor. His words were slurring more now, and he was leaning forward over the table, gathering urgency as he went along. He obviously felt a burning need to communicate something—something that was vitally important but essentially incommunicable.

"They were like *aliens* to us," he explained. "They talked funny. I mean, I know they just talked their own language and we probably sounded funny to them too. But it was more than that. I mean, it wasn't just the words. Their voices were, like—they were *pitched* different, you know? And they were a different *size* than we were too. I mean, I'm a pretty average-sized guy, that's all. But I was like a giant over there. A big man, you know?"

He took a long drink. It seemed to ease something inside him for a moment.

"Now I think about them people all the time," he said. "And none of this around here"—he made a sweeping gesture that encompassed the kitchen we were sitting in, the farm outside, and maybe the whole world beyond—"none of this seems real anymore. I keep thinking back, and it seems like An Doc was only *real* thing in my life ever."

He drained the bottle and immediately headed back to the refrigerator. He was definitely unsteady on his feet now. When he came back, he brought me another one too.

"All that bullshit I handed you before—all that 'What, me worry?' crap. I'm not stupid. I know there could be trouble when this comes out. Maybe serious trouble. But Jesus Christ, man! Enough is fucking enough."

"Why'd you decide to go public?" I asked.

"I'd been living with this thing for a long time. It seems like my whole life. For a long time I was scared shitless that people might find out. But then I realized I wasn't really scared at all. But I was almost *hoping,* you know? Hoping to get it over."

He took another drink, then sat quietly for a moment, pondering something.

I waited.

"I saw this movie," he said after a while. "It was a war movie. There was this guy who steps on a land mine. He's standing on it, and he knows that when he lifts his foot—and, sooner or later, he's *got* to lift his foot, you know?—when he does that, the thing will explode. You can tell he's scared out of his mind, but he can't do anything about it. He can't even move. But you know that sometime he's just *got* to move. Then the camera follows this other character who walks away. After a while, you hear this boom off in the distance. You know that the mine exploded, and somehow you know that the guy lifted his foot deliberately. Not only that—but when he did it, he was *relieved.* You know?"

"Yeah, I think I do," I said.

The two of us fell into an oddly companionable silence.

"Who the fuck are you!"

The outraged voice was loud but tremulous. The grizzled old man I'd seen sleeping on the sofa was standing in the parlor doorway brandishing a cane.

"Get out of my house!" he demanded.

With a shock, I realized that he was not addressing me but his son.

"It's all right, Dad." Andrew spoke softly, rising from his seat. "It's just me."

"How did you get in here? You get out right now!" The old man seemed to be on the edge of panic, his voice cracking into a kind of screech.

"Come on, Dad," Andrew soothed, slowly making his way across the kitchen toward his father.

"Stay away, god damn it!" the old man shouted. "You stay away from me!"

"It's just me, Dad. Andy. It's OK."

The son reached out his right hand toward his father. At first, the elder Mulroney eyed the open hand with deep suspicion. Then something in him seemed to click and, with a dawning sense of recognition, he looked up from the hand into his son's face.

"Is that you, Andy?" he asked hopefully. "Is that really you?"

The extended hand wrapped around the cane. "Sure it is, Dad."

Gently Andrew removed the cane from his father's hand, and the old man let the younger one enclose him in a clumsy embrace.

I had more questions I wanted to ask, but it was clearly time to leave.

The Mulroney farm wasn't far from the family homestead of a notorious Wisconsin murderer named Ed Gein who'd lived in a decrepit farmhouse outside Plainfield. When the police first entered his farmhouse, a female body gutted like a deer was hanging from an exposed beam in his kitchen and there was a pan on his stove with a human heart boiling in it.

I was only a small kid at the time, but I can remember a scary picture of the Gein home in a copy of *Life* magazine my mother left lying around our living room. The headline over the picture read: "HOUSE OF HORROR HAUNTS THE NATION." Well, I don't know about the nation, but Gein's horrors served to haunt my childhood.

The knowledge that such evils existed straight down Highway 51 from the corner of the block I lived on made them seem very real to me. At school, we kids titillated each other with half-understood tales of Gein's atrocities, and some of our parents used him as an all-purpose bogeyman.

"If you do that again," they threatened, "Eddie Gein will eat your insides and hang your hides up on the wall."

To her credit, my mother never said anything like that to me. Even so, I'd wake up doused in sweat from Gein-inspired nightmares.

When I got older, I discovered that the old ghoul was at least as pathetic as he was evil—a stunted soul, deeply in thrall to his dead mother. And, as serial killers go, he was pretty much of a piker. He hadn't even killed most of the people whose skins and vital organs he played with so much. They came from bodies he dug up from rural cemeteries.

By any objective standard, Andrew Mulroney was more of a monster than Ed Gein ever was. Whether or not Mulroney killed Jack Drucker, he had unquestionably done much worse.

I'd made my own moral judgment about Vietnam early, and because of that judgment I'd taken pains to avoid going over there. Having made that choice, and being very aware of what a morally equivocal choice it was, I respected the choices made by others. A big part of that was not judging the actions of those who went over there. God only knows what I might have done in the situations they faced. But Mulroney was something else. By his own admission, he had not only taken part in, but actually led, the slaughter of a village full of defenseless people.

And yet, although the phantom of Ed Gein haunted me for years, I'd just sat across the kitchen table from Andrew Mulroney and willingly drunk his beer. More than that, I'd actually found him *likable*.

How in hell was that possible?

28

YOU CAN'T ALWAYS GET
WHAT YOU WANT

—The Rolling Stones

Driving back to Pinery Falls, I switched on the car radio in the middle of a local news update that ran: ". . . discovered by a maid who entered the second-floor room of the motel believing it to be empty. The maid reported that the two were engaged in what Wausau authorities describe only as 'an obscene act.' A security guard at the motel detained the pair until the Wausau police could be summoned."

Unless they involve a case I'm working on, I'm not very interested in vice busts, so I was reaching for the preset buttons when a name in the report got my intention.

"Both Councilman Malik and his teenage companion reside in Pinery Falls," the voice went on. "The councilman, who is employed as a teacher at Pinery Falls West High School, denies engaging in improper activity of any kind. The young man, whose name is not being released because he is a minor, could not be reached for comment. A West High School spokesman announced that Malik has been put on paid leave until the administration has a chance to evaluate the situation. Although the Marathon County district attorney Martin Arnsbach acknowledges that the police relied solely on the maid's evidence in making the arrests, he states that neither the young man nor Pinery Falls councilman Malik could give satisfactory reasons for their presence at the motel. Both have been released on bail, pending a hearing, which is expected early next week. Central Wisconsin weather is next, immediately following this word—"

I could see the central Wisconsin weather through my windshield, so I punched the preset for a local golden oldies station. That old Wisconsin redneck Dave Dudley was rolling down the eastern seaboard, passin' everything in sight and tryin' to make it home tonight. *Roll on, old Dave. Roll on!*

It looked like Eugene Malik had a thing for boys. But what *age* boys? I wondered. "Teenage companion" suggested that his playmate wasn't all *that* young, but he was obviously young enough to spell serious trouble for a high school teacher.

In my mind, I went over Malik's reactions when we'd talked two days before, trying to imagine the interview from his point of view. Everything had gone fine at first. Then, all of a sudden, Malik had gotten really upset when I'd said something about the fear of scandal. He must have feared that I'd gotten wind of his sexual proclivities.

Did he think I was threatening him with exposure? Or—since our conversation was in the context of the Tobacco Island votes—did he think I was accusing him of caving in to blackmail? More to the point, could that be exactly what he had done? If so, who was doing the blackmailing? And had Jack somehow discovered that fact?

It looked like I might have to rethink the Tobacco Island angle after all.

I picked Harry up at school and we drove straight home. As soon as we got there, he insisted on showing me a new trick he'd learned to do with his favorite video game. Once I'd pronounced myself suitably impressed, I was free to go down the hall to use the phone in my bedroom. I was still wearing the bulky winter jacket with the revolver in its pocket, so I took it off and hung it on a hook in the closet before dialing Keith Grabowski's home number.

"What's up?" he asked.

"Thanks," I said.

"For what?"

"For that little present in my car."

"I have no idea what you're talking about."

"I must have you confused with somebody else," I said. "Well, that's not what I called about anyway."

"Oh yeah, what is?"

"What do you know about the Malik arrest?" Newspapermen always know more about a story than they put in the paper.

"It's the first good sex scandal this town's seen in years," he said cheerfully. "It broke too late to make this afternoon's edition, but it'll be above the fold tomorrow. We've got guys going through Malik's dirty laundry even as we speak. Say, what do you think about 'pedophilic pedagogue'?"

"Only if you want to confuse people," I said. "Is he, by the way?"

"Is he what?"

"Pedophilic? How old is this kid?"

"Oh, I see what you mean. He's sixteen, I think. Maybe seventeen. Goes to East."

"So, Malik's not exactly a child molester."

"Nah. Except legally, maybe."

"And he teaches at West, so the kid's not even a student of his?"

"That's right," Keith agreed.

"Since you know all this, you probably know the kid's name too."

"They're not releasing it," Keith said.

"But you do *know* it."

"Of course I do. I'm a newspaperman, remember?"

I waited, but Keith was being coy. He was like a little kid sometimes, playing games and wanting to be coaxed.

"Well?" I prompted.

"His name's Chris Dietrich. The family lives on Crater Street not far from Menard."

"Thanks. Have you got anything else on Malik?"

"Nothing relevant at the moment," he said. "I'll give you a call if we turn up anything interesting. It's a little tricky. The cops are on this thing like a blanket."

"The Wausau cops?"

"The Pinery Falls cops, too. Everybody. There's something going on."

I thought about that for a minute.

"Hank, are you still there?"

"Look," I said. "That present I was talking about—I'd really like to use it."

"What *could* you be talking about?" he asked.

"I don't hear a 'don't,'" I pointed out.

"Hey, who am I to say you can't use whatever you've got? If I don't know about something, I've got nothing to say about it, right?"

"What are you telling me, Keith?"

"If I shared something with you my boss didn't want me to share, he'd be pissed at me. And if I *didn't* share it with the cops, they'd be *really* pissed at me. I mean, they might even accuse me of withholding evidence, and that's a serious crime."

"What if I got it somewhere else?" I asked.

"Hey, who knows?" he asked. "Jack might have written some story I didn't even know about. A copy of it could have been lying almost anywhere, I suppose."

"Thanks, Keith," I said.

29

I HEARD IT THROUGH
THE GRAPEVINE

—Marvin Gaye

What the hell do *you* want?" George Carlson's emphasis was on the "you" and his voice didn't sound friendly at all.

"How's the Drucker investigation going?" I asked cheerfully.

Carlson was eyeing the five pages of bond paper I was carrying, but he was damned if he was going to ask about them.

"That's police business," he snapped.

"Not going so well, huh?"

He glared at me, but he didn't throw me out of his office. That meant two things—one, his investigation was *not* going well, and two, those pages intrigued him.

"You said that when I had something for you, you might have something for me," I reminded him.

He didn't say anything, but he turned his glare down a notch.

"Did you ever hear of An Doc?" I asked him.

He scowled, as if he wasn't sure that he'd heard me right. "I don't suppose, 'Who's she?' would be the right question, would it?" he asked.

I looked at him with real suspicion. Had George Carlson just made a joke?

"No, it wouldn't," I said, handing him the manuscript. "This is the story Jack was working on when he was killed."

"Where the hell did you get this?" he snarled.

"I found it," I answered, telling a literal truth.

"Where?" he asked suspiciously.

This time I had to lie. "A corner of a page was sticking out from under a sofa in the Drucker house," I said. "It must have got kicked under there or something."

He shot me a dirty look to let me know that he didn't believe me, but he'd let it go for now. Holding the manuscript in his left hand, he began to read. When he got to the end of the first page, he reached out with his right hand and waved it in the direction of a chair in front of his desk. I took that as an indication that I should sit down, and so I did.

Carlson grimaced as he read, as though the words were offending him. When he finished, he set the pages down on his desk and looked up at me.

"Interesting," he admitted. "But I don't see that it's relevant."

"Well, if you've already got the killer wrapped up, I guess it isn't. But I thought maybe if you could use a motive . . ." I let it hang. I wasn't going to spell it out for him. Carlson could see the possibilities as well as I could. Maybe even better.

"We'll look into it," he acknowledged grudgingly.

I grinned. "You owe me now," I said.

"Something," he conceded. "What do you want to know?"

"Tell me about Malik."

"Malik?" He seemed genuinely surprised.

I nodded. "His name came up in my investigation of Jack's murder. All I know is that he was arrested with some teenager in a Wausau motel. What's the rest of it?"

"What does Malik have to do with Drucker?" he asked.

"One of the last stories Jack wrote dealt with possible corruption on the city council. Malik's a councilman who changed his vote on the Tobacco Island project."

"Oh, that." Carlson shook his head. "The Malik arrest doesn't have anything to do with that. It's a sex offense."

"Sex and corruption go together like brats and sauerkraut," I said. He shrugged.

"Come on, George. There's more to this. Motel maids don't just wander into an occupied room in the middle of the night. They don't go at all unless they're asked. And even then, they knock. The maid who 'discovered' them was a setup, wasn't she?"

Carlson looked like a man whose dentist just turned on the drill. He was going to have to give me something—maybe not all of it, but something—and he just hated that.

"All right," he said. "I'm not admitting what you just said, but you're right that there's more to this."

He made me wait.

"Well?" I asked finally.

"We've been on the alert for this kind of thing," he said. "High school kids and older men."

"We? But this was in Wausau."

" 'We' meaning the police in this entire area. The crime was committed in Wausau, but both parties came from right here. For quite a while now we've suspected that there's a teenage sex ring operating out of Pinery Falls."

"A teenage *sex ring*?" The idea was so ludicrous that I thought he might be joking.

"The customers are mostly middle-aged men with a taste for young meat. Lamb or veal. Sometimes, when the men are nervous about being recognized, the kids meet them out of town—in Wausau, or Stevens Point, or somewhere."

"Jesus Christ!" was all I could think of to say.

"It's pretty professional, really. We think a kid named Adam Black-halter runs the thing. At least, he recruits the other kids for it."

"You *think*?"

"Chris Dietrich, the kid who was arrested with Malik, must watch a lot of crime shows on TV. He was angling for a deal before we even brought the subject up. He threw out the name 'Adam' to get our attention. He won't give us any more than that until *we* give *him* something, but we think he meant Blackhalter. Blackhalter's a senior at East. We've had complaints about him in the past. One was from a younger boy who said Blackhalter beat him up. He probably did it, too, but the victim was the only witness and Blackhalter had an alibi. The other complainant was more interesting. She was a fifteen-year-old who said Adam pressured her to have sex with some older man. But it was all pretty vague and we couldn't prove that one either."

"You're actually telling me that a high school kid's been running a professional sex-for-hire operation? Here in Pinery Falls?"

Carlson made a snorting sound that might have been a laugh. "Gee, Toto. It looks like we're not in Kansas anymore, huh?"

"And what does Malik say about this?" I asked.

"That asshole's clammed up so tight he'd need the Jaws of Life to take a dump. At first, he said it was a misunderstanding. Then he shut up until his lawyer bailed him out."

"Did Malik's lawyer have to bail out Dietrich, too?"

"Hell, no. When we notified Dietrich's mother, she came down and bailed him out. That was really too bad, too. Another few hours and we could've had a deal already."

"You called his mother?"

"We always notify the parents when we pick up a minor. The father's out of town, so the poor woman had to come alone. Can you beat it? That was some scene, I can tell you. She was so mortified, I thought she'd keel over from sheer embarrassment. But she posted bail and took the little scumbag home." He shook his head. "These fucking kids. They never think about what they're doing to their parents."

"So, the kid doesn't have any lawyer?"

"He probably does by now," Carlson said. "But a lawyer's only going to tell him what he already knows anyway. He has to cut a deal, and the sooner the better. With or without a lawyer, we expect him to come walking through the door any minute now."

I was leaving Carlson's office when a possibility occurred to me.

"Was this Dietrich the young-looking guy who visited Anthony Mason the night Drucker was killed?" I asked.

"You get no cigar," he said, shaking his head. "But guess who was."

I raised my eyebrows expectantly.

"Adam Blackhalter," he said with a grin.

30

BACK STABBERS

—The O'Jays

C hris Dietrich was stretched out on his bed. It was the same bed, in the same room, that he'd slept in since before he could remember—at least since the time his parents took him out of the crib in their room and put his newborn brother into it.

Chris was lying on his back, with his head on a pillow and his hands resting flat at his sides. Beneath him, the bed was neatly made: bottom sheet, top sheep, blanket on top, and hand-cushioned quilt on top of that. The slips on both pillows matched the sheets. His mother had made the bed that morning, the same way she made it every day, usually within ten minutes after he climbed out of it. Most often she'd pick a moment when he wasn't there to bug her about it, which he'd sometimes do: "Hey, this is my bed. Why you keep messing with it?"

And, to tell the truth, he really did appreciate her effort, even though he'd never gotten around to telling her that. Especially now, when she was so upset with him and so heartbroken over his arrest. And, even more, over what he'd been arrested for.

But Chris wasn't thinking about his mother at the moment. He was thinking about Adam. Adam was the guy who'd gotten him into this mess, and he was the one who'd have to get him out. Either that or Chris would have to turn him in.

At least, he wouldn't have to turn in his real bros. He'd already told the cops and the Pinery Falls District Attorney Hollander that he didn't even know who the other kids were. He only dealt with Adam, and Adam never mentioned anyone else by name. That was pure bullshit, of course. He knew them all and they all knew him. Even the girls. They'd compare notes about the weirdos they encountered, and some of them would actually go out on jobs together sometimes. But Chris had told the cops he didn't know any of them, and the cops had bought it. In fact, the cops didn't seem to care much about the kids. They wanted bigger fish. They wanted the clients. And, of course, they wanted Adam too.

Adam was the contact, the center of the whole thing, but he had never been a bro to Chris. In fact, until he offered Chris the job, he'd been—just what, exactly? A fucking bully, that's what. If you were smaller than he was and you weren't a bodybuilder or something, you had to be careful around him. You could never be sure what was building up inside him and getting ready to explode.

At least, Adam had never made Chris a victim of his rage. In fact, he'd left Chris alone until that day after school when he'd sidled up and told him he was a good-looking kid and he knew a way for Chris to make real money out of that.

When Adam explained what he meant, Chris thought it was a joke or even some kind of insult. But Adam had assured him no and had him talk to Bobby Grady, who'd been doing it for a while already. Chris was amazed. Bobby had always seemed like such a straight-arrow dude.

Getting it up was never a problem for Chris, and when Adam assured him that there wouldn't be any rough stuff, he decided to give it a try. Altogether, he'd been on the job for four months now and had no real complaints. The money was good—shit, the money was terrific!—and what he had to do for it wasn't all that bad. He never got to like it exactly, but he didn't mind it nearly as much as he thought he would.

Even so, none of that made Adam a friend. He was just an employer. And no matter how good an employer was, all you really owed him was your job. Well, Chris had done his job, and it looked like doing it could end him up in jail.

As Chris saw it, if one of them had to go to jail, it should be Adam. The employer is responsible for the employee, isn't he? And, if you're running what the district attorney called "a criminal enterprise," you have to expect to take the shit for it.

Hollander and that Arnsbach guy in Marathon County had both been clear about that. Chris might avoid naming his friends, but he'd have to give up both Adam and all his clients. The district attorneys were excited about that because the one client they knew about was a city councilman and they hoped some of the others might be even more important than he was. Dirty old men were pretty unpopular right now, and some kind of war against perverts was getting pretty big in politics.

All this made Chris a lucky young man. If he could identify some of those dirty old men, he would not only get off, he would become a star witness.

Earlier that afternoon, Adam had used a pay phone to call Chris and arrange for them to meet in a special place. Somewhere private, where they wouldn't be seen together. Chris figured he owed the guy that much. And besides, he thought that Adam might tell him something that would change his mind about dealing with the district attorneys. Maybe Adam could give him some better choice than jail or ratting on people.

Maybe.

But Chris doubted it.

He wasn't really looking forward to that meeting. Not forward at all. Checking his watch, he made himself a deal. He'd have to leave in about ten minutes to make the meet with Adam, so he'd close his eyes and lie here peacefully for all those minutes. If he fell asleep, so be it. If not, he'd get up and go to the meeting.

He opened his eyes three times before the ten minutes were up to check his watch. Then it was finally time and he was still awake.

His mother was in the hallway when he came out of the bedroom. She was headed toward the bathroom with some folded towels in her arms. She looked surprised to see him, and it hurt him to see how wary she had become of him since he'd been busted.

"I've got to be out for a while," he announced.

She seemed to hesitate. He knew that she was afraid to ask where he was going because he might lie. Or, even worse, he might tell her somewhere she didn't want to know.

He started crossing the hallway; then he turned back.

"Hey, Mom," he said.

She stopped and looked at him.

"Thanks for making my bed. It feels real good."

There was a flash of pleasant surprise on her face, quickly followed by wariness, as if she suspected that he was making fun of her.

"Really, Mom," he assured her. "I mean, I never say anything 'cause it's sort of lame, but I really do appreciate it. Honest I do."

And then, because he saw tears start in her eyes, he rushed on through the kitchen and out the back door.

He left in such a hurry that he forgot to grab a jacket. He was wearing a heavy sweater, but he still felt cold outdoors. He wasn't about to go back, though, not with his mother in the state she was in.

Adam had picked the place for their meeting and given him strict instructions on how to get there. He was to walk the three blocks from his house to Menard Avenue, then north on Menard until he came to the bridge where the avenue crossed over the railroad tracks. If no one was following him, he had to climb down the hill and walk west along the tracks for half a mile. Adam said that he'd be coming from the other direction. They'd meet at a place where the tracks ran through a kind of canyon that had steep slopes on both sides that closed you in where nobody above could see or hear.

Once an important branchline servicing several local factories, that stretch of track had lain unused since the last of those factories had closed down years ago. The slopes above it were sparsely wooded, but they were thick with underbrush all the way down to the graveled roadbed. It was about as private a public place as you could find in Pinery Falls

Adam said the chances of anybody else being down there were slim, and according to him, there was no way for anyone to follow either of them without being seen. But Chris had to be careful to make sure nobody was watching him. If anyone followed either of them, or even if someone else just happened to be walking along the tracks, they'd have to abort the meeting. If they did, Chris should wait at home. Adam would find some way to get in touch.

Chris thought the whole thing was a little stupid. He was pretty sure the cops hadn't been following him before, so why should they follow him now? And besides, what did it matter? So what if they saw him and Adam to-gether? A lot of people had seen them together, lots of times. Big fucking deal.

Nonetheless, he followed Adam's instructions the way he always had.

He walked up Menard with his hands in his jeans pockets against the cold. When he reached the bridge, he spun around, feeling like somebody in a bad action movie.

There was no one on the sidewalk behind him.

There were two girls on the other side of the street, but they were just kids, younger than he was, and besides, they were walking in the opposite direction, so they couldn't have been following him.

The traffic was heavy, and he waited long enough for all the cars in sight to clear the bridge. As far as he could see, none of the drivers who passed by showed any particular interest in him. For sure, none of them stopped or even slowed down.

When he was satisfied, he scrambled down the embankment.

Reaching the bottom, he ducked underneath the bridge, where he couldn't be seen from above. There, just as Adam had instructed him, he checked his watch and waited for a full five minutes in case anyone came scrambling down after him. No one did.

He began walking west down the tracks. He stepped easily from one railroad tie to another, with one in between. Most of the ties had black streaks on them, and he wondered where those came from. Did train en-gines drop oil like cars in parking lots?

He could tell that people came down here sometimes because there were scraps all along the tracks. Bits of broken glass. The tattered remains of an old T-shirt. An empty, but unbroken, Wild Turkey bottle. A used condom. And, most mysteriously this far from any road, a new-looking hubcap from a car! He tried to imagine how each of them might have gotten there.

Every thirty steps or so, he looked over his shoulder to see if anyone was following him, and, from time to time, he searched the rims of both embankments for signs of anyone watching from up there. He saw no one anywhere.

He was alone.

To tell the truth, it was beginning to creep him out. Particularly after the tracks swung around a wide curve and he found himself out of sight of the Menard Avenue bridge. It was nearly five in the afternoon and the sun was starting to set. Down here, it had more or less set already, and you could almost see the movement of the darkness closing in on you.

It was colder down here, too. He should have gone back for his jacket.

Pinery Falls was still right above him. He could hear distant traffic sounds, and once he heard the barking of a dog. But he felt cut off and isolated down here, as if he was off in the woods someplace.

Suddenly there was a rustling noise in the underbrush and Chris literally jumped in the air. He caught his foot on an iron rail and nearly fell on his face.

"Shit!" he exclaimed, mostly for the relief of hearing his own voice.

Once he'd regained his balance, he felt foolish. It must have been a rabbit or a squirrel. Maybe even a rat. Jesus! he thought. I must really be spooked.

He wasn't sure how far he'd come from the bridge, but it must have been half a mile at least. The banks were pretty high here, too. This could be the canyon that Adam had been talking about. But if it was, where was Adam? There was a curve some way ahead. That could be where Adam was waiting. Probably so paranoid that he was hiding in the undergrowth, waiting to make sure that Chris wasn't being followed.

Chris had just glanced back over his shoulder when somebody punched him in the stomach.

That was what it felt like, anyway. The force of the blow knocked him backwards off his feet. But how could anybody have punched him? There was nobody there.

He'd fallen onto the ties between the metal rails. He braced his right elbow on a rail and pulled himself up into a semisitting position. Suddenly a pain slammed into him that was much, much worse than the blow itself had been.

He looked down at his body and saw the blood. That was when he knew that he hadn't been punched at all. He'd been shot.

Oh shit, *he thought.*

He brought his left hand up to his stomach to try to stop the bleeding. The blood felt hot against the cold skin of his hand. He noticed a strange thing about the way the blood was flowing. It would gush and then stop and almost seem to try retreating back into his body. Then it would gush out again. With a shock, he realized that he was seeing the action of his heart. For sixteen years, his heart had been pumping blood through his body. Now it was pumping blood out of his body and onto his lap.

That was when Chris knew that he was going to die.

The shooter was stretched out on his stomach in the underbrush at the entrance to the curve. Sighting through the scope on his rifle, he saw Chris looking down at the wound in his belly and watched as the boy's face contorted with pain. The next shot would be a kindness.

Taking a deep breath, he willed his hands to stop trembling and carefully squeezed the trigger.

Chris's body jerked, then settled back motionless against the railroad ties.

The killer closed his eyes. He didn't want to look anymore.

The silencer—handmade from detailed instructions in The American Mercenary Magazine—*had worked perfectly. He'd hardly heard the muffled shots himself. No one up above could have heard a thing.*

Even so, he knew that he should get away from there as fast as he could. The trouble was, he felt too weak to get up. He felt nauseous, too, but he told

himself that he mustn't throw up. He'd seen a TV show where they identi-
fied a killer from DNA in his vomit. He didn't want that to happen to him.

After a while, both the weakness and the nausea passed. He stood up
and was relieved to feel his legs solid beneath him. Carrying the rifle barrel
down at his side, he set out walking along the curve of the railroad tracks
in the opposite direction from the body.

He felt a little bad about what he'd done, but he wouldn't have undone
it, even if he could. Chris had been a likable kid, and it was a shame that he
was dead, but there was no doubt he would have made a deal with the
prosecutors. Making a deal had been the only sensible thing for Chris to do.
Ironically, that had made killing Chris the only sensible thing for him to do.

One crime had led him to another and there was no turning back. Once
he had killed, he was committed to keep killing as long as necessary. He
had embarked on a road that had no end. One crime always led him to another one, and there seemed to be no turning back.

Worst of all, there was no statute of limitations on murder, no point in
time that he could look forward to when he would be safe. For the rest of
his life he would live in some degree of fear, always on guard, always wary,
always frightened of an unexpected knock on the door.

31

STIR IT UP

—Bob Marley

K eith called me around nine o'clock that night to tell me about the Dietrich murder, if I hadn't heard about it already. Or, if I had, to find out if I knew any more about it than he did.

Harry had just settled down for the night and I'd just popped my first can of Point Special when the phone rang. Keith said that some kids had found Chris Dietrich's body lying on the railroad tracks about two hours earlier. He'd been shot twice from some distance away. According to Keith, that was all the police knew about the actual killing, or at least all that they were willing to say.

Although they wouldn't call him a suspect yet, they were looking for a kid named Adam Blackhalter, but they hadn't found him yet.

I returned Keith's favor by telling him what Carlson had said about Blackhalter and the suspected "sex ring."

"Are you serious?" Keith asked. "And that kid was working both girls and guys?"

"According to Carlson."

"*Teenage* girls?"

"Yep."

"How come nobody ever gave me this ring's phone number?"

I laughed.

The phone rang again around ten thirty. It was Sarah calling from Paris, and the reasonable hour told me that this was more than a nuisance call.

"Congratulate me, Hank," she said.

"Consider yourself congratulated," I obliged. "What for, by the way?"

"I did it!" she exclaimed. "I made the deal, Hank. I actually pulled it off."

"Wow." I didn't know anything about the cheese business, but the uncharacteristic little-girl excitement in her voice told me I should really be impressed.

"And it's a *good* deal, Hank. Mueller's going to be thrilled."

"That's great," I said. "I'm really proud of you, Sarah." It was only after I said it that I realized, with some surprise, that it was true.

"All the papers are signed and everything. So, I'm taking tomorrow to see some sights, and then I'll be flying home on Saturday."

"Terrific," I said. "Harry'll be thrilled to have you back."

"He's not still up, is he?"

"Nope, he's sound asleep. Should I wake him?"

"Oh no," she said. "Let him sleep. But give him a big hug and kiss in the morning, will you? Tell him I miss him."

"You bet," I said.

After I hung up the phone, I sat on the sofa drinking Point Special and thinking about the case. It felt like a Dave Dudley song—*I'm sitting here just drinkin', a-drinkin' and a-thinkin', a-thinkin' and a-drinkin' a-bout yoo-ooo-uuu.* The idea was not to think too hard. To let elements of the case drift through your mind, while the beer clears some new neuron paths among your synapses.

Some nights that process helps, and some nights it doesn't. That night, it did.

I had two brainstorms while I was sitting there, both of which I should have had a lot earlier. They came in the form of possibilities, which, if true, would explain things that had been puzzling me about the case. I knew I might be able to check out one of them with a phone call, but it was too late at night to make it. I might be able to verify the other one on the Internet, but I'd already had too much to drink to do that very efficiently.

The morning would be soon enough for both.

After taking Harry to school on Friday morning, I stopped off at the Chippewa State Bank building downtown.

Mason's secretary was just as attractive, trim, well tailored, and carefully coiffed as she'd been before. I didn't get to see her smile this time, though, because I walked straight through the reception area without stopping. She was about halfway out of her chair in protest when I opened the door to Mason's inner office, stepped inside, and closed the door behind me.

I wondered if she'd open it and follow me, but she didn't.

Mason took it well. I saw a flash of irritation in his eyes when he looked up from the papers on his desk, but his voice was friendly enough.

"What can I do for you, Mr. Berlin?"

"I wanted to ask you about something," I answered, crossing the room toward him. I stopped two feet in front of the desk, so as not to loom.

He looked pointedly at his watch.

"I'm sorry if it's inconvenient," I told him. "But this won't take long."

"That's good," he said. "I don't have long."

The last time I'd been there, he'd asked me to sit down. This time, he didn't. I sat anyway, taking the same cushy armchair I'd used before.

"You've heard about Chris Dietrich?" I asked him.

He frowned. You got the feeling that Mason's facial expressions, like those of a bad actor, didn't so much reflect anything actually going on inside him as indicate some reaction he wanted to convey. This frown, for example, indicated uncertainty.

"Is that the boy who was murdered?" he asked. "Yes, I heard about it last night on the news."

"Did you know him?"

"Well, no," he said, as though he found the question odd. "I don't believe I ever met him. Why?"

"No reason," I said, waving it off. "The guy I really want to ask you about is Adam Blackhalter."

Mason wasn't a lawyer for nothing. His expression didn't change at all. But some of the color left his face.

"He's the kid who visited you the night Jack Drucker was killed, right?"

"That's right," he admitted.

"A client?" I asked.

"In the matter he came to see me about, yes."

"Well, I know you can't discuss a client's affairs, but do you happen to know where he is? He's disappeared."

"Disappeared?" This time, he couldn't hide his surprise.

"Well, 'disappeared' might be a little strong," I admitted. "When the police went to his home looking for him, he wasn't there. His parents say he never came home last night. I called East this morning and he hasn't shown up there either."

Mason gave me what he probably thought was a wry grin, indicating tolerance for the wayward young. "Kids that age are notoriously irresponsible," he said.

"Yeah, they can be a real handful all right," I agreed. "Playing hooky. Staying out late. Smoking pot. Selling their bodies."

The grin vanished.

"Selling their bodies?"

"That's one of the things the police want to talk to him about—that and Dietrich's murder. They think Blackhalter was running a string of teenage prostitutes."

"Adam? That's ridiculous." He tried to chuckle, but it came out more of a choking sound. "I don't mean to disparage a client, but the boy never struck me as particularly bright."

"We seem to be thinking along the same lines," I said. "At first, when I thought about him visiting you so late—with your wife gone for the night—my thought was that things could be the other way around. Maybe he wasn't your client. Maybe you were his."

"That's just absurd!"

"You know, I think it probably is," I acknowledged. "Like I said, that was my *first* thought. My second was, How could a high school kid run an operation like that? I mean, it sounds pretty sophisticated to me. These kids don't work the streets. They even meet some of their johns out of town. Besides, I hear that most of the customers are middle-aged men. Now, a teenager could easily appeal to them, but how could a teenager line them up?"

"This whole idea is—" Instead of finishing the sentence, he settled for a grimace that meant something like '*too ridiculous for words.*'

"It occurred to me that Adam needed help," I said. "More than help, probably. Advice and direction, at the very least. Then it occurred to me that he might be getting it from you."

He'd had plenty of warning, so he was ready with a really convincing expression that indicated appalled disbelief.

"You must be out of your mind!" he said.

"But hey," I said lightly. "It's just a thought. It's probably not even true. But if it *is* true, the evidence is bound to be around someplace. All I'll have to do is look for it."

For the first time in our short conversation I saw what I recognized as an honest emotion flit across his face. That emotion was anger.

I got up from the chair.

"I know you're busy," I said. "So I'll get out of here. I've just got one more question to ask you. What's the first name of Adam Blackhalter's mother?"

"*What?*"

"The kid has a mother. What's her name?"

"What the hell are you talking about? How should I know?" His voice was the impotent snarl of a caged dog.

"Well, I thought that you might." I grinned at him. "When I was here the first time, you claimed you were an old friend of the Black-halter family."

32

DESOLATION ROW

—Bob Dylan

Back at the office, I set out verifying the brainstorms I'd had the night before. First, I called Tony Carelli at the number he'd given me on Monday and asked him some questions. He couldn't answer them, but he promised to get back to me. Then I got busy on the Internet. It took me less than an hour. When I was done, I sat there for a long time, just staring at the screen and taking in the implications of what I had learned.

That goddamned war never ends, I thought. *Maybe no war ever does. They just go ricocheting down the ratholes of history, causing more misery and pain forever.*

I drove out to the Town of Dunoon that afternoon. It was a mild Fall day, and I decided to leave the jacket with the Bearcat at home. I no longer regarded Mulroney as a threat.

He was working the overnight shift. I didn't know his exact hours, but I assumed that he'd be home in the early afternoon, and he was. He didn't look particularly surprised to see me. Or particularly thrilled.

"You sicced the cops on me," he said accusingly.

"I just showed them Drucker's story," I said.

"Yeah, well, I guess that's fair enough," he agreed, stepping back and ushering me inside.

Once again we faced each other across his kitchen table.

"Why didn't you tell me about Jack?" I asked.

"What about him?" he answered.

"Andy!" The querulous voice came from the parlor. "Who's out there? Who is that, Andy?"

"It's just a friend, Dad. Go back to sleep."

A friend.

A whimpering sound from the parlor tapered off into silence. I pictured the old man lying on the sofa, clutching a cushion or a blanket and listening fearfully to the voices from the kitchen. What did he imagine? That his son was making arrangements to send him to an institution? That the police had come to take his son away?

"So what do you want?" Andrew Mulroney asked.

"'B' Company, Second Battalion, Twenty-fifth Infantry, Twentieth Light Infantry Brigade," I said.

"Yeah, that was my outfit. So?"

"It was also Jack Drucker's outfit on March 6, 1972. He was there, wasn't he? At An Doc?"

Mulroney frowned. I got the sense that he was deciding how he was going to handle it. Then he shrugged.

"Yeah, he was there," he admitted.

He jumped up suddenly, driven by an urgent imperative. "You want a beer?"

I shook my head. "I just want answers."

He looked at me speculatively, trying to decide if my refusal meant a fundamental change in my attitude toward him.

"Well, I'm going to have one," he said.

He went to the refrigerator and took out a longneck bottle of MGD. He grabbed a church key from the counter and came back to the table. When he popped the cap off the bottle, it clattered against the table and bounced off onto the floor. He ignored it and took a healthy swallow of the beer. Then he set the bottle down and looked at me, as if he were the one waiting for an answer.

"Why didn't you tell me that Jack was part of it?" I demanded.

"I told you, I wouldn't give you names. If you wanted them, you'd have to go somewheres else."

"Not even *Jack's* name? Even after he was murdered?"

"He and I had a deal," he said.

"What kind of deal?"

"He'd write the story, but he wouldn't say that he was there. I wouldn't either." He took another swig from the bottle.

"Why did you choose Jack to get the story out?"

"I didn't. I told you. We don't get the *Torrent* out here. Some of the neighbors get a paper out of Wausau, though. That's where I went first. They weren't interested. I thought maybe they were nervous because they were so small, so I went down to the *Journal Sentinel* in Milwaukee. Then over to the *Star* in Minneapolis. But nobody'd touch it."

"Why not? It seems like a hell of a story to me."

"*Hell* of a story," he repeated bitterly.

"So, why didn't they jump at it?"

"Nam's old news, man. Nobody cares anymore. Besides, they didn't believe me. They said they needed at least two sources. With something like this, maybe they'd need more. I didn't have no other sources. Nobody who's willing to talk."

"So you went to Jack?"

"Shit, no. I didn't know anything *about* Jack. I just went to the *Torrent* 'cause I'd been everywhere else. I asked to talk to somebody about a story. They asked what kind of story and I told them something that happened over in Nam. They pointed me to this guy I recognized from An Doc. And of course that was Jack."

"So, you guys weren't buddies from over there? You hadn't kept in touch?"

"Hell, no. I mean, he was a new guy when it happened. He just got there a week before An Doc and I left Nam a few weeks later. I didn't even know he was from Wisconsin, much less from around here."

"How did he react when he saw you at the *Torrent?*"

Mulroney snorted. "He went white, man. The blood just drained out of his face. The only other place I ever saw that happen to anybody was in Nam."

"So what happened then?"

"We went to a bar. We got drunk and talked about things."

I waited.

"It was one of those taverns out in the country, you know? About five miles out of Pinery Falls." He grinned. "I don't think he wanted to be seen with me, which was pretty weird. I mean, nobody knows me around there anyways. When I told him I wanted the *Torrent* to tell about An Doc, he freaked out. He didn't get it. As far as he was concerned, An Doc was dead and buried." He gave a bitter laugh. "Just like those fucking people."

"So, he didn't want to write about it?"

"Hell, no. He asked me why I wanted to ruin everybody's life."

It seemed like a reasonable question.

"What did you say?" I asked.

"I told him it wasn't *about* ruining other people's lives. It was about *me*. I was tired of feeling like an animal hiding in the dark. I just wanted people to know, that was all. I told him if he didn't write about it, I'd keep going till I found somebody who would. After that, he sort of came around. We started talking about it—how he could write about it without sounding like he was there. I think he agreed to write it so that he could control the story, and make sure he was kept out of it."

"But both of you must have known that once the story was out, anybody could find out who was there. I mean, *I* did."

He shook his head. "It ain't that easy. You only *know* because I *told* you. All you actually found out yourself is that we were in the same unit. Only some of us went to An Doc, remember, and there was never any official record of exactly who was there and who wasn't. Besides, why should anybody check if Drucker was there? He was just the reporter who wrote the story."

"Wait a minute. You said the other papers turned you down because you couldn't give them a second source. What about the documents?"

"I didn't have any documents."

"But you said—?"

"I know what I said. But that was just because Jack was going to write it that way."

"Then how did Jack get the documents?" I asked.

"He didn't. There *aren't* any documents, man. Drucker was his own second source."

"You mean the Army never investigated An Doc at all?"

"Oh, they investigated all right. But if they've got any documents, they're buried in the Pentagon or someplace. Nobody ever showed them to me."

"So Jack was lying to the paper? *In* the paper?" That really surprised me. Somehow I'd always assumed that Jack's adolescent sense of honor would have demanded absolute journalistic integrity.

"*Did* he lie?" Mulroney asked. "You're the one who read his story, not me."

"I'll send you a copy," I told him.

Mulroney got up again, slower this time, and went to the refrigerator. He turned back toward me and looked a question. I shook my head.

He came back to the table with another bottle of beer.

I took a deep breath, then let it out.

"Did Jack participate in the massacre?" I asked. "Did he fire on those helpless people?"

Mulroney smiled bitterly. "*Everybody* participated, man. It was like a fucking party."

"So Jack went along too?" I persisted.

"Went along? Yeah, you could say that. He wasn't the first one to fire, but he did as much as anyone."

I'd been hoping that Jack had held back. That he'd been there but hadn't actually taken part in the atrocity. Now that hope was gone.

"What about afterwards?" I asked, hoping that Jack had at least recoiled. "How did he react?"

"Afterward?" Mulroney was grim. "That was funny, man. After all that noise, everything got quiet. It started to sink in on us, you know? Most of us sat around like zombies. We looked at the ground or we looked away. Some of us threw up. But he was different. First of all, he was one of the two guys who walked around finishing off all the wounded. Then he walked around staring down at all the bodies. It was like he was looking for something that he thought would be there. Like he was really *interested*, you know?"

Walking down the steps of the Mulroney porch, I could hear, even through the closed front and storm doors, the reedy voice of Andrew Mulroney's father calling to his son. It sounded half-petulant and half-terrified.

It occurred to me that Andrew might have a second, maybe even subconscious, reason for wanting the An Doc story to come out. Was some part of him hoping that when his part in the massacre was revealed he would be seized and taken from this rotting farmhouse, and finally relieved from the crushing responsibility for this querulous, demanding, and ultimately irremediable old man?

33

STAYIN' ALIVE

—*The Bee Gees*

I knew that I'd been having an unpleasant dream, but I had no memory of what that dream was about. In the same way, I knew that I'd been wakened by a noise inside the house, but I had no idea what that noise was or where in the house it had come from.

I lay there listening in case it came again.

Nothing.

Maybe the noise had been part of the dream.

The bedroom was very dark. It must have been a cloudy night, because the shades drawn over the windows were only faintly brighter—that is, grayer—than the room itself. I pressed the button to illuminate my watch. It was 1:08 a.m. I was just about ready to roll over and go back to sleep when a sharp noise came from downstairs—a scraping sound of the kind a chair makes when you bump against it on a wooden floor.

Houses as old as mine make noises. So do furnaces and refrigerators. But none of those things *scrape*. Not all by themselves, they don't. And I didn't have any pets who might be running around bumping into furniture either. But something had moved down there. *Someone.*

The noise had seemed to come from the kitchen. My house has three doors opening to the outside. The one on the west side of the house—which happens to be the only one that can't be seen from Red Maple Street—enters into a little hall just off the kitchen.

What woke me could have been the sound of someone breaking into the house. Someone forcing the chain lock on the west side door? Or breaking the glass in a window?

My mind moved on to the more important questions of *who* the intruder might be and *what* he or she might want. The most obvious answer was that it was a burglar, looking either for valuables or for information about one of my cases. Either way, he would be interested in my office and the safe I kept in there. That might give me a little time to figure out what to do.

My first step was to alert the police. I picked up the handset of the phone next to the bed and listened for a dial tone. There wasn't any. The bastard had cut the phone line. *Would a burglar do that? For that matter, would anyone looking for confidential information do that?*

All of a sudden it felt very cold in the room. It occurred to me that nobody in Pinery Falls had been burglarized lately, but two people had been murdered. If this was a killer, it seemed very likely that he had come to kill again.

I thanked God that I'd been unusually tired that night and only had a few beers before hitting the sack. I tried to ease off the bed as slowly and quietly as I could, but there was something in my way. When I rolled against it, that something moved.

Harry!

He must have climbed in with me in the dark. His breathing was so light and so muffled by the bedding, I hadn't even noticed he was there. Guilt flooded over me. In the troubled moments after waking, I had forgotten he was even in the house.

Another noise came from downstairs. It was a creak this time, and I was pretty sure it was the sound of the bottom step on the stairway leading up to the second floor. Whoever was down there wasn't taking any time to search my office. He was coming straight upstairs. He seemed to know where he was heading. Maybe he'd been watching the house and taken note of the window where the last light went out.

I gently covered Harry's mouth with one hand and pinched his nose with the other. The breathing difficulty woke him, as I'd intended it to do. He grunted in protest, a sound I muffled with my hand.

"It's OK, Harry," I said, whispering as softly as I could and removing my fingers from his nose. "This is important. You have to be really quiet, and do exactly what I say. OK?"

My eyes don't adjust as quickly as they used to, but things were starting to become visible to me. I could see the whites of Harry's eyes widen, but he made no sound.

There was another creak on the stairs.

I took my hand away from Harry's mouth.

"Get under the bed," I whispered. "Do it now. Don't ask why. Just lie flat on your tummy and stay there. No matter what. Just *stay there* until I tell you to come out. Will you do that for me?"

"Yes." His voice was small and frightened in the dark. I longed to hold on to him and keep him safe.

"So do it," I told him sternly. "Right now."

Then, before he could move, I hugged him to me and kissed him on the cheek.

"Now move it," I whispered.

He scrambled off the bed and I followed him down, crouching beside the bed while he crawled under.

"Don't make a sound," I whispered. "No matter what."

I got to my feet. My eyes were well enough adjusted by now to make out the familiar objects in my room. A narrow band of yellow light showed at the bottom of the closed door to the hall. It was the hall light, which I'd left on in case Harry woke up during the night, and then, because it was on, I had closed my bedroom door.

This was good, I told myself. If the intruder came into the bed-room, the light would be behind him and he'd be looking into dark-ness. His eyes wouldn't be adjusted to the dark the way that mine were already. I took some comfort from that, but I wasn't sure that it would matter. If the intruder was the killer, he would certainly be armed. How was I going to overcome that?

When I was a kid, I used to lie awake sometimes planning what I'd do if a kidnapper broke into my room. I thought of places to hide, like under the bed or hanging by my fingers out the window. The best hiding place I could think of was under the dirty clothes in the ham-per at the back of the closet. Nobody would see me there, I told my-self, and who would want to rummage through smelly socks and dirty underwear to search for me?

When I got a little older, I decided that I was too old to hide. I couldn't leave my mother alone and undefended, so I'd have to stand and fight. I developed elaborate plans of action, using ordi-nary objects as weapons. The protractor on the desk where I did my homework became a dagger I could plunge into an intruder's eye. The detachable cord on my portable 33 record player became a gar-rote I could use to strangle the intruder after leaping on him from behind.

The trouble was, I hadn't been a kid for a long time and all my plans were out of date. I wouldn't fit in a clothes hamper these days, and I no longer owned either a protractor or a portable record player.

I suddenly remembered that I had something better. I had a gun. I'd worn a bulky jacket to Mulroney's that day, and left the jacket with the Bearcat in its pocket hanging in my closet. I'd been planning to lock the gun in the office safe when I got back from Mulroney's the other day, but I hadn't gotten around to it. Maybe my brain cells were starting to go on me. And maybe—at least in this case—that was a very good thing.

I crossed to the closet door. It was even darker in there than in the bedroom proper. Feeling around, I found the jacket and, reaching into the inner pocket, removed the gun. I pulled back the hammer the full three clicks. Then I stood in the dark, partly shielded by the open closet door from the view of anyone entering the room.

After a moment, I heard a clicking sound from the hall. At first, I thought it was the intruder cocking his gun the way I had cocked mine, but then, peering around the edge of the closet door, I saw that the band of light underneath the hall door had disappeared. What I had heard was the light switch in the hall being flipped off. That switch was near the bedroom door. The bastard was right outside the door, not ten feet from where I was standing.

There were no more sounds from the hall and I realized that he must be waiting for his eyes to adjust to the dark. It seemed like an hour that we stood there in the darkness, but it was probably only three or four minutes. During that time, I did something I hadn't done for a while. I said a quick prayer. The prayer wasn't for myself—that seemed too hypocritical at this point—it was for Harry. I prayed that he'd come out of this all right.

I heard the doorknob turn and, at the same time, a floorboard creak. They sounded as loud as gunshots in the dark.

Someone was moving into the room now. *Life or death, man. When it counts.*

Absurdly, I realized that I didn't know what to do. I'd just spent an eternity waiting and I hadn't even made a plan!

There was a thumping sound, followed by a swallowed curse. The intruder had bumped up against the bed. His eyes must not have been fully adjusted to the darkness after all.

Oh, Jesus! I thought. *He must think I'm lying in that bed. What if he does have a gun? What if he just starts blasting away? Harry is under there!*

I reached behind me with my free hand, feeling for the cord that hangs from the light on the ceiling of the closet. Feeling it, I grasped it between my fingers and yanked.

The light flashed on.

A man was standing at the side of the bed with his back to me. He did have a gun. It was some kind of automatic and it was pointed toward the center of the empty bed. The sudden brightness startled him, not least because the light had appeared in two places at once— behind him, where the closet was, and in front of him, where a full-length mirror stood against a wall. It was the mirror in which Sarah had always checked herself before venturing out into the world. As the man's eyes fought to adjust to the sudden glare, they spotted my image in the mirror. It must have looked to him as if my revolver was pointed right at his chest.

He had good reflexes. The gun he held in his hands came up and fired in the same movement. It was a large-caliber gun, much bigger than my .22. The blast of it roared in that enclosed space, and my image shattered into a thousand pieces.

"Don't move!" I shouted. But, of course, he did. He spun toward the sound of my voice with the gun extended in both hands in front of him. He fired again as he came around. I heard the roar and felt something go by my ear.

I pulled the trigger of the Bearcat.

It was not a good shot—I still couldn't see very clearly and my hand jerked when I pulled the trigger—but I was lucky. Or, more accurately, he wasn't. The bullet must have caught him in the carotid artery. The blood squirted out of his neck like a stream of red water from a miniature garden hose. It made a traveling arc across the bed as his body continued to turn with the momentum of his spin toward me. He collapsed in a slow corkscrew motion, landing on his back on the floor at the foot of the bed.

I stood over Anthony Mason and watched the blood continue to spurt from his neck for a moment before it weakened to a trickle and then stopped altogether.

Mason was dead.

There you are, Jack. I've finally killed somebody. Are you happy now? Have I passed your fucking test?

"It's OK, Harry," I said, trying to make my voice as reassuring as possible. It was an effort, because my heart was pounding dangerously and I was doused with sweat. I moved quickly to the side of the bed, away from the body, and knelt down on the floor.

"You can come out now," I said.

Harry came scrambling from under the bed and into my arms. I maneuvered myself to make sure that my body protected him from the sight of the corpse.

We held each other very tight. He felt heartbreakingly fragile in my arms.

"Come on, Harry," I said after a while. "Let's get out of here."

I carried him down the hall to his room and set him down.

"Will you be all right here by yourself?" I asked him. "Just for a minute."

He looked up at me. "You'll come right back?"

"Of course I will," I said.

" 'Cause you wanna know why?" he asked.

"Why, Harry?"

" 'Cause I was really scared," he said.

I knelt down and hugged him tight.

"I know," I said. "Me, too. But it's all over now. You're safe."

After a moment, I got back to my feet.

"I'll just be gone a minute," I said. "I'll be right down the hall, so if you need me just call out."

"Sure, Dad," he said manfully. "No problem."

I went back down the hall to the bedroom and knelt by Mason's body. He was wearing a lumberjack jacket. It gave him an older, rural look, which was not his style. That was probably why he was wearing it. If anyone saw him in the neighborhood, the description would throw off the police.

Fighting my distaste, I felt around in his pockets. What I was looking for was in the right-hand pocket of his pants. I had figured he was the sort of self-important asshole who'd carry a cell phone everywhere he went, and he was. He'd even taken it on a murder trip. At least he'd had the sense to turn the ringer off.

34

AFTER MIDNIGHT

—Eric Clapton

Two EMTs got there first and went straight upstairs. A couple of uniforms arrived a few minutes later. One of them was in his midtwenties and the other maybe ten years older. The younger guy had a mustache. I greeted them at the door, gave a brief account of what had happened, and told them where the bedroom was, explaining that I'd left my gun on the table beside the bed.

They wanted me to come upstairs with them, but I told them that I wasn't about to leave Harry and there was no way I was taking him back up there. They discussed it and decided that I could stay where I was. The younger of the two policemen would stay downstairs with Harry and me.

Before he went upstairs, the older one bent down to Harry and asked him if what his daddy had told the policemen was true. Harry, who hadn't said a word since the cops got there, seemed puzzled by the question, but he nodded yes.

"You sure, son? You can't think of anything that happened different?"

"No, sir," Harry said.

"Way to go," the older cop said. "You're a brave boy, son."

Then the cop looked up at me and winked.

I could have punched him.

George Carlson arrived about fifteen minutes later and the medical examiner half an hour after that. Shortly after George got there, he stuck his head in at the living room door and called for the young policeman to come upstairs with him. Before they left, he warned me to stay put. He didn't acknowledge Harry at all. Maybe he didn't even see him there.

For the first hour or so, the police busied themselves upstairs in the bedroom—*my* bedroom, *their* crime scene—while I did my best to comfort Harry downstairs in the living room. Both of us seemed to be in some kind of shock.

Harry was calm enough, but unnaturally quiet and a little wide-eyed. It was the way he'd acted one day when we were in the park and he got whacked on the forehead by a swing. The blow had opened up a cut. Head wounds bleed a lot, and the blood spurting from his forehead had covered his face. I rushed him to the emergency room where they stitched up the wound. During all that time, and for a couple of hours afterwards, Harry had behaved exactly like this. After that, he fell asleep, and when he woke up he was fine.

As for me, I felt as if I was watching myself from the other side of the room.

After a while, my brain started working a little. Sooner or later the cops would want to grill me, and Harry shouldn't be around for that. (They'd probably want to talk to him, too, but that was just too fucking bad.) I used the phone in my office to call Rachel. I apologized for waking her and told her what had happened. Once I'd assured her that Harry and I were both all right, she took the call in stride and agreed to come and get Harry. She said she'd be over as soon as she got dressed.

She made it in under fifteen minutes.

Before she got there, I told Harry that he'd be going to Rachel's for a while. He threw his arms around me and pleaded to stay with me. I told him that he didn't have a choice and neither did I. The police needed help with their investigation, and Daddy would have to give it to them. That's what Daddy did for a living.

I assured him that I'd come to get him as soon as I could. In the meantime, he and Rachel could play *Snakes and Ladders*. "And I'll bet she has some ice cream in her freezer, too. How about that?"

Well, maybe that would be all right.

As soon as Rachel's car pulled into the driveway I opened the side door to welcome her. She didn't look like a woman who'd been rousted out of bed with the insane news that someone close to her had just killed a man in a gun battle. In fact, she looked like sanity personified.

She hugged each of us in turn. Harry first. Once I had my arms around her, I didn't much want to let go.

I took her aside and told her that what Harry really needed was sleep. She ventured that he'd probably fall asleep in the car on the way to her place, and I thought she was probably right.

"Now, how are *you*, Hank?" she asked, touching my cheek and then my forehead with the back of her hand. "You feel clammy, and you look a little pale."

You oughta see the other guy.

"I'll be fine," I said.

Carlson was seriously pissed when he found out that Harry was gone. He was angry at me, but even more at the uniforms he blamed for letting Harry get away. Of course, George was in charge, so I suppose most of his anger was really directed at himself. I told him that Harry had been through a truly bad experience and needed some time to deal with it. The police could talk to him tomorrow, couldn't they? Grudgingly, he agreed to leave Harry alone. At least until morning. He wasn't nearly as considerate with me.

He had me drive my car to the police headquarters on Splinter Street where he interrogated me for over three hours. Ordinarily, when the police want to grill you the only sensible thing to do is re-

fuse to talk to them and call your lawyer. But this was an old classmate, and, although he wouldn't hesitate to nail me if he thought I
was nailable, I knew he would be fair.

Besides, the Bearcat was licensed and I was confident that the
physical evidence would show that I had acted in self-defense. Of
course, a lot of innocent people are behind bars because they'd been
similarly confident, but what the hell?

All interrogation rooms look alike, even the one in the basement of
the Pinery Falls police station. Bare walls and a table. You can see the
prototype any night on TV. Carlson had me sit on a metal folding
chair on one side of the table while he sat in a similar, but cushioned,
chair on the other. There was a mirrored surface on the wall behind
him that allowed us to be observed and videotaped from the next
room.

Before getting started, he asked me if I wanted a cup of coffee. "No
thanks," I told him. "I never touch the stuff, but I'd love a cold beer."
He didn't respond to that at all.

Carlson's questioning style was skeptical and relentless, but the
strongest emotions he displayed were irritability and impatience, and
I'd seen both of those many times before. I got the feeling that his
heart wasn't in this at all.

Another cop, a big guy named Grennauer, was in and out for a
while. He acted tough and he probably was, but it was a standard
bad-cop act and it didn't bother me any. After about two hours, he
left the room for the third time and never came back.

Carlson spent a lot of time trying to shake my story, but there was
nothing there to shake. At first, I thought he might be having trouble
seeing a big-time attorney like Mason as a burglar and a killer, but
that wasn't really Carlson's problem at all. What he was having trouble with was figuring out why Mason would want to murder *me*.

I told him about my visit to Mason's office the day before.

"I must have spooked him," I said. "He probably thought I knew
more about his involvement with the Dietrich charge than I really

did. As a matter of fact, I didn't know *anything* about it. It was just a guess."

George gave me a speculative look. Then he looked at his watch. I looked at mine. It was almost five thirty. He covered his mouth with his hand and let out a huge yawn.

"What the hell," he said, with the air of a man giving up on an effort that hadn't been worth making in the first place. "Let's get out of here."

It was the same thing I'd said to Harry.

He led me out of the interrogation room and upstairs to his office. When we passed a Pepsi machine on the way, he reached in his pocket for some change.

"Want a pop?" he asked me.

"I'll take a Diet Pepsi," I said.

He pumped in thirty-five cents, which is all the Pinery Falls cops have to pay for a can of name-brand soda. Then he pressed a button and a cold can of Pepsi dropped down the chute.

"Go ahead," he said.

I reached down and took the can.

"Thanks," I said.

He put in more change and got himself a Mountain Dew.

We took the drinks into his office.

"Why the change in attitude?" I asked him once we'd gotten seated.

He shrugged. "Hey, you've had a rough night, and I guess the last few hours of it have been my fault."

I'd understood that he'd had to grill me. After all, I had just killed a man, and a pretty prominent man at that. But it had been obvious that I'd acted in self-defense from the moment Carlson arrived at my house. So maybe George *was* feeling a little guilty for what he'd put me through. But I suspected that there was more to it than that, and it turned out there was. His competitive juices were flowing.

"I hate to admit it," he began, "but you probably did the taxpayers a big favor."

"How's that?" I asked.

"It costs a lot of money to keep a guy in prison for life," he said. "And that's where Mason was headed even before he broke into your place."

"For life?" I asked. I wouldn't have thought that procuring—or whatever crime Mason would have been nailed with—carried that stiff a penalty. Of course, the procurees *had* been minors.

"So you haven't figured it out yet?" He grinned at me. "Well, in that case, I've got a little present for you. And for Elizabeth Drucker. You'd better hurry and pass it on to her, though. We're having a news conference about Mason's death at ten this morning. We'll probably announce it then."

It had been a long and stressful night and I was feeling tired. "Announce what?" I asked.

"That everybody can relax. Pinery Falls' little murder spree is over. The killer of Jack Drucker and Chris Dietrich is dead."

I must have looked as surprised as I felt.

"Gotcha!" he said, his face cracking into a self-satisfied smirk.

"Are you sure?" I asked stupidly. That wasn't the way I'd figured it at all. I suddenly realized that I hadn't even begun to think through the implications of Anthony Mason's attempt to murder me.

"You didn't really think there was more than one homicidal maniac running around Pinery Falls, did you?" Carlson was suddenly in a rare good mood. He was obviously enjoying the hell out of conquering what was clearly a landmark case in Pinery Falls.

"Of course, I did have an advantage over you in figuring this out," he explained. "I've been talking to Adam Blackhalter."

"You found him?" I asked.

"Seems he took off Thursday night, as soon as the news about Dietrich hit the TV. That kid was scared shitless. He stole a car from his neighbor's driveway and headed south. Some troopers spotted the car on the interstate south of Madison yesterday morning and pulled him over. We sent a car down to get him this afternoon."

"So he ran because of the Dietrich murder?"

"You could say that. But he wasn't running from *us*. He was running from *Mason*. Mason was the real entrepreneur in this sex business. Seems that Mason knew every dirty old man in town. Older guys with a taste for the young stuff. Even business lawyers meet a lot of real scumbags."

"*Especially* business lawyers," I put in.

"Maybe," he acknowledged. "Anyway, Mason saw a business opportunity. He met Blackhalter when the kid made the mistake of trying to interest Mason's daughter in some Ecstasy after a high school football game a couple of years ago. She told Daddy about it, and he threatened the little prick with jail unless the kid recruited some of his friends for the operation. Whatever else Mason was, he was a good judge of character. And of talent. Blackhalter took to the job like a wino takes to cheap Chablis. Before long, he'd lined up a stable of willing kids. Only about three or four of each sex, but that was plenty. Mason used them mostly as a way of keeping some of his clients—and a few people who could help his clients—happy. The kids did it for the excitement and the money. Perverted sex pays better than McDonald's."

"Probably pays better than detective work, too," I said.

"No doubt. So anyway, Mason recruited Blackhalter and Blackhalter recruited the other kids. At first, Mason recruited all the clients, too. Then, after a while, the clients started recruiting more clients. Turns out a lot of the freaks know each other. It was actually getting to be a lucrative sideline for Mason." He grimaced with disgust. "Jesus! Who would've thought there'd be so many real degenerates in a town like this?"

"In any town, I suppose."

"Makes me sick," he said. "Anyway, about a month ago, some of the kids started telling Blackhalter about a reporter who was nosing around. That was Jack, of course."

I remembered what Jack had told Charlie Cleveland about blowing the lid off the town's power structure. My assumption had been that he meant something to do with Tobacco Island. Now I knew better.

"When Jack was killed out on Little River Road, Adam figured that Mason did it, but he couldn't be sure. Then the Dietrich kid got arrested and the shit started flying all over the place."

George was obviously enjoying explaining my case to me. He was like a wide receiver spiking the ball at a cornerback's feet.

"Everybody involved thought Dietrich would cut a deal." he went on. "He'd give up Adam for sure. Hell, he practically already had. Dietrich had never met Mason, and the other kids weren't supposed to know anybody beyond Blackhalter. But Mason couldn't be sure that they didn't. Besides, once Chris started talking, the whole thing was bound to unravel. So he got Adam to arrange a meeting with Chris at an isolated spot along the railroad tracks. Of course Mason went instead. After that, Adam knew that Mason was willing to kill anybody who might expose him. And that meant Adam himself."

"So he ran?" I asked.

"Right." He smiled a cop's smile. "But not very far."

"OK," I said. "Mason killed Jack because Jack was looking to expose his involvement with this sex ring, right?"

"Obviously."

"But why that night? And why would he do it in front of his own house? I still don't understand what Jack was doing out there anyway."

"Mason must have looked out the window and seen Jack sitting out there. By that time, Adam and Mason knew Jack was sniffing around, and Mason must have worried. He had a lot to lose. Maybe Jack had even questioned him. Maybe he spooked him like you did yesterday. Anyway, something snapped in him when he saw Jack out there, and he really panicked. The man was obviously going off the rails. After that, the fever was in him."

"You're saying Jack just sat there and let Anthony Mason walk up to the car and shoot him? He even rolled down the window to give him a cleaner shot?"

"He probably never suspected what Mason had in mind. Besides, can you imagine that arrogant son of a bitch being *afraid* of somebody like Mason?"

He had a point.

"Mason was taking a big chance, though. One of the neighbors might have been looking out a window."

"Not likely," Carlson said. "Remember the time of night. Mason probably knew the Holzmanns were gone and Mrs. Schneider was an early sleeper. Anyway, like I said, something snapped in him. It turned him into a homicidal maniac, remember. Jack was the start of it. Then Dietrich. And next, it was supposed to be you."

"What about the gun?" I asked.

"Mason must have had it in his house. Turns out he was something of a gun nut. I mean, he set out to kill three different people with three different guns, didn't he?"

"The gun that killed Jack was unusual," I persisted. "Where did Mason get it?"

Carlson shrugged. "Who knows? We can't really trace it, but it probably came from some criminal. Maybe he got it from a notorious client." That wasn't a great explanation, but then the gun had been a wild card in my theories too.

One thing still bothered me, though. "So what was Jack doing out on Little River Road in the first place?"

"He was reporting, of course. Specifically, he was trying to catch Mason and Blackhalter together."

"What do you mean?"

Carlson yawned. Apparently, he was getting tired. I wasn't surprised. Even proudly sharing information must have been tiring for him. He wasn't used to it.

"OK," he said. "I'll give you that, as well. Then this party's over, all right?"

"Aw jeez," I said. "And here I've been having so much fun."

"Adam has a girlfriend," he explained. "A girl named Shirley

Petorski. When I haven't been talking to Blackhalter today—yesterday, that is—I've been talking to her. It seems that Shirley didn't like Adam being wrapped up in the sex business. It wasn't the morality of the thing. She just thought it was taking up too much of his time. He didn't have enough left over for her."

Carlson was warming to his story.

"She kept nagging at him to quit, but he wouldn't do it. He was pulling in too much money. So she decided she'd make things too hot for him to stay. She didn't want to come to us because she didn't want to get him in any real trouble with the law. He'd be no fun at all if he was in jail. But she decided to put some heat on him. She thought that if she could get the *Torrent* to expose the operation, Adam would have to quit. So she went to Drucker. As you can probably tell, this girl's not the brightest bulb in the chandelier, but she did get Jack to promise he wouldn't identify Adam in his story."

"And you're saying that Adam put up with his girlfriend blowing the whistle?" I asked disbelievingly.

"No way. He would have done her some serious damage if he'd known about it. She only talked to Jack in absolute confidence. She'd call him on the phone, or he'd pick her up in some parking lot, and they'd drive out in the country where no one would see them together."

"Does Shirley Petorski have long black hair?" I asked.

"That's right," he said, looking surprised. "She calls herself Nightshade, and wears black lipstick and nail polish, too. She's into Goth."

That explained the black hairs that had been found on the passenger side of the Stingray.

"You know her?" he asked suspiciously.

That was when I remembered that I'd heard about the hairs from Augie and Carlson wasn't supposed to learn about that. Exhaustion and shock must have fried my brains. I did my best to put him off. "Somebody mentioned seeing a black-haired girl riding with Jack once, that's all. For a while, I wondered if he had a girlfriend on the side."

Carlson seemed to accept that.

"Jack and Nightshade?" He chuckled. "I don't think so. What Jack was hot for was exposing the sex ring. What he was *most* interested in was the clients. He kept pushing Shirley to get their names. She could only get a few of them, but they included some big surprises." *I'm gonna blow the lid off the whole damn thing, Charlie. You're gonna be surprised what's under there.*

There was a hunter's gleam in Carlson's eye. "With a little luck there'll be some valuable prosecutions coming out of this," he said.

"From what Shirley says, Jack believed her, but he needed corroboration. The trouble was that most of what she knew was just hearsay from Adam. She tipped Jack to some of the kids involved, but none of them would open up to him. Mason was the real key. At the very least Jack needed evidence that Adam and Mason were connected. Which brings us to the night of Jack's murder."

Carlson interrupted himself for a yawn that revealed the fillings in his back teeth. I glanced at my watch. It was almost six.

"Adam and Shirley were at a party that night—the one that got busted later. At one point Adam said he had to leave. Shirley asked why, and he said he had to go do some things and then he had to go over to Mason's house to see about some business. Sometime after he left the party, little Shirley got the idea that this might be the chance for Jack to connect Mason and Adam. She called him and told him that Adam was going to be at Mason's place. Jack must have gone out there hoping to catch them together—and at a compromising time of night to boot. As it turned out, Adam must have left by the time Jack got there. Mason looked out the window, and . . ." He let it hang.

I had to admit, it sounded good. The case against Mason was nailed down tight, particularly now that I'd saved Carlson and Hollander from having to prove it in a court of law.

George yawned again. Yawning is contagious and I yawned too. All of a sudden, I felt exhausted. The night's events were coming down on me.

"So it's all wrapped up?" I asked. "You're going to make an announcement this morning?"

"The exact timing will be up to Hollander," Carlson said. "He and Arnsbach were setting up for a power struggle over jurisdiction in the Malik case, but with Dietrich dead, that case is moot. Besides, the murders take precedence. So now it'll be up to Hollander to decide how to handle the sex part of it. But we'll make an announcement about Mason today for sure. The media already knows that Mason's dead, and we've got to reassure people that we no longer have a killer loose in Pinery Falls. Except for you, of course," he added with a grin.

"Jesus Christ, George."

"Hey, I'm only kidding," he said. "You don't have to worry. We'll make it clear that it was self-defense. Hell, you'll be a hero. You're the man who shot Liberty Valance. You could run for the Senate."

"Ha-ha-ha."

"Honestly, Hank." Carlson was suddenly serious. "You've been through a lot. It must have really shaken you up to have to kill a guy. You know, all the time I've been a cop, I've never had to do that." He sounded almost envious. "Why don't you go home? Call Liz and tell her the good news. Then just crash for a while, OK? You could use some sleep. And don't worry about Harry. We'll talk to him later. Maybe even tomorrow. And when we do, we'll make sure that a parent's right there with him. All right?"

I must have gawked. In all the years I'd known him, George Carlson had never once been solicitous for my welfare.

As I approached the double doors of the police station, Augie Bendorf came walking through them dressed in his uniform. He must have been working the weekend.

"Hey, man, I heard what you did," he said.

I just kept on walking.

"Nice going," he said, giving me the thumbs-up sign as we passed each other.

When I pulled the door open, I was hit with a draft of freezing air. I trembled with a sudden chill, followed by a wave of nausea. My stomach churned ominously, and then, like many a lost soul before me, I threw up in the entryway of the Pinery Falls police station.

35

PURPLE HAZE

—Jimi Hendrix

Harry was probably sound asleep at Rachel's place. As soon as I got home, I'd call and see if she could keep him long enough for me to get a few hours' sleep. Weak from the bout of nausea, and with my head swimming dangerously, I really needed some sleep. It would feel so good to just lie down on my bed and to let myself drift—

Halfway down Menard Avenue, I realized that there was no way I could do that. The cops would be all over my bedroom, and they wouldn't let me anywhere near my bed. Remembering how the blood from Mason's neck had sprayed across its surface, I wouldn't want to lie down there even if I could. Not now, and maybe not for a long time either.

I turned left on Cherry Street, planning to run up Fifth to Williams and then west over the bridge to Rachel's. I was still on Fifth when the frantic blast of a car horn shocked me into the realization that I was cruising down the left side of the street.

Jesus!

I jerked the wheel to the right, turning the Sentra straight into the path of a pale green SUV that was coming in the opposite direction.

What the hell is that doing over here? Then I realized it must have swung out of my path.

Time was fragmented. Things were happening in slow motion and the speed of light at the same time. Straight ahead, I could see the elderly driver of the SUV fighting to keep control of his unwieldy vehicle.

I jerked the steering wheel back to the left and the Sentra veered crazily in that direction.

I saw the old man's panicked face with an eerie clarity as the SUV skidded by, missing me by inches. His eyes were unnaturally wide and he was screaming curses at me. I didn't blame him. He was scared shitless and so was I. I thought that I might be screaming something too.

Getting the car under control, I pulled to a stop at the right-hand curb. Thank God it was early Saturday morning and there was so little traffic. If it had been a weekday, the street would have been crowded with people on their ways to work at that hour. I would probably be dead by now. And some other people too.

I'd been awake most of the night, but what I was feeling was not a natural tiredness. It was more like the way I'd felt in the hospital once after stomach surgery, when they put me on a morphine drip. There was no way I should be driving a car, but the shock had jerked me awake and I decided that I could make it as far as Rachel's house.

By the time I got there, the wooziness was starting again.

Parking at the curb, I walked to the door. I rang the bell, then leaned against it until she answered. It didn't take her long, a fact that I greatly appreciated. She was wearing a bathrobe, and I was so out of it I didn't even wonder if she had anything on underneath it.

"Hank!" she exclaimed. "You look really terrible."

"I admire your honesty," I muttered.

"Come on in."

"I've been at the police station," I explained, walking into the familiar living room. "Sorry about this, but I didn't want to go home. The cops'll be there, and the bed's a—a mess."

"Don't be silly. I was expecting you."

"I need a bed. I was hoping—"

"Of course," she said, helping me off with my jacket.

I felt absurdly relieved, as if I'd half-expected her to send me back out into the cold.

"I could probably use some sleep," I said.

"You probably could," she agreed with a smile.

"Where's Harry?" I asked.

"He's in my bedroom. You can have the bed in the guest room."

"I need to talk to him," I said.

She shook her head. "Not now," she said. "Let him sleep. He fell asleep in the car on the way over here."

"Me too," I said.

She looked at me questioningly, but I didn't explain and she probably decided it had been a mindless non sequitur.

She led me into the small guest room, which I'd seen before but never slept in. The few nights I'd stayed over at Rachel's, we'd slept together in her room. The guest room looked very different now, seductive and inviting. There was a double bed with a blanket and a quilt pulled up over two pillows that lay side by side. She turned down the covers and the bed called to me like a berth in Paradise.

I laid down on my back with my head on one of the pillows. My shoes felt tight. My feet must have been swollen, and I knew that the shoes would interfere with the circulation in my feet if I fell asleep. I was debating whether it was worth the effort to remove them when Rachel read my mind. She leaned over and untied both my shoes, then gently pulled them off one at a time.

"Bless you," I said.

She held them up to her nose and made a face. "You owe me," she said.

"Oh, God!"

"What is it?"

"Sarah. She's coming today. She'll worry about Harry . . . and, uh—I don't know. Maybe—"

Surrendering to an irresistible imperative, I rolled over onto my side and pulled a pillow under my cheek. It felt wonderfully cool. And soft. And almost loving.

"This feels so good," I muttered. "Just let me rest awhile and I'll be fine."

That's what I intended to say anyway, but somewhere in the middle of it, I fell asleep.

36

KNOCKING ON
HEAVEN'S DOOR

—Bob Dylan

Pressure weighed in on me from every side. With incipient terror, I realized that I couldn't lift my arms. When I tried to sit up, my upper body wouldn't budge. I was restricted—not pinned down exactly but completely enclosed in something that was incredibly strong without being palpable. It was as if gravity had been amplified to the point where it took on a physical dimension.

With an effort born of swelling terror, I fought against this ineluctable force, building up an energy of will until, not gradually but suddenly, I managed to propel myself upward toward the surface of whatever was oppressing me. With a kind of bursting, I not only attained that surface but broke blissfully free from it, like a dolphin rising high out of the water, arcing and twisting in the air until I returned to rest on my back, spent and exhausted as if after a long struggle.

I was on the bed in Rachel's guest room. The sheet and blanket were twisted and thrown aside, half-dragging on the floor. I lay there, breathing hard.

What had just happened? A formless nightmare? Rampant anxiety? A heart attack?

Was I dying?

Probably not.

The morning thoughts of a middle-aged man.

Jesus!

Then I remembered.

Rachel had pulled down the shade in the guest room and closed the nearly opaque drapes, so I that had to press the Indiglo button on my watch to check the time. It was one fifty in the afternoon.

I switched on a light. My shoes were on the floor beside the bed. I put them on and tied them. For the first time in a long time I didn't feel an urgent need to piss on waking up. Of course, I'd only drunk one can of Diet Pepsi in the past—how long? Fourteen hours or so.

I could use a sink and a toothbrush, though. And a whole lot of mouthwash.

Rachel was sitting at the table in the half-dining room, dressed in slacks and a turtleneck sweater, working on student papers.

"Thanks for not undressing me," I said.

She smiled. "And I was *sooo* tempted."

"Where's Harry?" I asked.

She rose from the table with a look of concern.

"I'm sorry, Hank," she began. "Sarah came and got him. You said she was coming in, so I called the airport and left a message for her to call here. That was so she wouldn't go to your place and find the police there."

"Thanks," I said sincerely. "It was good of you to think of that."

"I tried to wake you when she came, but you were completely out."

"It's probably just as well. Was she very angry?"

She made a wincing face. "You could say that."

"I'll bet," I said bitterly. Then I felt ashamed of myself. Sarah had every right to be angry. However unwillingly, I had placed Harry in mortal danger. And although he hadn't been physically harmed, he might still be seriously, if not permanently, traumatized. This would undoubtedly make her even more hesitant to leave him with me in the future.

"How was he?" I asked.

"Oh, Harry was fine," she said. "He really was. He was bursting to tell his mother all about it, as if it had been a great adventure."

"Thank God," I said.

"You want some lunch?" she asked me. "It's a little late for breakfast."

I shook my head. "I'm hungry, but I don't think my metabolism's working yet."

"There's Diet Pepsi and beer in the fridge," she said. She knew me well. I was usually in the market for one or the other. "And you know where the bathroom is," she added.

I went into the kitchen and got a cold can of the Diet Pepsi. As always, it cut through the toxic sludge in my mouth.

"This is your fifteen minutes," Rachel said as I came back to the table.

"How's that?"

"You're all over the TV. 'Local Investigator Kills Murder Suspect.' 'Courageous Private Eye Defends Self and Child.'"

"Jesus. Has the press called here?"

"Just your friend Keith from the *Torrent*. The rest of them don't seem to know about me yet."

"They'll learn," I said. "I'd better get out of here pretty soon."

"I don't mind a little nuisance, Hank."

"I do," I said.

Once I was fully awake, I called Sarah's place. I wanted to explain to her what had happened—God knew what she'd been hearing from the cops and reporters—and also to find out just how mad she was. Most of all, I wanted to talk to Harry and see how he was doing.

The phone rang eight times before she picked it up.

"Hank's not here!" she said angrily. It seemed that the newspeople *did* know about my ex.

"I know," I said lightly. "As a matter of fact, I'm right here."

She hung up.

I called Keith and gave him the details of the shooting. I owed him that much.

"Sorry this isn't in time for today's edition," I said. "Once the police were done with me, I just conked out."

"Are you kidding me?" he asked. "We're putting out a late extra. This is the biggest thing to hit Pinery Falls since the Wal-Mart opened up. And by the way, Hank?"

"Yeah?"

"This is an exclusive, right?"

"You bet," I told him. "After this call, I'm going into hiding for at least a day."

After about ten minutes, I called Sarah again. I figured she'd had some time to calm down and decide how to deal with me.

The line was busy.

Ten minutes later, I tried again. Still busy.

Her phone must have been off the hook. From her point of view, I guess that was as good a way to deal with me as any.

This time, instead of taking me to his study, Wes Drucker led me to the living room that had once been the showroom of the big house on The Hill. One wall was a large window that flooded the space with afternoon light. In my youth, that room had been the pinnacle of taste and luxury. Now it looked smaller than I remembered and the furniture had an indefinably old-fashioned, almost tacky, look.

Although I smelled alcohol on Drucker's breath when I passed by him in the front hall, he didn't offer me a drink. He just pointed me to an easy chair while he took a seat on one end of an out-size sofa. He sank down into the cushions and I was struck again by how small he was. A phrase came to mind that Pat uses when he's in one of his Celtic moods. Wes had become "a wee little man." Maybe he'd always *been* a wee little man.

"You want me to thank you?" he asked. "Well, I do. If you came for a reward, you can just name it."

I couldn't believe he'd said it.

"You think that of me? That I'd take money for killing a man?"

"Why not?" He chuckled comfortably. "I would, if the circumstances were right."

"That's not why I came here," I said.

"No? Then why?"

"I've read the story Jack wrote about An Doc," I said.

A flash of anger appeared on his face.

"Where did you get it?" he snapped. "Was it someone who works for me?"

I ignored that. "More important, I know why you spiked it."

He went pale.

I waited. He seemed to be trying to gather himself.

When he spoke, he sounded like a man with a damaged throat. "Oh, you little *fuck*," he said. "Why couldn't you just leave it alone?"

"Don't worry," I told him. "I'm not going to do anything with it. The police know about the story, but not about Jack. Carlson has no interest in An Doc now that his case is closed."

Wes's eyes closed and his chin dropped to his chest.

"Thank God," he said as the color started coming back into his face. "Thank you, sweet Jesus Christ."

I gave him a moment.

"I still don't understand why you didn't show the cops the story yourself. Nothing in it incriminates Jack."

"Bullshit," he said. "Jack *was there*. Once they started questioning the other men, that fact would have come out. There was no way I would willingly risk such a thing. My boy is not going to be remembered for *that*!"

"Not even if the story was the reason for Jack's murder and concealing it meant the killer would escape?"

"The story had nothing to do with Jack's murder," he asserted.

"Nobody knew the story even existed except Jack and that Mulroney boy. It was Mulroney who wanted it published, not my son. There was no motive there."

"But how could you possibly know that for sure?" I persisted. "How could you know that they hadn't talked to some of the others? How could you know what the others thought about it? Or what they might have done?"

Drucker just shook his head with stubborn finality. He was not prepared to consider the possibility, so he simply refused to do so. I suppose the whiskey helped.

He peered at me through narrowed eyes, as if he was trying to read something that was written on my face in very small letters.

"Why did you come here?" he asked.

It was a good question. I thought that I'd come to verify his reason for spiking the story, but I'd already done that and I still felt unsatisfied.

"I don't know," I said honestly. "But there was a time when I thought of Jack as a kind of brother, so I guess I thought of you as a kind of father, too."

There it was—my childhood secret. *Why had I told him that?*

He responded with a look of alarm. His head moved slightly from side to side, as if he were shaking it no.

"Maybe I came for some fatherly advice," I said, trying to give the words an ironic spin. "But, like I said, I don't really know."

"Sweet Jesus Christ!" With an air of decision, he freed himself from the embrace of the sofa and thrust himself to his feet.

"Do you want a drink?" The offer sounded like a demand.

"Yes," I told him. "Yes, I do."

He crossed the room to a sideboard.

"Whiskey?" he asked.

"Fine," I answered.

There were several bottles lined up on the sideboard, but no Bombay Sapphire gin. Maybe he saved that for his study. He picked up an open bottle of Jack Daniel's Black Label, half-filled two glasses with whiskey, and brought one over to me.

"Thanks," I said.

He returned to the sofa, where he wolfed down about half the contents of his glass before putting it down on an end table and fixing me with his eyes.

"All right, little Harry," he said, with the air of a man who was committing himself to something. "Let me tell you something about fathers. Fathers have a lot to do with what their sons become. That's a cliché these days, but like most clichés, it's perfectly true. Let me give you an example. I knew a man named Benjamin Standard. He's dead now. He ran the Linotype machine down at the paper, back in the days when we *had* a Linotype machine. He worked at it for thirty years, and we were friends of a certain kind—the kind you can be when a man works for you. But we'd known each other from when we were children, the way that you and Jack knew each other."

He watched me sharply from under his unruly eyebrows. That last had been a not-so-subtle reminder that I had never been Jack's brother and that I had always entered this house on sufferance. When he saw that I'd gotten the message, he went on with his story.

"I knew Ben's father, too. He was a vicious and self-hating drunk. Ben had two brothers and one sister, and that miserable bastard beat them all when they were children. I mean 'beat them' literally. In those days, what a man did with his own children was his own business. He used to pummel those kids with his fists so hard—my God, you wouldn't believe it! Ben's nose was broken in three different places, every one of them his father's handiwork. One of his sister's arms was broken, too. Just here—" Using his right hand, the old man patted his left arm above the elbow. "The only thing that saved their lives was the fact that each of them had two siblings. If that man had confined his beating to just one, that child would've been dead for sure."

He took another sip of whiskey and I followed suit. I don't much like whiskey, but it felt warm going down.

"Ben Standard *learned* from his childhood," Mort continued. "He had eight children of his own and he never laid a hand on them. Not on one. He was the gentlest, sweetest father you could ever meet. And he never drank, either. You know why? Because of his father, of course. Seeing what his father had done to him and to his siblings, he resolved never to do such things to his own children."

Drucker closed his eyes for a moment. Then he took a deep breath and let it out.

"But it doesn't always work that way," he said quietly. "The truth is, it almost *never* works that way. Mostly it's the other way around. When a boy has a bad father, he becomes a bad father himself. A bad man. I've seen it a thousand times. Oh, they all try to fight it at first. 'I'll never be like my old man. No way!' But the seed is there, and the seed grows."

He pursed his lips and his forehead ridged as if he was in pain. But when he spoke, his voice was soft and almost tender. "*Une fleur de mal*," he said. "Do you know what that means, Harry?"

"I know what it means."

He nodded. "Well, maybe that's what Jack was. Do you think so?"

Fathers have a lot to do with what their sons become. My own father was mostly a myth to me. What did that mean for what *I* had become?

And what *had* I become exactly?

"Do you?" he asked, almost imploringly. "Do you, little Harry?"

I stared at him aghast.

"How the hell do I know?" I asked with my voice coming out louder than I intended. "I don't know what kind of man you are. I never even knew what kind of man Jack was."

Getting up from the chair, I carried my glass to the sideboard I gulped as much as I could take in one swallow and set it down firmly. I was sweating, and my heart was beating faster than it should.

"I can't judge you, Mr. Drucker."

Turning away from him, I left the room and walked straight out of the house.

It felt like an escape.

There were snowflakes in the air. They were the big, soft kind that make you think of childhood and Christmas. I looked straight up into the hypnotically shifting patterns as they drifted down from the sky. As I remembered doing as a child, I stuck out my tongue to catch them. They were exquisitely light, making tiny bursts of coolness as they landed on my tongue. Then they were gone. Intimations of mortality.

A different kind of movement in the sky caught my attention. It was the bald eagle, gliding down from some impossible height in the sky to perch on the tall turret that made Drucker's house the highest building on The Hill.

Herman used his massive wings as a parachute, so that his descent resembled a huge dark snowflake floating to earth. Having touched down on the turret, he gracefully raised and then lowered his wings to balance himself before folding them back against his body. Once settled there, he sat perfectly still, looking off into a far distance that only he could see.

I watched him for a while, hoping absurdly that he'd look down and our eyes might meet. When that didn't happen, I got in the Sentra and drove away, leaving him posed like an imperious omen against the winter sky.

What I had told Wes Drucker was true. I didn't know enough to judge him. More than that, I had no right to do it. And yet, heading back down The Hill, I felt as though I had just failed in some important way.

But how? And who?

Wes Drucker? Jack? Myself?

I had no idea.

37

ANOTHER SATURDAY NIGHT

—Sam Cooke

I took Interstate 39 to Wausau, where I planned to hole up for the night in a motel. There were decisions I had to make, and I didn't want to have to deal with either reporters or the Pinery Falls police.

The snow picked up a little on the way, and by the time I got there it had accumulated to the point where traffic was slowing down for it. It was almost four o'clock in the afternoon by then, and I was finally getting hungry. I hadn't eaten since supper time Friday. *By God, that was less that twenty-four hours ago!* In that time, I'd actually gone to sleep and then awakened to the sounds of someone breaking into my house. Then I had killed Anthony Mason. Then Carlson had grilled me. Then I'd nearly smashed up the Sentra. Then I'd slept. And *then* I'd wakened to discover that Sarah had returned and taken Harry away. Could all of that have happened in less than twenty-four hours? Or had I missed a day somewhere? It felt more like a week.

I stopped at the Culver's drive-through restaurant on Wausau's Bridge Street. According to the nutrition guide they gave me, their pork tenderloin sandwich had less saturated fat and cholesterol than a Butter Burger, so I ordered the pork.

After eating, I stopped at the local Save 'n' Smile, where I picked up a toothbrush, some toothpaste, a phone card, and a cold twelve-pack of Point Specials. Then I drove to the Ramada Inn. Checking in, I used a phony name and paid in cash. Maybe my ego was showing, but Keith had told me that Anthony Mason was big news, and I didn't want some eager desk clerk calling me in to the local news hotline.

I filled the bathroom sink about two-thirds with ice from the ice maker in the hall and stuck in as many beer cans as would fit. My plan was to see how many I could drink before passing out, but first I had a couple of phone calls to make.

The first was to Sarah. Because I hadn't used a credit card to pay for the room, I had to use the phone card I'd bought at the Save 'n' Smile for the call. She answered after three rings.

"Hello."

"Sarah, this is Hank."

Silence. But she didn't hang up.

"I wanted to find out how Harry was doing," I said.

Nothing.

"And I wanted to explain to you."

"Harry's good, Hank. I think he's going to be all right." Her voice was steady but affectless. "As for the rest, not now. I'm just not ready to listen."

"OK," I said. "I understand. The only thing—"

Now she hung up.

I felt enormous relief. Sarah had said that Harry was doing well, and if he wasn't, she wouldn't hesitate to let me know about it. What's more, she'd said she wasn't ready to listen, which implied that she *would* be ready sometime in the future. It might be a while before she'd trust me with Harry again, but that time would come.

My second call was to Tony Carelli.

"This is Tony."

The piping voice sounded as incongruous as ever.

"Hank Berlin."

"What's going on?" he demanded. "A cop answered when I called this morning. He said there'd been a shooting, but he wouldn't tell me who shot who."

"I was the shooter," I told him. "The guy I shot was no one you knew."

"I didn't think you were the shooting type," he said drily.

"I didn't either," I said. "Why did you call? Did you have the information I asked for?"

"Yeah, I got it," he said. "A Python .357 Magnum."

"With a combat stock?"

"That's right. *And* he taped the handle, just like you thought."

So, I'd been right after all.

"Thanks, Tony. You've been a big help."

"Yeah. But now it is over, right? I've done my Hail Marys for what those jerk-offs did to you."

"It's over," I agreed. "And you don't have to worry. The cops think they've got it all wrapped up, so they won't be bugging you. They're satisfied they've got their guy."

"The one you shot?"

"That's right," I said.

"Then, thank *you!*" he said, and hung up.

At six o'clock, I sat down on the bed and flicked the TV's remote. The motel's cable didn't carry any Pinery Falls station, but the murders were big news all over central Wisconsin. I found a Wausau station that was running highlights from the morning's press conference on their news show. The report opened with a video of Mayor Mulkowski, Vern Hollander, and Police Chief Randolph Muerrette, all gathered at a podium in the Pinery Falls City Hall. At least ten microphones were taped to the stand, which indicated a lot of interest in the story.

I spotted a glum-looking George Carlson in the background of the shot. Maybe he was sulking because he wanted to be up front with the big boys.

Mulkowski formally announced that an attorney named Anthony Mason had been shot to death in the act of burglarizing the home of a local citizen. With a start, I saw my house appear on the screen. Yellow crime scene tape was stretched over the front door.

"While any death is unfortunate," Mulkowski was saying, "we believe that Mason's demise marks an end to the recent wave of murderous violence that has plagued our community. Pinery Falls residents can once again rest easy, secure in the knowledge that they, live in a safe and law-abiding community."

A stern-looking Muerrette appeared: "Mr. Mason was shot to death while breaking into the home of local private investigator Henry Berlin." As he said my name, an old video of me testifying in a Marathon County court case came on the screen. Maybe I should have worn shades and a false beard at the check-in, as well as used a phony name.

"Berlin was investigating the deceased's alleged involvement with teenage prostitution. The gun with which he shot Mr. Mason is registered, and our preliminary investigation indicates that Berlin's shooting was fully justified. Mason was armed, and he fired his gun while trespassing with evil intent. What's more, Mason shot first. Mr. Berlin was defending not only himself but his home and his six-year-old son as well."

Meurrette had more than fulfilled Carlson's promise to me. I was not only off the hook; Berlin Investigations had just gotten a free plug.

"Our department has been conducting its own investigation of Anthony Mason in connection with the recent murders," Meurette was saying.

The screen quickly filled with a beaming Vern Hollander. "Thanks to the excellent work of Chief Meurrette and his investigators," he said, "my office has received conclusive evidence that attorney Anthony Mason was responsible for the recent murders of both Jack Drucker and Christopher Dietrich. Furthermore, we believe that both murders, as well as the attempted murder of Mr. Berlin, were motivated by a desire to cover up Mason's activities as a procurer for Mr. Dietrich and, perhaps, for other young prostitutes as well."

The Wausau anchor wrapped up the story by quoting "sources" in Hollander's office who speculated that the "young offenders, who are also, in a sense, victims," would be charged as juveniles and "might expect" to receive probation.

When the anchor started talking about the Wausau school budget, I flicked off the TV and tossed the remote onto the table beside the bed.

The highlights of the news conference had been most interesting for what they didn't contain. For one thing, there was no mention of my investigation of Jack's murder. It looked like the cops were taking all the credit for connecting Mason to that. Well, they were welcome to it.

Most interesting of all had been the lack of any mention of a pedophilic aspect to the case. "Teenage prostitution," "procurer," and "young prostitutes." That was all. It was clear that Mulkowski and Hollander were going to downplay the sex-ring angle. Because it provided the motive for their killer, they couldn't ignore it altogether, but it looked like they were going to welcome guilty pleas from the kids (even Blackhalter?) and leave their clients out of it.

Maybe I was getting too cynical, but I didn't think that anyone—with the possible exception of George Carlson—would be looking for a list of Mason's and Blackhalter's clients. That list would almost certainly include several prominent citizens, and Pinery Falls' law enforcement officials have never been eager to lock horns with prominent citizens, much less to lock them up for statutory rape.

It looked like poor Eugene Malik was going to do the penance for all their sins. Jack wasn't going to get to blow the lid off the Pinery Falls power structure after all. Not even posthumously.

I'd done Carlson an injustice. This must have been what he was looking so disgruntled about. Well, that wasn't my concern, was it?

I got a beer from the bathroom sink and plopped down in the easy chair. The time had come to think about tomorrow—something I wasn't looking forward to. That's what the beer was for.

38

KYRIE ELEISON

—Mr. Mister

I passed out in the chair sometime between nine thirty and ten o'clock on Saturday night, about halfway through my seventh Point Special. Around 1:00 a.m., I woke up with an urgent need to piss and feeling as if someone had slipped a 50-pound weight into my brainpan. I felt my way to the bathroom (I couldn't face turning on the light), where I relieved myself, and then stumbled back to the bed where I slept until about nine fifteen.

If I had any dreams, I didn't remember them in the morning.

When I woke up, I just lay there for a while, taking stock of what I'd decided the night before. Sleeping around-the-clock had refreshed me and I realized that I no longer felt any signs of a hangover.

In fact, I felt pretty good.

After about ten minutes, I got up. Then I showered and brushed my teeth.

Just before I left the motel, I got out my phone card and called long-distance to the cop shop in Pinery Falls. George Carlson wasn't there, but they put me through to his voice mail.

"Hi, George. This is Hank Berlin. Look, I don't want to tell you your business, but if you haven't done it already, you might want to check Anthony Mason's phone records. After he was dead, I pressed redial on his cell phone. The last person he called was Vern Hollander. Then I star sixty-nined it. The last person who had called him on it was Vern Hollander too. What do you think they were talking about?"

I hung up feeling that I'd done my small part for the revolution.

Then I left the motel.

The full winter had arrived overnight. The temperature must have dropped twenty degrees. Nearly eight inches of powdery snow had fallen, and the world was astonishingly bright. The sky was blue and cloudless, and the sun glared off the snow's surface as it would off a mirror. It was the kind of winter day that could give you sunburn.

I swept the snow off the Sentra's windows and drove back to Pinery Falls through a vast pristine whiteness, letting the snow from the hood blow up and over the car like a cleansing spray. The freshly fallen snow covered the landscape like a thick white comforter. You could almost believe that there was nothing dirty or ugly in the world.

I got back to town in time for 11 o'clock Mass at St. Mary's. It had been a long time since I'd gone to church without the responsibility of taking Harry, but I felt some need of Mass today. I got there before the service started and knelt down in one of the back pews.

I had a lot to think about, and church is a good place for some kinds of thinking—particularly the kinds that are close to prayer.

Mostly, I had to think what I owed to people. To Liz, of course, and, in a very different sense, to Jack. Did I have an obligation to the past? And did An Doc change that obligation in any way? I still hadn't fully taken in the fact that my old friend wasn't just the victim of a murder. He was—*Jesus, Jack!*—a *mass* murderer himself.

Another question that troubled me was whether I owed anything to the man I'd killed, beyond whatever I felt about killing him? And what *was* that exactly? Regret? Remorse? Mason had come to my house to kill me. Worse, he might have killed Harry, either by mistake or, if he found him under the bed, in order to eliminate a witness. Better Mason than me. And infinitely better him than Harry!

And yet—

I looked up to the crucifix that hung above the altar. My thoughts were not very Christ-like. But then, I wasn't an all-loving God.

What about Mason's wife? And his now adult children, none of whom I had ever met? Did I owe *them* anything? Specifically, did I owe them the total truth about their husband and father?

Well, Mason was a pimp and a killer who'd died trying to kill again. *That* was the truth and nothing was going to change it. What did the details matter?

After a while, the priest came down the aisle flanked by two servers. One of them was a girl. Back when I'd served at Mass, the idea of a girl at the altar had been unthinkable. In those days we were called the altar *boys*. Even the nuns weren't allowed up there while the Mass was being celebrated.

I will go unto the altar of God, the Mass began.

Introíbo ad altaré Dei. The opening of the Latin Mass came back to me, a distant echo from what Harry calls the "olden days" of my youth, a time when I went to Mass every Sunday and many parochial school days too.

Confiteor Dei—I confess to Almighty God, and to you, my brothers and sisters . . . that I have sinned exceedingly, in thought, word, and deed. In what I have done, and what I have failed to do.

Oh yes, my brothers and sisters, I have sinned. Exceedingly.

Through my fault, through my most grievous fault.

I tried to make a sincere Act of Contrition to clear my way for Communion. I felt bad about killing Mason, but I didn't feel guilty about it. I didn't feel that I was to blame. But I did feel guilty about other things. I had messed up my marriage, or at least had not worked hard enough to preserve it. I had failed as a father, living apart from my son as much through my fault as through Sarah's.

I clung to the fact that I loved Harry deeply and wanted only the best for him, but I knew I'd been a hypocrite for not trying harder to make sure the best would come about.

Lavabo inter innocéntes manus meas. I will wash my hands among the innocent. But it had been a long time since I was really innocent. Since anybody was.

I thought about what I was going to do when the Mass was over.

The priest held up the Host.

For this is my body.

I felt a deep and complicated sense of loss. Loss of something associated with my childhood. Loss of old friends and, maybe even more, loss of the future we had once expected to have. Maybe, most of all, loss of the certainty I had once felt that in this moment the bread was being transformed—in some way that I didn't understand but believed in absolutely—into something that was the essence of God himself.

For this is my blood . . . which shall be shed for you, and for all men, so that sins may be forgiven.

If I didn't still believe this, why was I even here?

Lord, I am not worthy to receive. You, but only say the word and I shall be healed.

I prayed that I was making— or rather, had already made—the right decision.

Behold the Lamb of God . . . Happy are we who are called to His table.

I felt a small but very real pleasure as the priest recited those words, as if a blessing really did reside in them. As if I were coming home. At least for a visit.

When the Communion procession arrived at my row, I joined it and made my way down the aisle. I took the Host in my left hand, then raised it to my mouth with the fingers of my right. Walking back to the pew, I knelt and waited for the Host to dissolve, as I'd been taught to do as a child.

While the priest completed the ceremony, I had an uneasy feeling that time was running out. It wasn't just the Mass that was ending or the case that was being wrapped up but a large part of my own past that was sliding rapidly and irrevocably to a conclusion.

The priest gave us his final blessing.

May Almighty God bless you, the Father, the Son, and the Holy Spirit.

The thinking and the praying were over. The decision had been made, and I was committed to it.

Go, the Mass is finished.

It was the time.

39

ONE TOO MANY MORNINGS

—Bob Dylan

Liz came to the door dressed in a white turtleneck sweater and black slacks. As soon as she saw me, she threw open the door and embraced me, her body trembling in my arms.

"Thank God you're all right!" she exclaimed. "George Carlson came yesterday and told me what happened. I went to your home, but only the police were there and they didn't even know where you were. I've been calling and calling ever since."

"I'm fine," I told her, moving out of her embrace.

She took hold of my hand and drew me inside.

"Let me hang your jacket," she offered.

"That's all right," I said. "I won't be long. I'm here to make my report."

She took a step back and looked at me searchingly.

"Where's Tommy?" I asked.

"He's at the Y," she said. "His basketball team's got a Sunday practice."

"Good," I said.

I walked past her into the living room and she followed me.

The space between us was suddenly a palpable thing.

"Would you like something?" she asked uncertainly, pausing in the entryway. "Coffee or anything?"

"No, thanks," I said.

She seemed to reach a decision, then walked across the room to the sofa and sat down. She leaned forward with her elbows on her knees and clasped her hands in front of her. She looked as vulnerable as a frightened animal peeking out of its burrow.

"What *is* it, Hank? What's the matter?"

I remained standing.

"You're my client and I'm here to report on my investigation," I said. "I suppose Carlson told you that Anthony Mason killed Jack and the Dietrich kid, and then he tried to kill me too."

"Yes," she said.

"Well, it's not true," I said. "Mason did kill Dietrich, and he did try to kill me, but he didn't kill Jack. Of course, if I'm right about things, you already know that."

Her face, which had been open and vulnerable, had changed while I was speaking. Something seemed to close. She was steeling herself to take a blow, and the overstiff set of her body revealed the electric emotions that were running through her. She knew that a critical moment had arrived—a moment she had been both waiting and dreading for a long time. She was the patient whose doctor had just entered the room with the X-rays. Depending on what was said in the next few minutes, her life might never be the same again.

"How would I know that?" she asked, her voice oddly flat and strained.

I had come into the house charged with a certain amount of energy for what I had to do. Now that energy was draining out from me. Suddenly I felt like a bully towering over her. I moved to an easy chair across the room from the sofa and sat down on it.

"Because you were the one who killed Jack," I said.

She opened her mouth to speak.

"Don't," I said. "Please don't."

She stopped, looking a question.

"I don't want you to lie to me," I explained.

"I wasn't going to lie," she said.

"Then it's even more important that you don't say anything. Right now, I've only got a theory. I'm pretty sure that it's right, but it's only a theory. If you confirm it, then it's not just a theory anymore. Then I've got *knowledge,* and we've both got a serious problem. Do you understand that?" I asked.

"I think so," she said.

"Good. Now, my theory fits some important facts that the police theory doesn't," I explained. "The police are so happy with what they've got, they're willing to ignore what they don't have. That's normal for them, by the way. There are loose ends in every investigation. But in this case, the loose ends are critical.

I took a deep breath, then let it out.

"The most important loose end is the gun," I said. "The police can't explain it because they don't know that it came from this house."

Her infinitely changeable eyes grew brighter and more intense. They seemed to be searching for something in my face. I wondered if they were finding it.

"Jack was killed with the gun he took from a hood named Mattiacci down in Milwaukee several years ago. I can't prove that, and maybe the police can't either. But it's true. The police must have assumed that all of Jack's guns were on display here in the house, I think that they weren't, though. Jack would've kept that one out of sight because it was illegal. It was a hit man's gun with its identifying marks filed off, so he couldn't register it. Worse, he didn't know what crimes it might have been involved in. I'm sure that the police ran a ballistics check since the killing, and the gun must have come up clean. But Jack couldn't have known that it would do that."

I knew that there was another, more important, reason that Jack had kept the gun hidden. He had taken it away from a professional killer in a face-to-face confrontation. For Jack, it was the equivalent of a scalp—a proof of manhood. It was a badge of honor in a way that nothing from Vietnam could ever be. Not after An Doc. And that had made it a sacred thing, not something to be put out on display for strangers to gawk at.

"The fact that the gun came from this house meant that the killer was probably either you or Tommy. It didn't *have* to be, though. Someone else could have stolen the gun from here. It was even possible that Mattiacci came up here, stole the gun, and then killed Jack with it. I sort of liked that theory for a while. It had a kind of poetry to it. But why would Mattiacci *wait* so long? No, it was almost certainly either you or Tommy. Only, I didn't see how it could have been Tommy."

The mere suggestion spurred an indignant protest. "Of course it wasn't Tommy!" she exclaimed.

"I couldn't think of any realistic way he could have gotten out to Little River Road," I went on, ignoring the interruption. "Granted, it was so late that everybody might have been asleep at the Keeler's, so he could have snuck out without anyone noticing. But I checked and the Keeler's house is about five miles from Little River Road. He could have ridden a bike or something, but how likely is that? And besides, how would he know that Jack would be out there anyway? Jack didn't know himself until that late phone call from Shirley Petorksi—that was the girl's name, by the way—the caller you must have overheard. I could think of only one logical way for Tommy to have gotten out there. That was if he went with Jack. But why would Jack take him? And, if he had, how did Tommy get back to the Keelers' after the murder? No, it wasn't Tommy. That meant that it must have been you."

Liz's expression hadn't changed. She was still sitting in the same spot on the sofa, in the same stiff position, but she seemed to be shrinking a little.

"The other loose end is the button from your winter coat that the cops found in the Stingray. That was the clincher really. The cops weren't troubled by it because they assumed that you were a regular passenger in that car. But you told me that the car offended you and you'd refused to ride in it since just after Jack bought it last summer. Well, it was a really hot summer, and nobody wears a winter coat in the summertime anyway. Unless you were lying to me, you must have lost the button when you killed Jack.

"It was on the passenger side, so it must have been torn off with some force. My guess is that Jack grabbed for you—or maybe for the gun—and that's when the button went flying."

She ran her tongue over her lips, but her mouth was so dry that it failed to moisten them.

"This couldn't have been a spur-of-the-moment decision," I said. "I don't believe you killed Jack on a whim. You must have already decided to do it, but not figured out exactly *how*. Then Shirley Petorski called and presented you with an opportunity. You heard the phone ring, and you picked it up and listened. You probably didn't understand all of it, but you got the important part. She told Jack about some kind of meeting at a house on Little River Road. She must have given him the address, and said something like, 'If you go out there and wait, you'll see him come and go.' You knew then that Jack would be out on a fairly isolated road. And he'd be alone for at least some length of time."

Her head seemed to dip twice, just slightly, and maybe even unconsciously. It wasn't quite a nod.

"This was the perfect chance," I continued. "Or at least it was as good a chance as you were likely to get. Tommy was away at a friend's house. That, I think, was vital for you. You didn't want him around when his father was killed. What's more, Jack's murder"—she flinched at the word—"wouldn't happen here. He'd die somewhere that had no connection with you or Tommy. That would throw off police suspicion, but more important, there would be nothing to haunt Tommy with images of his dad's murder *here*. Not here where he lived."

Again, that almost nod.

"I don't know how long you took to think about it, but sometime after Jack left the house you got dressed and went out to Little River Road yourself. You took the Sable, and, of course, you took Jack's hidden gun."

My throat was starting to get dry. I wished I'd taken her offer of a drink.

"I'm not sure how you knew about the gun," I continued. "Maybe he showed it to you when he got back from Milwaukee and told you how he got it. Even if he didn't, a wife knows where her husband hides his treasures. I also don't know if Jack kept the gun loaded. But, knowing him, he probably did. Most likely with the same rounds it had in it when he took it off Mattiacci. You must have figured out in advance that it would be the perfect murder weapon. It was untraceable—at least, not back to you or Jack."

She wasn't denying any of this. She wasn't admitting any of it either. But then, I had warned her not to do that.

The day she hired me, I'd told her she was a good client because she knew how to answer questions. Now she proved that she knew how to ask them too.

"And why would that be, Hank?" she asked, her voice sounding strained with tension. "Hypothetically speaking, assuming that you were right. Why did I . . ." She hesitated and started over. "I'm trying to follow your goddamned jesuitical rules here. Why *would* I kill Jack?" Her voice got very quiet. "I really loved him, you know."

"I know you did," I said.

"Then *why,* Hank?"

"Because of Tommy," I answered. "Because of what Jack was doing to him."

She closed her eyes and her body seemed to relax. For the first time since she'd sat down, she adjusted her position, sitting farther back on the couch.

"He was abusing Tommy, wasn't he?" I went on. "Not sexually. And not *just* violently either. Psychologically, I mean. You saw happening to Tommy what your parents did to you. Or at least you thought you did."

I remembered what Wes Drucker had said about *une fleur de mal*. "Maybe you were right, and maybe that was what Jack's father had done to him too. But you couldn't let that happen to your son. This couldn't keep happening generation after generation. It *had* to stop. And that meant that you had to stop it."

She looked enormously relieved, as if her most devout wish had been granted by a merciful God. Some part of her must have feared that she had only imagined all this—the destructive effect that Jack was having on their son. Now she felt validated by the simple fact that someone else had seen what she had seen.

But the truth was, although I understood her motive, I had no real understanding of her situation as it looked—and felt—to her.

"What I don't understand, Liz, is why you didn't just leave him. In theory now, why would you have to *kill* him?"

"He would never have let us go," she said simply. "*I* could have left, but not with Tommy. He swore that he'd fight me in court, and that would have just torn Tommy apart."

"Are you hearing yourself?" I asked. "You're saying a custody battle would have been worse for Tommy than you killing his father."

She looked as if she was in pain. "But I would have lost!" she said. "Don't you see? With his father's backing, Jack could have hired the best lawyers in the state."

"His father?" I asked. "What did Wes have to do with it?" Even as I spoke, I realized that Wes Drucker had everything to do with it.

"Jack's father made it clear that he'd pay for a custody fight. No one was going to take the only Drucker heir away from the Druckers. He could afford the best lawyers, and who could I get on my side? I make enough to hire a competent attorney, but nobody who could match what the wealthy Wesley Drucker could buy."

"Lots of good lawyers work on contingency," I protested.

She shook her head vigorously. "But there *wasn't* any money," she protested. "You have to remember that Wesley has all the real money in the family. No topflight lawyer would take my case on contingency because there was no hope of a big settlement. You can't get a divorce settlement from a father-in-law."

She had a point. I was beginning to understand the nature of the trap she'd felt herself in and to sense the desperation that she'd felt.

"Even so," I protested. "You've been a good mother. You make a decent living and you could provide a good home. Even with the best lawyers, Jack couldn't have taken Tommy away from you."

"Maybe not," she said. "But he would have gotten joint custody, at least. Don't you *see*, Hank?" Her stunning blue eyes were feral now, and she spoke with a gathering intensity. "He didn't have to take Tommy away from me, but *I* had to take Tommy away from *him*. As long as he had a big part in Tommy's life, the damage would be done. He'd keep making Tommy feel that he was a great disappointment to his father. Make him feel ashamed. Unloved. The way *he's* always felt. Eventually Jack would *destroy* Tommy, the way he'd been destroyed himself."

There was something obsessive in the way she spoke about the harm that she'd seen done to Tommy. It was the fierce irrationality of a lioness defending her cub, but it was more than that too. It was clear that she wasn't just talking about her son. What she was describing so fervidly was a pain she felt herself.

For the first time since I had known her, I realized that the mysterious quality I had always sensed in her—the quality that had drawn me to her when we were young and that had haunted me ever since—was a kind of madness. Once that thought occurred to me, I wondered how it could have escaped me for so long.

And yet, wasn't all parental love obsessive? A little crazy, even?

"Nothing I could do would make up for what was happening," she said. "A mother loving a child can't make up for a father *not* loving him. Hating him, even—using him as a whipping boy for his own self-contempt. I couldn't let him keep Tommy," she insisted. "I had to—"

"No!"

I raised my hand to silence her. We were walking very close to the edge of my conscience here.

She nodded, to show that she understood.

"I loved Jack," she said. "I really did. But I loved Tommy more. I couldn't go to court and risk Jack getting custody. And there was no way I could get Jack declared an unfit father. The things he was doing to Tommy didn't show. What evidence did I have? The fact that our son had once been happy but was becoming sullen and withdrawn?"

"All adolescents get sullen and withdrawn sometimes," I protested. "It could be just a normal part of growing up."

She shook her head.

"You didn't know Tommy when he was younger," she said. "He was born to be the happiest child in the world. You should have seen him, Hank! As a baby, he almost never cried. He gurgled, and he *laughed*. Really. As a little baby, he just laughed and laughed. He was filled with delight."

I felt strongly that she was wrong about this—about the extent of the damage that had been done, about her inability to compensate for it, and, most of all, about the necessity of killing Jack. But there was no way I could argue her out of it now. And what was the use? At this point, to convince her that what she had done had been unnecessary, even pointless, would be a kind of cruelty.

"My theory's pretty good," I said. "Some of the evidence wouldn't mean much in court, but it's convincing to me. For instance, I can't prove the gun was the one taken from Mattiacci, but it matches the description perfectly. The most important thing—for me, not for the cops—is that it *feels* right. You said something like that when you hired me. Remember? You said that it felt right, somehow, to come to me. Well, when the evidence started coming together, that felt right to me."

"So, why *did* I come to you?" she asked. "What's your theory about that?"

Her tone had changed. The tension was gone now. But those amazing eyes were fixed on me, as if she really wanted an answer to her question. As if she really didn't know.

I remembered the day she had come to my office and I remembered what she'd said. *I want you to find out who killed Jack. And I want you to find out why.*

"I think you came to me for the same reason that you used to come in the old days. You came because you were conflicted. You felt justified in what you'd done, but you felt guilty too. You wanted someone to judge you—and maybe to tell you what to do. I had been close to both you and Jack, and I was your confessor. Who better to judge what you had done?"

"But then," she said tentatively, as if she was only now working this out, "if I wanted you to judge me, why didn't I just tell you what I'd done? *If* I had done it," she added quickly.

"I don't think you dared," I said. "Not in this case. There was too much at stake to come right out and confess. I don't mean just your freedom. I mean Tommy's future, too. That most of all. But you still felt guilty and conflicted, so you rolled the dice. You decided to leave it up to me. If I couldn't figure it out, and the cops couldn't either, then you'd just have to live with what you'd done. If I *did* figure it out, then it would be *my* problem and not just yours anymore. Just like old times."

She nodded thoughtfully. Then, incredibly, she smiled at me. It was a fleeting and bittersweet sort of smile, but it was real. "So, what about it, Hank? You say it's your problem now, so what are you going to do with it?"

The time had come.

"Nothing," I said.

Once again, she closed her eyes. This time, she didn't open them right away.

"I won't tell the cops what I know. What I *think*," I corrected myself. "Let them keep their neat little theory—and let Tommy keep at least one parent. He needs that and I'm not going to take it away from him."

Everything she had said about Jack and Tommy might be true, or it might be a nightmare fantasy. Certainly I'd seen and heard enough to know that Tommy was a troubled kid and that Jack had a lot to do with making him that way. I also knew that Jack had hit the kid, and done it more than once. More than that, I knew that if the truth came out now and Tommy's mother was taken away from him and sent to prison, his life would be, if not destroyed, at least severely and irreparably damaged. That was a responsibility I wasn't ready to take. (Would my decision have been different if I hadn't found out about An Doc? That I thought, but didn't know.)

Liz's lower lip began to tremble, and I thought that she was going to cry from the sheer release of tension.

"*Unless,*" I added.

Her eyes opened and she looked at me warily.

"Unless the police decide they were wrong about Mason being Jack's killer, and try to nail some innocent person for it. Then I'd have to give them what I know."

"*You* wouldn't have to," Liz said.

I believed her. If that happened, she'd confess herself.

"I don't think you have to worry," I said. "They've got a solid case. It'll hold up."

She nodded.

"About your bill—," she began.

Jesus Christ!

"Good-bye, Liz."

I headed for the front door.

She jumped up from the sofa as if to head me off, but about halfway to me she saw something in my face and stopped.

"I was fair with you, Hank," she said earnestly. "I never lied to you. Not ever. Not directly."

Looking back, I thought that was probably true. But so what?

She stood in the middle of her and Jack's living room, looking lost. Then she raised an imploring hand in my direction.

For Christ's sake, what else did she want from me?

"If you want anything else from me," I said, "absolution, for instance, I can't give it to you. I haven't got that power."

She bit her lip.

"And I *won't* give you my approval."

I was just about to start for the door again when I remembered something.

"One thing I'd like to know, Liz. Did you know about what happened at An Doc?" The puzzled look on her face was more than enough answer for me.

Oh, Liz, I thought. *It could have been so easy. With that information, any halfway decent lawyer could have made sure that Jack never got within a mile of Tommy.*

But I didn't say it out loud.

As I said before, that would have only been cruel.

Y*elping with delight and filled with a wild exhilaration, we took to the forest as eagles take to the air.*

The white-eyes' bullets ripped the air around our ears. They tore at the leaves all around and slammed into the trunks of trees ahead of us. We, who had known the thrill of the hunt, now found that the prey feel a joy of their own.

Branches lashed at our bodies and brambles caught at our feet, but the forest was only playing with us. The same branches that lashed us on our way would grab at the white-eyes and held them back. The underbrush obstructed them; hidden thorns cut their flesh; the exposed roots of basswood trees lay in ambush, snagging their feet and sending them tumbling them over each other.

Jack was in the lead, but the two of us together were pulling steadily away from our pursuers. We had no need to look behind to track their progress; we could hear them crashing through the underbrush, their bloodlust audible in the shouted curses and the inarticulate tumult of their rage.

We flew through the woods like spirits. Almost without effort, we dodged the trees and bushes that seemed to spring up in our path, leaping over the roots of oaks and birches and the rotting trunks of fallen maples. We had crossed some invisible border into a more exultant universe, a place that was entirely separate from the world of time. For that brief moment, we were safe and free and timeless.

We were young!

The urgency of our breathing joined with the rush of the wind generated by the speed of our running and filled our ears with a sound like laughter—a resonance that was as soft as a whisper and as loud as a roar.

Our feet pounded the forest floor, but the sounds they made were lost to us. It was as if we were outrunning even our own footsteps.

We had a kind of magic that summer afternoon.

We knew that unless the white-eyes had a magic of their own, they could never catch us. And yet they refused to give up the chase. Their pursuit seemed as relentless as it was surely hopeless. Our hearts rose in our chests as the sounds of the white-eyes became fainter as the distance between us increased.

Jack was in the lead as we burst out of the cool darkness of the forest and into the eye-shocking brightness of a large clearing on which the hot sun beat down.

Our hearts rose even higher.

It was an omen.

Escape was certain now.

But no!

Not even the bravest warrior can escape his fate. Not even the fastest runner can outrun the bullets from the white-eyes' guns.

Crack!

Something rammed my back with the force of a charging buffalo. Thrown to my knees, I pitched forward onto the ground. Twisting an arm behind me, I could feel warm blood leaving my body. I knew that I was doomed.

On the far side of the open clearing, Jack glanced back in alarm. When he realized what had happened, he stopped and turned back toward me.

He seemed to hesitate.

Frantically I called to him to run, to save himself, but he ignored my warning.

Calling out to reassure me, he charged to my rescue, just as he had on the first day we'd ever met.

Crack!

Jack's body was thrown backwards by the impact. Fighting to keep his feet, he staggered for a few steps, only to collapse across the trunk of a lightning-felled tree.

The chase was ended.

We were at peace.

The two of us lay there for a while, taking in great gulps of air until our breathing and heart rates slowed to normal. Gradually, the warriors vanished and we became young boys again, playing in the woods.

The sun was hot on my back.

The forest smelled of pine.

A stick insect crawled across my hand.

I looked over at Jack, and he looked back at me.

He grinned.

I grinned back at him.

It felt good to be alive.